TWICE AS DEAD

AN ODELIA GREY MYSTERY

TWICE AS DEAD

SUE ANN JAFFARIAN

THORNDIKE
C H I V E R S

This Large Print edition is published by Thorndike Press, Waterville, Maine, USA and by AudioGO Ltd, Bath, England.

Thorndike Press, a part of Gale, Cengage Learning.

The text of this Large Print edition is unabridged.
Other aspects of the book may vary from the original edition.
Set in 16 pt. Plantin.

LIBRARY OF CONGRESS CATALOGING-IN-PUBLICATION DATA

Jaffarian, Sue Ann, 1952–
   Twice as dead : an Odelia Grey mystery / by Sue Ann Jaffarian.
      p. cm. — (Thorndike Press large print mystery)
      ISBN-13: 978-1-4104-4063-1 (hardcover)
      ISBN-10: 1-4104-4063-X (hardcover)
      1. Grey, Odelia (Fictitious character)—Fiction. 2. Overweight women—Fiction. 3. Legal assistants—Fiction. 4. Large type books. I. Title.
PS3610.A359T87 2011b
813'.6—dc22
                                     2011020842

BRITISH LIBRARY CATALOGUING-IN-PUBLICATION DATA AVAILABLE

Published in 2011 in the U.S. by arrangement with Midnight Ink, an imprint of Llewellyn Publications, Woodbury, MN 55129-2989 USA.
Published in 2012 in the U.K. by arrangement with Llewellyn Worldwide Ltd.

U.K. Hardcover: 978 1 445 86041 1 (Chivers Large Print)
U.K. Softcover: 978 1 445 86042 8 (Camden Large Print)

Printed in the United States of America
1 2 3 4 5 6 7 15 14 13 12 11

For Lynne DeVenny Craig,
the paralegal's paralegal.

ACKNOWLEDGMENTS

Thanks again to the usual suspects, who were never more than a phone call or e-mail away during this journey:

Whitney Lee, my agent
Diana James, my manager
Terri Bischoff, my acquisitions editor

And thank you to all the wonderful people at Midnight Ink/Llewellyn Worldwide who have worked very hard to make every book a dream come true.

ONE

I eyed the thick wooden coat hanger with suspicion, poised as it was to do serious damage to my skull.

"Put that damn thing down before you hurt someone," I demanded. "Namely me."

"I'm warning you, Odelia." My assailant's eyes were glazed with menace. "You take one step outside this room, and I'll knock you unconscious. I swear I will."

The door to the cloakroom flung open, surprising both of us. From beyond the door, we could hear the band playing "Achy Breaky Heart." Even though I'm as uncoordinated as an elephant in a tutu, at that moment I would have given a kidney to be on the dance floor doing the Electric Slide with assorted bridesmaids and wedding guests.

"What in the hell is going on here?" demanded Seth. He snatched the hanger from his wife's hands. "Zenobia Washington, have you lost your ever-loving mind?" His question was presented in the hushed voice of a really ticked-off librarian, not that of an experienced lawyer. Behind him was Jacob Washington, Seth and Zee's college-age son. Now as tall as his father, he stood looking at his mother and me like we were circus freaks — which might not be that far from the truth, given the current circumstances.

"Actually, Seth, her insanity is a *teensy* bit justified." I held up my right hand with my thumb and index finger about an inch apart to add emphasis to my words.

Seth's mouth dropped open. "She was about to club you, and you're *defending* her?"

After straightening up from my defensive crouch, I smoothed the wrinkles out of my ice-blue lace cocktail dress and studied Zee. She looked fabulous in her champagne silk tea-length mother-of-the-bride dress, though I doubt the designer foresaw the dress being accessorized with a weapon. Now Zee had her hands on her ample hips in her signature stance of intimidation, which ruined the flowing lines of the garment. Since we're both short and fat and wear a size 20, I wondered, not for the first time, if she'd let me borrow the dress for my in-laws' fiftieth anniversary party in two months. Something told me now would not be a good time to ask.

"Of course I'm defending her." I kept my own voice down in case someone was passing in the hallway. "She's my best friend, and she had her reasons." I glanced over at Zee, who hadn't moved a muscle. "Even if her method was a bit barbaric. Still, I'm not so sure I wouldn't have done the same."

Seth shifted on his feet and pulled at the collar of his tuxedo shirt. He looked from his wife to me, waiting for an explanation. "Are either of you going to tell me what this is about?"

Jacob started to say something, but his mother cut him off. "She was going to ruin Hannah's wedding." Hannah being Seth and Zee's daughter.

I felt my hackles rise. "I would never dream of doing such a thing, and you know it."

Seth turned to Jacob. "Go find Greg. Tell him I need his assistance. Don't say why."

"And miss this?" Jacob crossed his arms in front of him, settling in for the show.

Seth leveled his paternal glare at the young man. "I said, go find Greg. Do it now."

After a few seconds' hesitation, Jacob caved, giving in to years of good upbringing. "Okay, but don't move the body till I get back."

11

As Jacob dashed out the door, Seth turned to me. He started to say something, then his open mouth clamped shut so hard I heard his upper and lower molars collide. He turned to his wife, his dark face incredulous, silently begging her to say it wasn't true. Zee's dark eyes met his. She nodded, confirming his worst fears.

When Seth turned back to me, I took two steps to my left and cast my eyes slightly behind me. Seth's eyes followed mine.

There, half hidden, was the dead body of a woman.

We were at a local private club, standing in a fair-sized room with no windows. During cooler months, the room was used as a cloakroom. Portable clothing racks, their sturdy wooden hangers dangling like soldiers at the ready, lined the walls on either side of the door. The room was slightly L-shaped, with a small alcove to the right. Against the back wall of the alcove stood several stacks of large plastic storage containers. From the view afforded by the opaque plastic, most were full. The only entry into the room was a Dutch door — a door split in two horizontally so that the top portion could be opened with the bottom half remaining shut. Right now, the top and bottom portions were latched together.

Seth had closed the door after Jacob had gone in search of Greg Stevens, my husband.

Hmmm, my husband. It was anyone's guess what he was going to say about this latest turn of events. Dead bodies find me like flies zeroing in on dog poop, though it *had* been over a year and a half since I'd stumbled upon the last body — a point I was ready to make if the subject came up, as I was sure it would.

Without stepping forward, Seth leaned the top part of his torso toward the stiff. "You sure she's dead? Maybe we should be calling 9-1-1."

The dead woman was sitting on the floor, her back against a stack of containers. Her legs were spread in a V, the straight skirt of her bronze silk suit hiked up mid-thigh. She'd been neither slim nor fat, with long, muscular legs. Her feet, clad in open-toed high heels, ended with toes painted a muted rose. The same colored lacquer adorned her fingernails. Around her neck was an expensive-looking gold necklace. At her ears, diamond studs. On her wrist, a designer watch. Whatever had happened, it was easy to see it hadn't been a robbery.

The woman's dark blond hair contained pale highlights and was nearly shoulder-length, the ends turned under in a slight pageboy. It partially hid her face, which was square-shaped with a slightly crooked nose. She would have been described as a handsome woman — the term used when a woman isn't necessarily pretty but is still very attractive. Her brows were carefully cultivated. Her makeup was meticulous, though a bit on the heavy side for my personal taste. She could have been taken for anywhere between thirty-five and fifty years old. It was clear that in life the woman had taken very good care of herself and had spent considerable time and money in salons of one type or another.

But was she dead?

One look into her cornflower-blue eyes, wide and staring at nothing, and her slack jaw, open in silent song, and there was no doubt that any call to 9-1-1 would be in vain.

"I checked for a pulse," I told Seth. "Nothing." Pointing down to the floor, I indicated the small pool of blood she was sitting in. "There's a knife in her left side, just under her breast. But I don't think she's been dead very long."

A soft knock sounded at the door. Seth opened it with caution, relieved to find Greg on the other side. After opening the door as wide as it could go, Seth stepped back to make room for Greg to enter in his wheelchair. Jacob was behind him.

"Go back out there and keep an eye on things," Seth told his son.

"But Dad, I want to see what happens."

"We can't have your sister wondering why we're all missing. Go back out there," Seth ordered again. "Act like nothing's wrong. Say nothing to anyone. You got that?"

When Jacob hesitated, Zee stepped up to him. "You want your sister's wedding ruined?"

With reluctance, Jacob left to keep the party going and his sister in the dark.

"What's going on?" Greg asked after Jacob left and the door was shut tight again. I had stepped in front of the corpse, hoping to ward off the initial shock and outcry from Greg on seeing it for the first time.

"We have a situation, Greg." Seth forced his voice to remain calm.

Zee looked at Greg, then at me, her soulful eyes full of unspoken but loud explanation.

Greg looked up at me. "What's going on?" His voice wasn't tender but direct, like he knew what was coming and didn't want to hear it.

"I had nothing to do with this, Greg. Honest." I stepped aside. When his eyes found the body on the floor, he went white.

"Not again," Greg said in a small voice. He looked up from the body to me. "I thought this was all behind us, Odelia. It's been so long since . . ." His voice trailed off.

"Since I found that body in the cornfield? Yeah, yeah, I know. I thought it was over, too."

I looked at the three faces of the people I loved most — Greg, Zee, and Seth — and felt like I was on trial. Odelia Patience Grey, aka the corpse magnet. I was feeling compelled to plead my case, and not liking it one bit. The gloves came off.

"Hey, it's not just me, you know. Zee was with me when I found the body. She's just as involved."

"Me?" Zee pointed a finger at herself. "The only time I see dead bodies is when I'm with *you,* Odelia. Couldn't you have waited until tomorrow?"

"Waited?" I couldn't believe my ears. "You think I *planted* this corpse?"

"No, but you're the one who wanted to call the police, and right in the middle of my baby girl's wedding." Zee's voice cracked during the last three words, letting us know she was barely containing hysteria.

16

"Okay, everyone," Greg said, wheeling deeper into the middle of the room. He looked down at the body. "You're sure she's dead?"

"Yes!" came a trio of muffled shouts.

"Zee and I came in here," I started to explain, "to get away for a few minutes. She was exhausted and needed some downtime away from everyone. The ladies' lounge was packed, then I remembered this cloakroom." Before continuing, I swallowed the bile invading my throat. "We were here a couple of minutes before I smelled something not right. When I poked my head into this little niche, I found the body, just as it is now."

"She wanted to call the police!" Zee told them in horror, like that was the real crime at hand.

"But we have to call the police, Zee." I pointed toward the door. "Someone out there probably killed this poor woman."

Zee looked even more horrified. "Certainly you don't think one of our guests did this?"

"Not necessarily, but *someone* did — and there are almost three hundred suspects out there right now. The police need to get here ASAP."

"More than three hundred if you count

the band, waitstaff, and caterers," added Greg.

"You're not helping, Greg," Seth snapped at him.

Greg looked from Seth to Zee. "I'm afraid I have to side with Odelia on this. The police must be called."

Zee started tearing up. "But not at this very minute. Can't we wait until Hannah and Rob leave the reception? It should be very soon. When Jacob found us, it was to tell me Hannah was changing into her honeymoon clothes."

Looking at Seth, Greg asked, "What do you say, Counselor?"

Seth hemmed and hawed. "This is my daughter's wedding. You can hardly expect me to be objective."

Greg pressed, "But what legal obligations *do* we have?"

Seth took a deep breath and ran a hand over his ruggedly handsome face, which now sagged with weariness. "We don't have to report it. But as Odelia said, someone out there probably killed her. The sooner the police get here, the better."

There was a soft knock, followed by Jacob opening the door a few inches. "Hannah's looking for you, Mom." As he spoke to his mother, he craned his neck to glance at the corpse. "She's changed, and they're about to leave. They want to say goodbye to you and Dad."

Zee looked at Seth. "As soon as they're gone, we can call the police. We can ask everyone to remain — tell them it's for a final toast or something."

Seth thought it over, then turned to me. "Odelia, instead of calling the police, why don't you call Detective Frye directly? Tell him what's happened. We're in Newport Beach, so it's his jurisdiction, and I'd feel better having someone we know handling this from the beginning. By the time he rallies his troops, we'll have Hannah and Rob on their way." He looked at each of us. Greg, Jacob, and I nodded, on board with his plan. Only Zee looked unsure.

"I feel awkward calling Detective Frye," Zee said. "After all, I didn't invite him to the wedding."

Her husband stared at her like she'd lost her mind for the second time in less than twenty minutes. "I don't think the good detective will hold a grudge, dear."

As Seth guided Zee and Jacob out to play their role as the happy family sending off the newlyweds, I pulled my cell phone out of my evening bag and turned it on. Greg wheeled close to me and rubbed his hand up and down my back in comfort.

"The sooner we turn this over to Dev," he said, almost in the tone of an order, "the sooner we can get out of the middle of it."

I nodded in agreement as I scrolled through my phone's address book.

Greg let out a short, sad chuckle. "Here's a story the wedding planner won't soon forget."

I tossed my head toward the body. "Meet Shirley Pearson, the wedding planner."

TWO

Detective Devin Frye is a homicide detective with the Newport Beach Police. I met him the same time I met Greg, when my friend Sophie London was murdered. Over the years, the three of us have remained good friends. Dev is as chagrined over my penchant for finding dead bodies as Greg is, if not more. You see, Greg has finally adopted the "if you can't beat her, join her" attitude and often sticks his nose into things right along with me. Dev, on the other hand, being a homicide detective, faces the horror of murder every day and doesn't find it one bit funny that it follows me like a pesky shadow. As he has often said, with a shake of his grumbling head, now he worries about the two of us instead of just the one.

It was just after ten o'clock in the evening when I called Dev about the murder at Hannah's wedding. Just to make sure we gave the bride and groom time to make a getaway, Jacob agreed to tell us when the limo was about to leave the club. As soon as his knock sounded on the door, I punched the speed dial. For the past couple of years, Dev, a widower, had been seeing a lovely schoolteacher named Beverly. It being a Saturday night, there was a good chance they might be together, or even out. But this wasn't something that could wait.

Dev answered on the first ring. He sounded neither sleepy nor annoyed. I gave him a brief rundown of what we'd found and where and about the delicacy of the situation. After barking at me to not let anyone leave, he hung up, no doubt dialing the station house for backup as he ran to his car.

Right before the departure of the bride and groom, and before too many people could get away, Seth had made an announcement that he and Zee had a special toast to make and asked people to remain. Once the happy couple's limo was gone, fresh champagne was poured all around. Seth even invited the catering staff and the band to join in. He said a few words about Hannah and Rob, the young man Hannah had met while attending Stanford, and thanked everyone for contributing to their happiness.

I waited by the front door of the club for Dev. Just as glasses were tipped in a final salute to the newlyweds, the police showed up, and all exits were blocked. We'd been right to wait until Hannah had gone. It wouldn't have done the bride any good to see her wedding reception turned into a prison lockdown.

Dev Frye arrived almost at the same time as the police cars and took charge. I showed him to the cloakroom, where I'd left Greg to stand guard. The Orange County coroner had arrived with everyone else and followed us. Greg and I were quickly shuttled out of the way so they could work.

The questioning of the guests and wedding staff went into the wee hours. Some of the guests had left earlier, and Zee had to produce a guest list so that they could be contacted. The police were about to head to the Four Seasons Hotel, where the newlyweds were bunked down for the night before leaving on their honeymoon the next day, but Zee's tearful pleading moved Dev to wait until morning.

Eventually, Greg and I were allowed to leave, but we stuck around until the police let the Washingtons go home. It was almost four in the morning when we dragged our sorry asses home. While Greg texted a buddy of his to let him know he would not be making their basketball game later that day, I fed our two cats, Seamus and Muffin, and Wainwright, our dog. It was way too early for their breakfast, but if I didn't feed them, they'd be driving us nuts in a couple of hours. Mommy and Daddy needed their beauty sleep. Well, Mommy did.

"Did the kids get off on their honeymoon?" I asked Zee as I chopped vegetables for a salad.

It was Sunday evening. As soon as Greg and I had woken up, we'd had the idea of firing up the grill and inviting the Washingtons over for supper later. They'd been so wrapped up in the wedding preparations and now the stress of the murder, we thought they could use a little pampering. Seth and Zee readily accepted, but Jacob had plans with his friends. It was a simple meal of fresh vegetables and salmon cooked side by side on the grill and served with a large salad, followed by fresh strawberry shortcake — perfect for a warm June evening.

Zee was sitting at the kitchen table, watching me work. I wouldn't let her lift a finger. The men were chatting around the grill, beers in hand.

"Yes, finally." Zee let loose with a deep sigh of relief. "Good thing their plane to Maui wasn't early in the morning, or they would have missed it."

"How did they take the news of Shirley Pearson's murder?"

"Hannah was very upset." She took a drink from the glass of lemonade I'd placed in front of her. "Detective Frye was so nice to let us break the news to the kids first. We called them around eight this morning. They met the police at our house shortly before ten. They made their plane in plenty of time."

"I'm so glad." I had just halved some baby corn and added them to the big salad bowl. "I hope Hannah, um, doesn't blame *me* for this."

From the way Zee looked at me, then cut her eyes away, I knew the topic had come up amongst the Washingtons.

"Come on!" I slapped the knife down on the counter. "You can't be serious?"

"Odelia, honey," she started, then paused. Zee had put on her motherly comfort tone — the sort of voice used for telling a kid his guinea pig had just bitten the big one and gone to the eternal wheel in the sky. If she reached out to pat my hand, it just might end up in the salad. Her hand, not mine.

"We know you had nothing to do with Shirley's murder," she continued, wisely keeping her fingers to herself. "But."

There it was — the *but* — and she wasn't referring to my big butt. Or hers, for that matter.

"But what?" I turned toward her and leaned against the kitchen counter, arms crossed, waiting. Zee had her intimidating stance, I had my own.

"But why do bodies always show up around you?"

My nose twitched in annoyance. "Maybe you should have invited Dev Frye to the wedding after all? He could have taken my spot. Think how handy *that* would have been."

"Now, Odelia, don't be like that."

Turning back to my work, I started fussing with a nearby tomato. It was round, red, and ripe, waiting patiently for its execution under my knife. I knew how it felt. Knife poised over the bright orb, I shifted my eyes to Zee. "It's not like I killed the woman myself."

"No one is saying you did, Odelia." Zee's body rose and lowered as she emitted a another big sigh. "It's just . . . well, it's just that sometimes I wonder if somehow, someway, something unseen has chosen you to find these bodies."

I looked at my friend as if she had sprouted two heads. Zee Washington was a devout Christian, and I wasn't quite sure where she was going with this. Me, I'm a fence sitter on spiritual things. "Are you saying God has me on some sort of ghoulish scavenger hunt?"

She shrugged and drank some more lemonade. "You do help people in an odd, creepy way." She paused, then added, "This never happened to you before Sophie died, did it?"

"You know it didn't."

Zee knitted her brows in thought. "It's almost as if Sophie's murder opened some sort of door linking you to finding murderers."

"Show me the door, Zee, and I'll gladly slam it shut. And lock it. And throw away the key." I sliced into the waiting tomato, glad I couldn't hear vegetables scream.

She looked at me in earnest. "But what if it's your destiny to help these people?"

Huh? I stared at my friend and wondered when she'd gone bananas. Had a year of wedding planning turned her brain to mush? "But I thought you weren't thrilled with my being a corpse magnet."

"I'm not. It puts you, and often the people around you, in danger. But in the end, some real good comes out of it. Think about it, Odelia. Murderers are brought to justice. People who have lost loved ones get some sense of closure."

I finished dissecting the tomato and threw the chunks into the salad bowl. "So you're okay with it as long as good is accomplished?"

Another shrug was thrown my way.

Turning to face Zee, I locked my eyes onto hers. "What if, one day, the bad guy wins?"

The men called us out to the patio. Dinner was ready. Zee scampered out without responding to my question. Relieved, no doubt. After giving the salad a quick toss, I picked up the bowl and followed.

We were just sitting down to eat when our front doorbell rang. Wainwright started barking and dashed for the door. I got up and followed, noting when I reached the door that Wainwright's tail was wagging with enthusiasm. On the other side of the door had to be someone we knew.

"I hope I'm not interrupting anything," Detective Dev Frye said when the door opened. "But I have a few more questions." Wainwright whined with pleasure. Dev was one of his favorite people. Instead of his usual suit, the detective was dressed in chinos, and a dark blue knit shirt slightly strained across his muscular chest.

"Come on in, Dev." I unlocked the screen door and pushed it open, kneeing the big golden retriever out of the way so the even bigger detective could come into the house.

"We were just sitting down to dinner," I told Dev. "Please join us."

As Dev grinned, the skin on his neck turned pink. "It's no accident I dropped by around your usual dinner time, Odelia. Hope you don't mind." He bent down and playfully roughed up the dog around his ears and head. Wainwright was in doggie heaven.

"Zee and Seth are here, too. And there's always plenty."

Dev stopped playing with the dog and straightened. "I'm sorry, I don't want to intrude on guests. And I think the Washingtons may have had their fill of me today."

"Zee and Seth aren't guests, Dev. Like you, they're family." I lowered my voice for my next comment. "But as far as discussing the murder goes, let's see how they feel before mentioning it. Let them lead the way."

He nodded in agreement and winked at me. "Anything for a good meal."

I hooked an arm through one of his and tugged him toward the patio. "Hope you like grilled salmon."

"Love it."

Seth and Zee joined Greg in welcoming Dev to our dinner table. Dev declined a beer in favor of iced tea. When I returned to the patio after fetching an extra place setting, the topic of Shirley Pearson's murder was in full swing, with Seth pumping Dev for information. So much for tiptoeing around the Washingtons.

"We don't have much information on it yet," Dev told us between bites of food. "We're working through the guest list, questioning folks."

Zee groaned but said nothing.

"We're also talking to everyone who worked the wedding or at the club or with Ms. Pearson."

"Shirley owned the wedding planning service," Zee volunteered. "It was called Rambling Rose. They handled anniversary and special occasion parties, too."

Dev nodded. "We know she had an assistant. Not sure of any other employees yet."

"Amber Straight," Zee said. "That was her assistant's name, I believe. At least that's who we spoke to when we couldn't reach

Shirley directly. I think it was just the two of them. It was a small but well-respected operation."

"Who referred you to it?" asked Dev.

"Kay Lorraine, a friend of Hannah's, used Rambling Rose for her wedding. Hannah raved about how lovely it was, so when it came time for us to plan a wedding, we went straight to Shirley's company. Everything was perfect." Zee sighed and put down her fork. "Until . . . ," she trailed off.

"It *was* a perfect wedding, Zee," Seth assured her, placing a comforting arm around her shoulders. "In spite of everything." Zee smiled at her husband, but I could tell she wasn't convinced.

We fell silent for a few moments, eating quietly and enjoying the subtle ocean breeze from the beach a few blocks away from our Seal Beach home. Then Dev turned to me. "And how about you? How do you know Shirley Pearson?"

"I don't know Shirley," I answered, a bit surprised by the question. "I only just met her at the wedding. Greg and I didn't even go to the rehearsal dinner."

"We had a prior commitment with my parents," Greg added.

Zee shook her head. "I think you met her once before, Odelia. That time you came with me and Hannah to the bridal shop so Hannah could show you the dress she'd ordered. I think Shirley came into the shop while we were there."

I dug through my memory, replaying that day months before in my mind. "I think you're right. I only vaguely remember it, though."

"I'm not surprised," Zee added. "It was just a quick introduction, then we left."

Dev moved his eyes back and forth between Zee and me. "So you didn't know?"

"Know what?" I asked, going on alert. Zee had picked up her fork again, but it was now stopped halfway to her mouth as she waited for his response.

Dev cleared his throat but didn't speak. Everyone at the table was still, hanging in suspense.

"What is it, Dev?" Greg urged, his voice eager.

Finally, Dev wiped his mouth and made his announcement. "Shirley Pearson was a he — a man."

"No way!" Seth said loudly, his eyes wide with disbelief. He'd taken the words right out of my mouth and probably everyone else's.

"Are you sure?" I asked.

Dev looked straight at me to make his

point. "I think the coroner would notice a little something like that, don't you?"

Without thinking, I let loose with "Was it really that little, or did he pack it tight?"

Dev continued eating while the four of us snickered at my immature and tasteless remark. But in my defense, it did lighten the mood around the table.

"All that time I spent with her — him," Zee stumbled, "and I never noticed."

"Her," Dev corrected. "It appears Shirley Pearson was living her life as a woman and had been for quite some time."

Greg drained his beer. "Did she have a sex change?"

Shaking his head, Dev answered, "Not yet, but the coroner said it looked like the process was underway, at least hormonally."

With the rest of us still in shock, Dev took another bite of salmon, studying me while he chewed. Then he swallowed and took a long pull from his iced tea. "If you'd only met her that one time, Odelia, then why would she have your phone number? Did you give it to her at the wedding?"

"*My* number?" I pointed an index finger at my own chest in surprise.

"What's this all about, Dev?" asked Greg.

After wiping his mouth on a napkin, Dev reached inside his pants pocket and retrieved a folded piece of paper. He opened it to reveal a copy of a small handwritten note. He handed it to me to read. It was my name and cell phone number.

I looked up from the note. "What's this?"

"It's a note we found in the pocket of Shirley Pearson's skirt."

Greg took the note from my hands and read it.

I turned to Dev. "I know nothing about this, Dev. Shirley never said a word to me at the wedding."

I paused as a shard of remembrance knocked on my skull to come out. "Oh, wait." I held up a finger, giving pause until I could hook the memory and reel it in like a flopping fish. "There was one time, during the reception, Shirley came up to me and asked if I was Odelia Grey. Said the guest list had me down as Odelia Stevens but that my first name was so uncommon, she had to ask. She was about to say something else when someone called her away."

Dev leaned forward. "Do you remember who?"

I shook my head. "No. I only heard someone, a man, call Shirley's name. The next time I saw her, she was dead."

Zee held out her hand to Greg. He passed her the note, and she read it with Seth looking over her shoulder. "I don't think this is Shirley's handwriting."

"You sure, hon?" Seth asked.

"It's difficult to say because it's mostly numbers, but I'm almost positive. I saw Shirley jot down a lot of notes during the past several months, and I'm pretty sure this isn't her writing. Hers was smaller, more like printing than cursive."

She handed the note back to Dev after it had made a complete round of our redwood picnic table. Zee got up and went into the house. When she returned, she held her handbag and was rummaging through it.

"Great," she exclaimed upon pulling out a small notebook. From it she extracted a folded piece of paper, which she turned over to Dev. "This is a short list of things Shirley wrote down for me. Things I needed to remember for the rehearsal and wedding."

Dev held the list by its edges and looked it over. Zee stood at his side and pointed out several things. "See, her handwriting is much more concise than on that note. Even her letters are formed differently."

Dev nodded as he compared the list to the note found on Shirley's body. "Good work, Zee. They are totally different. May I take this list with me?"

"Of course." She returned to her seat next to Seth.

"What about the knife that killed the woman?" Greg asked.

"The knife belonged to the caterer," Dev told us. "We're processing it right now for prints. The owner of the catering company doesn't recall it missing or any of his staff being unaccounted for during the evening, but there was a lot going on. The knife was long and had been thrust in hard and deep, possibly wielded by a man or very strong woman. And there was little struggle on the victim's part. We believe she might have known her attacker and was taken by surprise. It looks like she was pinned against the storage containers, then slid down to the floor after the attack."

Greg looked at Dev with great interest. "You mean she might have gone into the cloakroom to meet whoever killed her?"

"Most likely. There was no sign of her being killed or wounded elsewhere, then being dragged into the room."

"Shirley couldn't have been dead long," I said. "When she spoke to me, it had been near the beginning of the dinner service."

"Do any of you recall seeing her after that?" Dev asked.

The four of us looked around the table,

each questioning ourselves silently about Shirley's whereabouts during the reception. All our faces were blank, then Zee spoke up. "The caterer came to me and asked about cutting the cake," she recalled. "I told him to find Shirley, but he said he hadn't been able to locate her. I didn't think much of it at the time and herded Hannah and Rob toward the wedding cake myself."

Dev finished eating and pulled his small notebook out of his pocket. He started writing down the information. "About how long was this after the dinner started?"

Zee shrugged. "About an hour, maybe a little more."

Seth shook his head. "More like an hour and a half to two hours. After dinner, the band started playing and people started dancing. The band had been playing awhile before the cake was cut. I remember because I wanted a piece of cake and had to wait."

Everyone at the table laughed except Seth. "Hey," he said, his brow furrowed. "If you knew what that damn cake cost me, you'd understand. I wanted to know what money tasted like." That brought more laughter.

"I feel your pain, Seth," Dev told him with a grin. "I married off a daughter myself."

"What about the photographer?" I asked. "It's a long shot, but maybe he caught something on camera." I turned to Zee. "Wasn't he taking both video and still shots?"

"Yes, he was doing both," answered Zee.

"The photographer is already cooperating," Dev assured us. "As is everyone else connected to the wedding we've contacted so far."

When I went inside to fix the strawberry shortcake, Dev offered to help. The others, sensing he had more questions for me, stayed on the patio.

"You're sure you can't think of anyone you know who might be connected to Shirley Pearson?" He rinsed off the dinner plates he'd brought in and started to put them in the dishwasher.

I stopped him. "Don't, Dev. I'll take care of the dishes later." I dropped a dollop of whipped cream onto a dish of fresh strawberries and sponge cake. "And yes, I'm sure. I can't for the life of me think of anyone who might give Shirley my number."

Later that night, when Greg and I were climbing into bed, I was still combing my tired brain for who could have given my cell number to Shirley Pearson.

"Quit worrying about it, sweetheart," Greg said, poking his nose over the top of his book. "You'll just drive yourself nuts. Not to mention the rest of us."

I settled in bed. Using one leg, I pushed Muffin out of my sleeping area so I could stretch out. It was a nightly ritual. Seamus was at Greg's feet. He was no dummy. With Greg paralyzed from the waist down from an accident as a young teen, the cranky cat could snooze undisturbed. Wainwright was settled on the rug at the foot of our bed. Everything and everyone was winding down for the night except for my thoughts.

"But I didn't know Shirley," I persisted.

"Or Steve or Sean or Bob," Greg teased. "Or whatever the hell her name used to be."

"Dev didn't tell me that, though I think he knew. He simply said they won't be able to confirm Shirley's legal name until her fingerprints come back."

"Whatever it is, it doesn't mean you didn't have acquaintances in common." Greg put down his book and took off his reading glasses. After turning out the light, he rolled to face me. "Now put that hornets' nest of a brain down for the night," he gently ordered as he planted a big goodnight kiss on my mouth. "With the police checking fingerprints, I'm sure whoever wrote that note will be revealed soon enough, and hopefully it will have nothing to do with

Shirley's death. That way, it will have nothing to do with you."

I kissed him back and turned over. Scooting back against Greg, I settled my body into his in a classic spoon position. He wrapped an arm around my waist and fell asleep instantly. I listened to the soft and not-so-soft sleeping sounds of my little family and wished my brain had an on/off switch.

THREE

Two days later, when Dev Frye showed up at my office, the mystery was still driving me nuts. Not the issue of who killed Shirley Pearson — although that was on my mind, too — but I was still racking my brain over the identity of who could have given her my number. It gnawed at me like an army of hungry termites.

Dev had called me around four o'clock, asking if I had time to meet with him to discuss some new developments in Shirley's murder. I found that odd; usually I have to pull information out of Dev. Then it occurred to me that he probably knew who had written the note.

"What time's good for you?" I'd asked him. Pulling up my Outlook calendar on the computer, I noted a meeting scheduled in thirty minutes with my supervising attorney Michael Steele, obnoxious pain-in-the-ass extraordinaire.

41

I am a paralegal for the law firm of Wallace, Boer, Brown and Yates, or Woobie as both its fans and not-so-fans refer to it. It's a medium-sized law firm in a high-rise office building near South Coast Plaza, one of the largest malls in the country. I've worked there since God wore short pants, and it was at Woobie that I first met Zee Washington. She'd been a secretary there years ago when Seth was starting his own practice and Hannah was just a toddler. *Wow,* I thought, remembering that bit of history. A few days ago, murder or no murder, Hannah, now a beautiful young woman, had gotten married. Time flies when you're not paying attention to details.

"Now," Dev said, his tone blunt and demanding. "I'm just pulling into the parking garage next to your building. I'll see you in a minute." The call ended.

I quickly tidied my desk, then thought it a lost cause. One of our clients was currently in the midst of a major and messy acquisition, and there were at least a dozen boxes of due diligence documents stacked in my office, some with files spilling from them in a lava flow of paper. Then there was the confidentiality issue of client documents being visible to an outsider, even though that outsider was a cop.

Recently the firm had moved me into a different office. The move had been both a blessing and a curse. While my new office was larger and had a window, it was next door to Steele's office. My other office had been down the hall. Some days it felt like Steele was in my office more than his own. There was also more room to store and spread out the documents I needed, but that meant a less shipshape office — and, again, more reason for Steele to be in here. He treated my office as an annex to his own. It was just a matter of time before he installed his own hi-tech desk chair.

I made a quick call to our receptionist and asked about the availability of a conference room. Joyce advised me that the small one a few doors down from my office was free. Damn. That also meant it was just a few doors down from Steele's office. I asked about the others, any of the others, but she said they were all occupied. If Steele saw me talking with Dev Frye, he'd decide it was his business to find out what it was about.

I grabbed my purse and headed for the lobby, nodding politely at colleagues along the way. I would cut Dev off and take him back downstairs to the small coffee shop on the ground floor of the building next door.

Dev was just getting out of the elevator when I corralled him.

"I'd rather talk here, Odelia," he told me. "It's more private."

Humph. Not when there's a prying attorney trolling the halls. But I gave in and told Joyce we'd be taking the small conference room after all. The problem with our conference rooms is that they all have floor-to-ceiling glass windows looking out to the hallway. Only one was completely closed in, and that one was upstairs and unavailable. I glanced at my watch. At this moment, Steele was on a conference call concerning the boxes of documents in my office. With luck, I could get Dev in and out before Steele freed up from the call and came looking for me for our meeting.

I showed Dev into the conference room and waved him into a nearby leather chair the color of ash. I shut the door as I addressed him. "Will this visit be a nice surprise or a not-so-nice surprise?"

"Hmmm, not sure." Dev ran a meaty hand over his heavy face. Dev Frye is a very large man, standing well over six feet and built like a linebacker. His voice is gravelly and deep, his short, curly hair more gray now than blond. "But it will definitely be a surprise," he added, raising a brow at me.

44

"More so than Shirley Pearson being a man?"

"Could be."

I stared at him, wondering what news could top what he'd spilled before.

Dev leaned back in his chair. "You have anything to drink, Odelia? It's hotter than hell out, and I'm parched."

I went to the small refrigerator built under the counter on the far end of the room and pulled out a can of soda for Dev. I knew how he took his poison — diet and full of caffeine. "Or would you rather have a bottle of water? We have both sparkling and still."

He reached out a hand for the soda. "Perfect. Thanks."

I grabbed one for myself and sat down opposite him. We popped the tops on the cans in harmony and took sips before Dev started.

"We got two sets of fingerprints off the note Shirley had in her pocket addressed to you and the list Zee gave me. One set of prints was common to both."

I laughed. "Not Zee's, I hope."

Dev showed a small smile. "No, not Zee's. Hers were only on the rehearsal list, which we expected." He adjusted his big body in the chair. "Shirley Pearson's prints were common to both, which we also expected.

And, by the way, Shirley Pearson used to be Doug or Douglas Pearson, that's been confirmed."

"Doug," I repeated, trying on the name. "I thought when people changed genders they usually chose a name that sounded like their original one — like Doug would be Donna or Dottie or something like that. You know, how Chastity Bono became Chaz Bono."

"Not sure there are hard rules about such things, Odelia," Dev grinned.

"Humph," I shot at him for his sarcasm. "So what was unexpected?" I motioned with my hand for him to keep it rolling while I kept an eye out for Steele.

"We had two big surprises," Dev continued, again smiling. He'd met Steele on many occasions and fully understood my lookout for my obnoxious boss. "Three, if you count Shirley Pearson not really being a woman. Seems Doug Pearson disappeared about fourteen years ago after being involved in a rather large armed bank robbery in Minnesota."

"What?" I nearly shouted the word at him.

Unfazed, he nodded. "There's more. A couple of years after disappearing, a body identified as Doug Pearson was found in a burned-out building following a gas explosion."

As much as I tried to wrap my brain around what Dev was telling me, it wasn't making sense. "Then how could Shirley's prints be his?"

"We're ordering dental records on Doug Pearson right now to make sure, but I'm guessing that Doug Pearson's death was staged. Then he came to California and began life as a woman named Shirley Pearson."

"But there was a body, correct?"

"Yep, at least according to the PD back in Minnesota. I've been on the phone with them all morning."

"So who was buried as Doug Pearson?"

Dev shrugged. "Dunno. But he wasn't buried. He was cremated — or what was left of him anyway. His ashes were scattered by his family somewhere."

"And what about the bank robbery? Did he act alone?"

"According to the Minnesota police, there were three people involved that they know of, but during the heist only Pearson was caught on the security camera. So far, none of the others have been identified, and the money was never found." Dev was feeding me information piecemeal, letting me connect my own dots. "Pearson was only about twenty or twenty-one at the time."

I shook my head in wonder. "How convenient is that? The cremation, I mean."

He laughed lightly. "How convenient, indeed. But that's not all." He leaned forward, resting his arms on the edge of the conference table. "Now we get to the part that involves you."

"Should I be worried?"

"Difficult to say, but I don't think so." He gave off a short laugh that sounded more like a cover to a small belch. "Who is Roslyn Beckworth?"

Like playing roulette, I rolled the name around the wheel of my brain, hoping it would stop on a winning number. "Roslyn Beckworth," I repeated, hoping it would snag on a hangnail of memory. "Sorry, Dev, I've got nothing. Should I know her?"

"It was Roslyn's prints on the paper with your phone number."

Rubbing a hand over my brow, I dug back into my memory, searching for a Roslyn Beckworth. Any Roslyn. Or any Beckworth. Again, I came up empty. I shook my head at Dev. "Still nothing. Anything more you can tell me?"

"Besides the fact that she's dead?" The words came out of Dev's mouth as dull as flattened cardboard.

"Dead?" My jaw nearly hit the conference table. "You mean since Saturday?"

"I mean for the past six years. Died in a car accident just outside of Chicago. Car was incinerated. So was the body."

"What?" I popped out of the chair as if it had zinged my heinie. "How in the world could a dead woman give out my phone number? And why would a dead woman have it in the first place?"

Dev shrugged and took another drink of his soda before responding. "Just as Pearson faked his death, so did Roslyn Beckworth. And from this evidence, she's alive and living in Southern California — although, unlike Pearson, she doesn't appear to have a criminal record. Her prints showed up because she once did some part-time security work for the University of Chicago back when she was a student. Probably a work-study situation."

I paced the length of the conference room. It wasn't very long, and I covered it in just under three strides. Reaching the end, I made a return trip. After another loop, I stopped once more in front of Dev and clutched the back of the chair I had been sitting in. "I still don't understand what this woman has to do with me, dead or alive." I spun the chair around, plunked down, and swiveled back to face Dev. "What more can you tell me about her?"

Pulling his little notebook from his suit pocket, he read off some details. "Beckworth would be about 33 or 34 by now. African-American, 5 foot 7, weighing about 135 pounds. Of course, the weight thing could have changed one way or another by now."

I ran down the very short list of women I knew who might fit that description, but I had known each of them more than six years, which put them in the clear. "Any idea why she took off?"

"Not yet. We're having trouble finding her family. I don't think she was from Chicago originally. We have calls into the university to check records or see if anyone remembers her, but so far we haven't been able to reach anyone. I've also put out a call to the Chicago PD."

"Wow," I muttered softly.

"It's interesting, for sure." Dev took another pull from his soda and put the can down on the table with a decided *clunk*. "But that's not your problem. I didn't come here to get you involved. I only wanted to know if you knew anything about this Beckworth woman."

I shook my head again. "Nothing. I can't imagine how she'd know me or why she'd give my number to Shirley Pearson."

Just then, a movement in the hallway caught my eye. I turned to look out the window to see Mike Steele standing just outside the conference room, arms crossed over his chest, observing us. In dealing with the living dead, I had totally forgotten to be on the alert.

Mike Steele had just turned forty. He's about six feet tall, slim, and athletic. Generally, his appearance is impeccable, but this afternoon the shirt sleeves of his light blue dress shirt were turned halfway up to his elbows, his tie was askew, his hair was limp, and his handsome face was showing signs of an early five o'clock shadow. He'd arrived at work this morning looking like a model straight out of a gentlemen's fancy clothing catalog, but the current deal was running him ragged, and it showed. His weary face was blank as his gaze moved between Dev and me. Dev noticed him, too.

"Can he read lips?" Dev asked.

"Wouldn't be surprised," I told him. "I'm also convinced he has some sort of unnatural radar. He always senses when I'm doing something non-work related."

51

Dev waved for Steele to come in and join us.

"Don't do that," I snapped. "It just encourages him."

"If I don't, he'll barge in anyway, won't he? So why not be gracious about it?"

I couldn't argue with that logic. Mike Steele, a partner at Woobie, believed nothing was private if it happened within the walls of the law firm, especially if it had to do with me.

"I hope I'm not disturbing you two," Steele said as he came into the conference room and closed the door behind him.

"That's exactly what you were hoping to do." I gave him a mild snarl. "So drop the act. Dev knows you too well."

Steele tossed a smirk my way, then held out his right hand to Dev. "Nice to see you again, Dev."

"Always an interesting pleasure, Mike." Dev completed the shake.

"So," Steele began as he settled into the chair next to mine and leaned back in cocky comfort. "Who's the stiff, and how is Grey involved this time?"

I looked at my boss and scowled. "Dev and I are friends. Can't he visit me without there being a murder involved?"

"Of course he can, Grey." Steele fixed me

with a slow smile. "But if this were simply a friendly visit, it would be over lunch or at your house with Greg firing up steaks on the grill. Not in a private conference room."

"Impressive." Dev drained the remainder of his soda in admiration. "Maybe you should have been a detective."

"Lawyers *are* detectives," Steele shot back with a grin. "Just paid better."

Dev looked around, unfazed by Steele's rude comment. "Nicer digs, too."

"He's just showing off," I said to Dev.

"He's good at it," Dev replied with a chuckle.

I turned to Steele. "As you pointed out, this is a *private* discussion."

Steele made no move to leave. He looked back at Dev. "If you're here in an official capacity, Detective, then Grey should have an attorney present." I couldn't tell if he was joking or serious.

"She's not a suspect in anything, Mike. I'm just asking her a few questions about the murder at the Washington wedding."

"The *what* at the *where?*" Steele's eyes popped out of his head like side by side turkey timers, and his weariness was replaced with keen interest.

Dev looked just as astonished as he turned to me. "He doesn't know?"

I shrugged. "Steele was in Cabo until the night before last." I shot a glance at my boss, whose womanizing was legendary. "Twenty-something lingerie model, wasn't she?"

Sitting straight as a lamp post, Steele ignored my dig and addressed Dev. "Are you talking about the wedding of Seth and Zee Washington's daughter?"

"The same," Dev told him, pointing in my direction like a tattletale. "Odelia here found a corpse in the cloakroom."

Steele stared at me like I'd just slapped his momma.

"Don't look at me that way," I demanded. "Zee was with me when I found the body. It's not like I killed the woman and planted her there for laughs."

Once Steele realized the body in the cloakroom wasn't a joke, there was no way Dev and I could get rid of him. And his presence wasn't just to protect my legal interests. Over the past few years, Steele had become morbidly fascinated by my ability to ferret out dead bodies. To him, it was just another positive tick on my résumé — a bullet point listed under *Other Interests.*

"How do you do it?" he asked me with genuine awe after learning the gory details.

I shrugged. "You know how some people

always manage to step in dog poop even if there's only one pile of poop within a one-mile radius?" I paused. "Well, that's me. If there's a dead body within a one-mile radius, somehow I'll find it, whether I want to or not." When neither man responded, I added, "What can I say, it's a gift. At least Zee's beginning to think that way."

"Zee?" Dev looked at me in disbelief. "The same Zee whose daughter's wedding was the scene of a murder?"

"Yes," I told him, wearing my attitude like bright orange lipstick. "That Zee. She told me Sunday right before you showed up at my house that she's beginning to wonder if it's my destiny, my calling, to help people through these murders."

Steele let out a groan that nearly shook the glass walls. "Now I've heard everything."

I swiveled in my chair to face my boss. "May I remind you, Mr. Steele, that I saved your arrogant behind a while back by getting involved with a murder."

It took Steele, a quick study, a full nanosecond to consider and digest that little tidbit. He turned to Dev. "I can't argue with the truth, Dev. She's got a gift, or maybe a helpful curse."

Dev inhaled, then blew it out. "Helping people by solving murders is *my* job, Odelia.

Yours is to answer my questions so I can do my job."

"I was just telling you what Zee said."

"And I'm telling you that one day your luck is going to run out. One day it won't be a bullet in your ass but a bullet in your chest or one to your brain."

My nose twitched at hearing the ugly possibilities. It was true. I had been shot in the ass. And I've had more guns pointed at me than a bakery has cupcakes.

I've heard that many women going through childbirth swear they will never have another baby as long as they live. Then time passes, and they forget about the pain. They look at the cute little buggers they already have and decide pushing out another might not be so bad.

That's called denial.

I guess it's the same with me and sticking my nose where it doesn't belong. After I've been shot, threatened, kidnapped, or nearly burned to death, I swear I'll never get involved with another murder again. Then someone dies and someone else says they need my help. I look back on my past death flirtations and think, this time it won't be so bad. This time it will be different.

That's called denial on performance-enhancing drugs.

FOUR

"Okay," Steele said to me, "now that we've dealt with your little problem, can we talk about mine, which isn't so little?"

We were in Steele's office, having just finished up with Dev and sent him on his way.

"Someone's death is a *little* problem to you?" I plopped down in a chair across from Steele's modern chrome and black lacquer desk.

Steele is usually obsessive about keeping his office clean. Most of the clutter for his cases is kept in my office or in his secretary's area. But this current case was different. Steele's desktop was nearly obliterated by files and binders and documents pertaining to the acquisition, which at various points in its history threatened to collapse in a heap of dead trees due to bickering by the parties involved.

"At the risk of sounding more callous than

usual, yes. At least if it doesn't pertain to this matter." Steele tapped one of the folders on his desktop. "As much as I find your Miss Marple act amusing, I need you, *all* of you, focused on this right now."

"I thought the deal was finally on track. How did your conference call go?"

"The seller's counsel is an idiot, that's how it went." He picked up a pen from his desk, fiddled with it, then tossed it back down in disgust.

I smoothed a hand over the wrinkles in my plum-colored skirt and frowned at a couple of spots near the hem caused by a coffee dribble this morning. "I've always thought Lori Ogle to be both knowledgeable and professional."

From the way Steele glared at me, you'd have thought I'd suggested he start buying his suits from Target. Without responding, he strode to the window and put his hands on his hips. For a long time, Steele stared down at the traffic below. If the window had been capable of being opened, I would have worried about him jumping.

I tried again, this time with more tact. "Seriously, Steele, Lori Ogle and her clients have delivered every document we've requested. You've finally come to terms for the sale agreement. What's the problem now?"

Without turning around, Steele raise his right hand in the air and shook it, signaling for me to shut up. At least he wasn't flipping me the bird.

"Who got his panties in a bunch?" a voice asked. I turned around to see Steele's assistant, Jill Bernelli, coming in with a stack of late mail, which she placed in Steele's in-box.

Jill is the first assistant Steele has been able to hang on to for more than a few months — and the first one for which there wasn't an office pool started on how long she would last. I'd won fifty dollars several secretaries back. Jill seems to be here for the long haul, and the entire firm couldn't be happier. She's smart, extremely competent, and totally calls Steele on his shit. She's also the partner of Sally Kipman, a high-school classmate of mine. And if that wasn't enough, Jill can bake like it's nobody's business. This morning, she'd brought in lemon–poppy seed muffins.

"Lori Ogle," I told her.

"Lori?" Jill was surprised. She ran a hand through her dark brown pixie cut, pushing her bangs out of the way. "She's a doll. Both she and her secretary."

I glanced at Steele. He was still facing the window, but I could see his shoulders bunch under his shirt as if he were lifting weights.

"I think," Jill continued, "she's one of the nicest attorneys we've ever worked opposite of on a deal."

Steele spun around. "Keep it up, Bernelli, and you'll be asking Ogle for a job."

"Oh, please." Jill shot Steele a coy smirk. "You know you'd miss my orange-cranberry scones too much to fire me."

I piped up. "I know *I* would."

Steele glared at me. I glared back. I knew he always ate at least three when Jill brought them in.

"Both of you," Steele snapped as he headed back to his desk, "out of here."

I didn't budge. "But I thought you wanted to talk to me about your conference call. We had a meeting scheduled."

"Out," he ordered again, with more force. "And shut the door."

"Wow," Jill said as she shut Steele's door. "He's crankier than usual. How is that possible?" She went to her desk, and I followed.

"I wonder what happened during the conference call?" I looked at Jill. "You have any idea?"

"I'm as puzzled as you are. I thought the deal was finally on smooth sailing and go-

60

ing to close. At least it sounded like it."

"Did you hear the call?"

Jill scrunched her brows in thought. "He buzzed me into his office near the end of it to make some copies, and the call sounded pretty jovial to me — almost celebratory. It sounded the same way when I returned a minute later with the copies."

"He wasn't arguing with Lori over something?"

"Quite the contrary. He was pouring on the Michael Steele charm for all it was worth." Jill turned serious. "Could it have been your meeting with Dev Frye that turned him around? I saw you in the conference room."

"I don't think so. If anything, that meeting seemed to act as a temporary diversion for whatever was on his mind."

As I walked back into my office, I tried to think of what could have made Steele behave snarkier than usual, especially when he hadn't been that way with Dev and me in our meeting. Excuse me — *my* meeting, which he'd crashed. And according to Jill, he hadn't been that way during his conference call.

I threw up my hands in disgust. Just what I needed right now, a schizo boss. It would go nicely with dead women giving out my phone number.

Unable to get Steele's behavior out of my head, I rewound the last twenty minutes in my memory. *Let's see, we went back to Steele's office and started talking about the acquisition. That's when the change occurred. But Jill thought his call had gone very well.* I was about to sit down when an idea struck me. Turning, I set my high heels back the way they'd come, toward Jill's desk.

"Have you ever met Lori Ogle?" I asked her.

"Nope. I've only spoken to her on the phone. You?"

"Same here."

Before I could say anything more, Jill's fingers were busy with her mouse and keyboard. She'd read my mind.

"Here she is," announced Jill.

She'd brought up the website for Lori Ogle's firm, Templin and Tobin, a very large law firm headquartered in Los Angeles. With a few clicks, Jill had located the firm's attorney bios and found Lori.

"You don't think he's slept with her, do you?" Jill asked, her voice poised to sound disgusted should the need arise. "Or maybe she's an old girlfriend?"

"No, I don't. Steele just met her for the first time on this deal, and he would never

62

poach on client time." I looked at Jill. "He may not have many ethics when it comes to women, but when it comes to the law and his clients, he gives 150 percent."

Staring back at us from the computer screen was a lovely and engaging woman probably in her mid to late thirties. Lori Ogle had long, shiny dark hair, a perfect nose, and flawless olive skin. In the photo, she was wearing a creamy white shell under a dark collarless jacket. The pieces of jewelry at her ears and neck were understated and elegant. But it was her luminous dark eyes and strong chin that captured my attention. They spoke volumes of confidence and accomplishment. Lori Ogle was very beautiful, but she was no idle plaything.

"Look here." Jill pointed at a spot on Lori's bio. "She runs triathlons for charity."

Quickly, I scanned the bio. The education and list of achievements were over-the-top impressive, rounded out by a great deal of charity involvement, both local and international. Reading it, I was ready to campaign for her in the next presidential election.

"No," I said, my green eyes latching on to Jill's brown ones in impish delight. "Steele hasn't slept with her, but dollars to donuts it's on his mind — and more dollars to donuts he's scared silly of her."

"Scared? Mike Steele?"

I chuckled. "Yes, scared. This woman is his perfect match, at least on paper, and he knows it. And he knows if he starts anything with her, he'd better be prepared to take it all the way."

We both turned back toward the computer screen and studied Lori's photo.

"I do believe, Jill, our Mr. Steele may be falling in love — or at least age-appropriate lust."

Jill chuckled. "I want a ringside seat for this."

FIVE

"No, Sally, I don't need your help. This doesn't involve me."

I had just arrived home and was kicking off my heels when my cell phone rang. It was Sally Kipman. Jill had told her that Dev Frye had been in to see me, and Sally had made the same assumption Steele had — that a dead body was involved. Ever since she and I had teamed up a few years before to solve the murder of a high-school classmate, Sally, an engineer, had been itching to get back into the sleuth game. In high school, Sally Kipman had been my nemesis. After our partnership in crime solving, we'd become good friends. Maybe *she* should be the one with the special gift and not me. I'd gladly sign whatever documents were needed to make the transfer.

"Ah, but Odelia," Sally said over the phone. "Somehow, someway, it will end up involving you. I just know it."

I was thankful I hadn't given Jill any details. She only knew that Dev had come calling. I'd just given Sally a thumbnail sketch.

"I didn't know Shirley Pearson," I assured Sally as I dodged the two cats trying to trip me in welcome. "Her being killed at Hannah's wedding was a fluke, a nasty coincidence."

"Uh-huh." Sally didn't sound convinced.

Our doorbell rang, followed by a soft knock on the screen door. Greg worked out a couple evenings a week at a gym with special facilities for men and women in wheelchairs, but on Wednesdays he met with his personal trainer and got home later. Wainwright, as usual, was with Greg.

"Believe what you want," I told her as I headed for the door. "Someone's at the door, Sal, gotta run."

"Keep me posted," Sally called out as I shut the phone.

Looking out the front window, I saw a woman standing on my doorstep. She wore a floppy straw hat. I opened the door half-way.

"Yes?" I asked, keeping the screen door latched.

"Odelia Grey?"

"Do I know you?"

66

"I'm a ghost from the past, Odelia." The woman took off her sunglasses and pushed the hat back a few inches. "It's me, Clarice Hollowell."

For the umpteenth time in one day, I was slack-jawed.

"May I come in, Odelia," the woman at my door asked with clipped superiority, "or have you gone stupid with shock?"

If I had any foggy remembrances of Clarice Hollowell, they now became crystal clear. While she looked different, her signature sarcasm had been burned into my brain like a brand. With reluctance, I unlocked the screen door and let her in, wondering what fresh pile of poop this was about.

I showed her into the living room, where she took a seat on the sofa and removed her hat, placing it on the cushion beside her. Without speaking, she put her sunglasses carefully away in a case inside her designer straw bag and set the bag next to her hat. Then she looked around my home, studying and observing everything within her gaze. The stalling movements told me I was in for another humdinger of a time with Clarice Hollowell. We'd recently bought a large sectional sofa. I took a seat on the smaller L-section. For a few minutes, we simply stared at each other, absorbing and measuring the vibes each sent out.

When I'd first met Clarice, she was a skeletal-thin, chain-smoking boozehound, disappointed by life and pissed off. She also had bobbed jet-black hair. Today her hair reminded me of a ribbon of sage honey, the way it looks when you try to pour the thick, gooey stuff from the jar instead of spooning it out. She wore it down to her shoulders, held back from her face by a thin headband. Doing the math in my head, I realized Clarice had to be approaching the sixty hurdle, if not having recently scaled it. She looked fabulous. During the years since our last meeting, her body had filled out. She was still slim, but not concentration-camp thin. The few extra pounds had also softened her face. Even her eyes were less flinty. She still dressed expensively, but she didn't smell of cigarettes. Maybe she'd stopped smoking. Or maybe not being married to John Hollowell had brought about these positive changes.

"You're married now," Clarice observed, her eyes resting on a large wedding photo on a nearby table.

"Yes. In fact, my husband and I met when Sophie London died. He was a friend of hers."

"Interesting." Clarice raised one crescent-shaped eyebrow. "Was he the same type of *friend* to the fat slut as my husband?"

I felt my eyes cross in growing anger. John Hollowell had had a penchant for bedding and taking advantage of plump women. He'd even tried to woo me. The years and a few pounds might have softened Clarice's appearance but not her acidic tongue.

"Greg was a true friend to Sophie," I informed her, my voice laced with warning. "He's nothing like John Hollowell."

A sardonic smile passed her lips. "Well, goodie for you, my dear." At this point, the old Clarice would have taken a drag from her cigarette and blown smoke my way.

"How did you find my home address, if I may ask?"

"You're not the only one who can dig for information." She tossed me a shrewd wink. "I found the guest list for the Washington wedding at the Rambling Rose office. I'm a silent partner in the business. You and your husband were on it, with your address."

Muffin jumped up on the sofa and tried to get chummy with Clarice. After a slight hesitation, Clarice reached out a hand and stroked the animal behind her ears. Muffin purred. The gesture surprised me. I would have bet Clarice would have shoved the cat away or demanded that I remove it. Seamus, always leery of strangers, was watching everything from under the buffet. A part of me wanted to join him.

"That's how I discovered you in the first place, you know, through Shirley Pearson," Clarice continued. "I dropped her off several months ago at a bridal boutique and saw you there with a short, round black woman and her daughter. I asked Shirley later who you were, and she confirmed your name." Another tight smile crossed her face. "She didn't remember your last name, but there are not many women named Odelia running around Orange County."

In spite of her innate rudeness, my manners yanked at my conscience. "Can I get you something, Clarice? Some iced tea, maybe? I'm afraid I'm fresh out of martinis."

She emitted a short, static laugh. "I gave up drinking right after I last saw you. But some cold water would be nice. No ice."

Going to the kitchen, I pulled a pitcher of filtered water from the fridge and poured it into a tall glass. When I handed it to her, she thanked me and drank like a thirsty camel, downing nearly half the glass before coming up for air.

"I've been out front waiting for you for a long time," she explained, sounding like she expected an apology.

Since she was dilly-dallying, I got down to the business that now inhabited my mind. "The police found my number on a slip of paper in Shirley's pocket when she died. Besides Shirley's fingerprints, it had prints belonging to a Roslyn Beckworth. Are you the one who gave Roslyn Beckworth my phone number?"

If Clarice was surprised by my question, she didn't show it. "Yes. I gave it to her to pass along to Shirley. Roslyn helped out sometimes at Rambling Rose, especially when Shirley took Amber, our assistant, into the field. I called the office a few weeks ago and Roslyn took the message. You might recall you gave the number to me when we last spoke several years ago. I'd kept it tucked away in my address book. Not sure why, but now I'm glad I did."

Clarice studied the flat-screen TV on the wall across from the sofa as if she were watching a movie. "So the police don't know anything about me?" She asked the question without looking my way.

"Not that I know of. Should they?" I leaned forward in my chair, remembering that Dev's theory included how Shirley knew her attacker. "Clarice, did *you* kill Shirley?"

She looked horrified and flashed her eyes

at me. "Of course not. Shirley was my friend."

"Friends have killed friends before." I thought about Zee trying to club me with the coat hanger. "It could have been an accident or done in a moment of rage."

"No," Clarice said, leaning forward herself until our faces were about a foot apart. "I did not kill Shirley. It could have been someone from her past."

I straightened myself in my chair. I didn't trust Clarice, but I was curious about exactly how close she was to Shirley. "Yes. I was told Shirley took part in a bank robbery years ago. She was known as Doug Pearson then, correct?"

Finally, a look of surprise crossed Clarice's face, then it quickly faded to bland. "So, you know about that, do you?"

I wasn't sure if she was asking if I knew about the bank robbery or about Shirley once being a man named Doug. I decided to assume she meant both.

"The cop who questioned me about my phone number being found on Shirley told me her name was really Doug Pearson, a man connected with a bank robbery in Minnesota years ago. I was also told that Doug Pearson died and was cremated."

"Once again, Odelia, you surprise me with

how much you know about things that are supposed to be private." Clarice took another drink of her water — a smaller, more dainty one this time.

"What can I say? The cop was chatty." I'd decided to leave Dev Frye's name out of the conversation. No need to alert Clarice that I was close to the detective on the case. She could find out on her own or when I was ready to tell her. She wasn't the only one who could play coy.

Ignoring my remark, Clarice continued, "Doug was Shirley's real name, but she hadn't used it in years, not since her death was faked." Clarice paused. "Her first death, that is."

"Had you known her a long time?"

Clarice nodded while she examined her perfect fingernails. "Yes, we met at a charity event about ten years ago and became good friends. She was working for an event-planning company, with dreams of having her own. I've never known her as Doug. To me, she was always Shirley, though I did realize soon after we met that she was really a man — a man who desperately wanted to be a woman."

I fought to hide my surprise. I'd never figured Clarice as being the open-minded type. But she'd met a woman who'd turned out to be a man and seemed to have accepted it with no problem. Maybe she wasn't the uptight bitch I thought her to be. Maybe she was just a bitch.

"So who do you think killed her? Any ideas?"

"A couple," Clarice told me without looking up. "I think it was someone involved with the bank robbery."

"That's just one idea. How about a lover, past or present?"

"No," Clarice slowly moved her head back and forth as she spoke. "Shirley wasn't seeing anyone. She wanted to wait until after the medical procedure. She thought it might be less complicated."

I didn't see how letting that cat out of the bag to a future lover would be anything but a major complication, but I kept my mouth shut. First of all, Shirley would never get the chance. Secondly, it was none of my business.

"Are you sure there wasn't someone who wasn't happy with Shirley's decision to change gender?"

"Everyone who knew Shirley was very supportive of her, even encouraged her. I'm telling you, I think it was someone from that robbery. It's the only thing in Shirley's past that was shady."

"Did Shirley tell you who was in on the robbery with her?"

Clarice looked up at me. "No. But I did get the feeling they were still out there, and that was one of the reasons she staged her death all those years ago."

That, I thought, *and to throw the police off her scent.* Getting up, I walked across the wood floor in my stocking feet. I had a lot of questions and wanted to sort them out. "Who was the dead guy they cremated?"

"The what?"

I stopped and faced Clarice. "The dead guy. Back in Minnesota. A corpse was passed off as Doug Pearson and cremated. Who was the dead guy?"

She looked surprised by the question. "I have no idea." Clarice gave a slight shrug. "Probably some body they got from a local mortuary or coroner's office."

"Who are 'they'?" I set my eyes like laser beams on her face.

"They," she answered, "is whoever helped Shirley, I suppose." Clarice frowned, but her face was so tight hardly a line showed on her forehead, in spite of her intent. "That was a long time ago, Odelia, and I didn't know Shirley then. How in the hell am I supposed to know that?"

"Shirley never discussed it? Never got in

her cups and boo-hoo-hooed about it just between you girls?"

"Never."

"And she never *ever* talked about the others involved with the robbery?"

Clarice shook her head. This time she put more effort into it, making her hair move like a curtain in a soft breeze.

I didn't believe her for a minute.

"I was informed that the money taken in the bank robbery was never recovered. Did Shirley have it? Is that how she got away and started her new life?"

Clarice crossed one leg over the other, smoothing the skirt of her dress over her legs. "I have no idea what happened to that money, but I doubt Shirley had it — or, if she did, that she had any left. Otherwise, why would she need me to help finance Rambling Rose?"

She made a good point, but I still wasn't satisfied. "It seems Shirley was in the medical process of becoming a man. I've heard that's very expensive. Who was paying for that?"

"Maybe she did have some of the robbery money," Clarice answered, her voice starting to crack with annoyance. "And maybe she didn't. But if she did, don't you think she would have had the operation years ago?"

"Maybe."

Muffin had hopped off the sofa and was dogging my heels. I picked up the gray cat. No longer a kitten, Muffin was still small, especially next to Seamus. I held the animal in my arms and stroked her behind her ears. She purred with delight.

"But maybe not," I told Clarice. "It could have taken Shirley years to make a decision of that magnitude. A sex change operation isn't like buying a pair of shoes or a handbag. You can't return it if it doesn't match an outfit."

"Rambling Rose was doing very well, Odelia. Shirley could have saved the money. Even if she did have all or even some of the money from the bank, it probably cost Shirley a bundle to disappear and start a new life. She also couldn't have flashed money like that around without notice, at least not at first."

Clarice switched legs, uncrossing one and crossing the other. "But I didn't come here to talk to you about Shirley — at least not entirely."

I put Muffin down and took my seat again, waiting while Clarice struck a pose right out of a 1940s crime movie. All she needed was a cigarette, and she looked like she wanted one. A cigarette with a long, dramatic holder.

"I want to hire you, Odelia."

Well, shut my mouth. I wasn't expecting that. "Hire me? You need a corporate paralegal?"

"What I need is someone to do some nosing about, on the computer and off. You obviously have the nosiness down pat; the paralegal part will cover the rest."

"I have a job, Clarice. A steady job that I like."

"This isn't a job offer, Odelia. It's a one-time assignment. I need someone to find some friends with whom I've lost touch."

My mouth made the leap before my brain and common sense could stop it. "You want me to hunt people down so you can kill them?"

Clarice's face flushed like a ripe berry, and she popped up, taking her own spin around my living room floor. "I did not kill Shirley! In fact, she and I were going to hire you together."

Walking back to the sofa, Clarice plopped down on it in a very unladylike way and stared at me. To my surprise, there was something in her eyes I hadn't noticed before — concern, genuine and solid.

"Some people I know have disappeared, Odelia. Absolutely vanished. They're people Shirley and I both know . . . knew. One of them was Roslyn."

"They owe you money or something?"

"No, nothing like that. They have simply disappeared. Their homes are empty. Phones turned off. Gone." She snapped her fingers, the sharp sound causing Muffin to trot over to Clarice. "Just like that. We tried to find them but couldn't. Then I remembered spotting you at the bridal boutique. I thought maybe you could help."

"Have you tried Facebook?"

The scowl Clarice shot me could have frozen Niagara Falls.

I leaned back in my chair, regrouping from the chill. "I don't think so, Clarice. They probably just got a great and unexpected job offer and left in a hurry. I'm sure they'll turn up once they're settled."

"It's not like that, Odelia." She paused but never took her eyes off me. "I'll pay you five thousand dollars to locate them."

Yowza! Did I hear right? Five grand to track someone down? But the offer also made me more suspicious.

"Something's not kosher about this, Clarice." I got up from the chair and stood looking down at her, ready in case she did something stupid. "Five grand just to locate some old friends? And right after the death of another friend? Not to mention, I know Roslyn Beckworth also faked her death a few years back."

Another short flash of surprise flittered across Clarice's face, and again she recovered quickly. "Someone needs to stick a cork into that cop."

I ignored her comment. "What's really going on here?" I demanded.

When she didn't answer, I put my hands on my wide hips and narrowed my eyes at her, hoping to give her a dose of my own stubborn bitchiness.

Again, she remained silent.

I pushed. "You don't think it was the bank robbers who killed Shirley at all, do you?"

Clarice raised her face and threw out her hands. "It could have been them. They could have found her after all these years."

"Could have, yes," I told her. "But more likely, you and Shirley started digging around into something, and someone didn't like it. Something's telling me you hope it was the bank robbers."

Clarice set her jaw. "I have to find these people. I have to know what happened to them before the same happens to me."

"Before what?" I dropped back down into

my chair, confused. "Are you afraid Shirley's killer might come after you now? If it were the other bank robbers, they wouldn't know anything about you, would they?" I switched my voice into a more soothing tone. "You need to go to the police, Clarice. The sooner, the better. Whoever killed Shirley could have killed those friends of yours."

"No, I don't think so. But I do think they ran."

"Wait a minute," I said, pointing an index finger at her. "Are these friends of yours also on the run like Shirley and Roslyn? What did they do wrong?"

Clarice fixed me with another arctic stare. "People don't always need a legal reason to disappear, Odelia."

My head was about to explode. *On the run. Not on the run.* Clarice, seeing my confusion, produced a folded piece of paper from her purse and handed it to me. On it were scrawled a couple pairs of names, two on each line — two lines, four names.

"These people, Odelia, for one reason or another started their lives over, like Shirley, and in some ways like me. They re-created themselves. Now they've scattered to who knows where."

Like roaches, I thought, but kept it to myself.

81

I looked up from the list to Clarice. "Is there some sort of club you all belong to? 'People on the lam, meeting every other Thursday at the public library.' "

"Don't be so sarcastic, Odelia."

I rolled my eyes. "Coming from you, that's rich."

"These people are not running from the law," Clarice insisted. "At least, I'm not. And neither was Roslyn. I just didn't want to pick up my old life."

"I'm not buying that, Clarice. You had money and position. I understand you were even cleared of any suspicion about John's murder. Seems he was killed by an international hit man."

"I still have money and position, Odelia. I just choose now to live under the radar."

"Didn't you have a daughter from your first marriage? The one before John Hollowell?"

"Leave Jackie out of this," she snapped. "She knows nothing of my life, and I want it kept that way."

Clarice was definitely afraid of someone or something.

I studied the paper in my hand, going down the list of names.

"The name on the left is the name they use now," Clarice explained. "The name on the right is their old name."

I noted the first name. It was for a Roslyn Stevens, who used to be known as Roslyn Beckworth. "Stevens is my married name," I said to Clarice without looking up.

"I know, though I doubt you're related." The remark was wrapped with a sneer. "This is her new name."

"And what is the name *you* use now?" I asked.

"That's on a need-to-know basis, Odelia. And right now you're better off not knowing."

She was probably right about that.

"I could understand one of the people up and leaving in a hurry," Clarice told me, "but not all of them. Something or someone is scaring them off. I want to know who is behind it."

Or killing them off, but I kept that to myself, too. I ran my eyes up and down the list again. Something about it was bothering me. I absorbed the names one by one. The second name pricked my brain like a toothpick testing a cake. The name to the left was Alfonso Nunez. The name to the right was Alfred Nunez. The third name was Scott Joyce, who now went by Scott Johnson.

It was odd, I noted silently, how the

people didn't steer too far from their original names. Maybe it was an identity thing — something about not wanting to give it all up entirely. A need to retain some shred of their former selves.

"You know the approximate ages of these folks?" I raised my eyes from the paper to look at Clarice.

Clarice gave the question some thought before answering. "Roslyn is thirty-something. Al is somewhere in his sixties. Scott is somewhere in between — probably his forties."

"How about a photo?"

Clarice hesitated, her eyes scurrying up and down my face while she made up her mind about something. Finally, with a sigh of submission, she dug into her purse and produced a photo. It was taken at a party in someone's back yard. In the background was a swimming pool. There were close to a dozen people. Some were were seated, and others were standing around them. Most were hoisting glasses and beer bottles toward the camera and appeared happy and having fun. I spotted both Clarice and Shirley right off. They were seated in the front.

Clarice pointed to a very pretty African-American woman. "That's Roslyn Stevens.

On the far left is Scott Johnson." She moved her finger over one spot. "And that's Al."

I couldn't take my eyes off of Alfonso Nunez. I knew him, I was sure of it. Several years ago, I had attended his funeral — or rather, the funeral of an Alfred Nunez.

Six

"I'm sure of it, Greg."

We had just finished eating and were cleaning up. Over supper I'd filled Greg in on both Dev and Clarice's visits — and my suspicions about Alfred Nunez.

"One hundred percent sure?" Greg was putting the leftovers into plastic containers while I loaded our plates into the dishwasher.

I hemmed and hawed. "Okay, maybe 85 to 90 percent sure." I shook the serving spoon in my hand for emphasis. "I'm telling you, I went to that man's funeral."

"But did you ever meet him in person?"

"Yes, a couple of times when he came by Woobie to see Joan or take her to lunch."

After putting the spoon into the utensil holder in the washer, I wiped my hands on a kitchen towel and picked up the photo Clarice had left me. It was still on the kitchen table, where it had been the centerpiece of our dinner conversation.

I showed the photo to Greg again and poked a finger at Alfonso Nunez. "I'm telling you, Greg. This is Alfred Nunez, Joan's father."

Joan Nunez is another paralegal at Woobie. She's a quiet and serious woman who specializes in litigation. Joan's been with the firm just shy of ten years. A few years after she started working with us, her father, Alfred Nunez, was killed in a car accident. He'd gone off the cliff on a winding road during a trip to Northern California and plunged to his death. The car had gone up in flames. Joan had been inconsolable. Kelsey Cavendish, another coworker at Woobie, and I are very close to Joan and had attended the funeral to support our friend.

"What's more, now that I remember, the car fire had pretty much cremated the body." I paused to link some information together. "Just like the body used as a stand-in at Shirley Pearson's first funeral and the one in Roslyn's case."

"What about these other people?"

"Clarice didn't mention them at all. She was only concerned with these three."

Greg took the photo from my hand and placed it back on the table. "Sit down, sweetheart."

With a deep sigh, I put my butt in a chair at the kitchen table. Here it comes, Greg's "be reasonable" speech. It's never worked, but you have to give my hubs an A for effort and persistence.

"Say this *is* Joan's dad — have you thought about the effect this might have on Joan? All this time she's thought him dead, only to have you charge in and say he's not."

"I wasn't planning on charging in, Greg." My nose twitched.

"There is no easy way to announce news like this, Odelia. And what about Mr. Nunez? If this is him, he's gone to a great deal of trouble and caused a lot of pain to his family. Don't you think he might have had his reasons? It's not like he's had amnesia all this time. If he had, Clarice wouldn't know his real name."

"And there wouldn't have been a body," I pointed out.

"Exactly," Greg said, with too much enthusiasm for my taste.

"Makes you wonder who *did* die in that accident, doesn't it? And who was buried in place of Doug Pearson and Roslyn Beckworth years ago?" A horrible thought occurred to me. "Greg, you don't think *they're* murderers, do you? Could they have killed the people who took their places in death?"

Greg wheeled over to the fridge and started loading the plastic containers into it. "Who knows, sweetheart. It's quite a puzzle. But it does sound a lot like someone else we know."

The same thought had crossed my mind. "I know. It sounds like Willie, doesn't it?"

William Proctor had disappeared on a boat years ago after embezzling millions from his own investment company, causing thousands of people to lose their nest eggs. When his boat was destroyed by a storm, he had escaped. His wife's body had been found, but not Willie's. For years he'd been assumed dead, but I had stumbled upon him doing follow-up on a client's sudden death. Since then, he's become a good friend to Greg and me, even though he's still on the run from the law.

"But," I continued, "Willie didn't stage his death. There was no substitute body. There really was an accident, and he was presumed dead."

"But," Greg said, seeing my *but* and raising me one of his own, "Willie did build a new life for himself and gave himself a new identity."

Everything Greg was saying was true. I rolled it around, giving thought to all angles.

"Remember when Steele disappeared?" I asked.

"Of course. It was right before we got married."

"I went to Willie for some advice on finding Steele, and he told me it's actually quite easy for a person to start over if they know how to do it. They just need to find someone who can provide new ID like a driver's license, social security card, passport, even college degrees and backgrounds. He said the higher the price, the more believable the new identity."

Greg went silent, weighing the information. "Makes sense," he finally said. "And if Shirley had all that money she stole from the bank, she'd have the money to start over."

"Clarice disappeared into thin air during that blowup with John Hollowell. Maybe Shirley still had the right connections and helped Clarice." Picking up a stray dirty paper napkin, I tossed it into the trash under the sink and leaned back against the counter. "Besides these folks being friends, maybe Shirley is the one common denominator. Maybe she was the person who arranged the new lives."

Greg smiled. "Well, she helped couples begin new lives as a wedding planner."

"Do you think someone in hiding killed her, Greg? Maybe a disgruntled client?"

He shrugged. "Maybe it was a disgruntled bride or groom? Maybe the caterer or someone in the band thought they got a raw deal? Who knows, it might even be that one of the guests recognized her and held a grudge."

"And, as Clarice said, it could even be her partners in the robbery finally tracking her down after all this time." I scratched my head using all five digits. "Doesn't seem to be any end to possible suspects, does there?"

Greg rolled over to where I stood and grasped my hands in his. "We're getting off-track, sweetheart."

"What do you mean?"

"Clarice only asked us to look into those missing people, not into Shirley's murder."

"What's this *us* business? Clarice asked *me.* You don't need to get involved. You have enough on your plate with the shop." Greg owned Ocean Breeze Graphics and had opened a couple of satellite shops in Phoenix and Denver. Even in the current slow economy, his business was going strong.

"You don't need to get involved either. In spite of the beating we took in the market when the economy took a nosedive, we're doing fine. We don't need the five grand."

I sighed and tightened my grip on his warm, strong hands. "I was about to tell Clarice no when I saw Alfred Nunez's name on the list. If that is Joan's father, Greg, then I must get involved. And the money has nothing to do with it."

Greg looked up at me. I knew that look. It was determination, as solid as a mountain and just as unmovable. "Then this is a project for *us*. As I've told you before, if you won't give up poking your nose into dangerous business, then I'm tagging along."

I nodded in agreement. Whether my inclination toward finding murderers is a curse or a gift, it was much more enjoyable doing it with Greg by my side. Not to mention I felt safer.

"And," he continued, "I propose we only look into the disappearance of Alfred Nunez. If we find him and he is Joan's dad, we can decide then how to handle telling her. If we don't find him, I think we should let it slide and let Joan continue thinking he's dead. Those other people mean nothing to us, and we have no idea what Clarice Hollowell's agenda is in finding them."

My husband is not only handsome and sexy, he's smart.

"Sounds like a great plan." I planted a big

kiss on his mouth.

"So you'll say nothing to Joan?" Greg persisted.

"I promise I won't say a word until we're sure."

"Cross your heart?"

"You don't trust me?"

Greg laughed. "Trust is not the issue, sweetheart."

SEVEN

In my defense, it was never my intention to say a word to Joan about her father. It just popped out like the little critter in Whac-a-Mole, and Greg wasn't there with a mallet to stop me. But, as always, I had my reasons.

It was the Thursday after Hannah's wedding. My nose was buried in a box of documents. Additional documents had arrived from Lori Ogle's office via e-mail, and I'd spent the morning downloading, printing, and organizing them so that Steele and whatever young associates he could wrangle could review them. I had just sorted the last batch when Joan Nunez showed up at my office door. She'd approached so quietly I hadn't even realized she was there until she spoke.

"Can I talk to you, Odelia?" she'd asked.

Surprised, I dropped the stack of documents I had been holding into the box, the edges of the paper slicing into my palm on the way down. "Ow." I lifted my hand to my mouth and licked the thin but painful cut. "Sure," I mumbled.

"You okay?"

"Fine." I gave one last lick to the tiny spot of blood. "By the time this deal is done, I'm going to feel like I've been attacked by Edward Scissorhands."

Joan gave my joke a forced smile. She entered my office, closing the door behind her. While she took a seat in the chair across from my desk, I lifted the box I'd been working with and moved it from my desk to the floor so I could see her clearly when I took my own seat.

Joan is a petite woman in her early forties. She's very quiet and serious and rather on the plain, dowdy side. Mousy, some would say. She's also very conservative in demeanor and in her beliefs, and she has never been married. When she first came to Woobie, we all thought she was in her forties because of her mature appearance, so when her mother threw her a surprise fortieth birthday lunch a couple of years ago, we were rather shocked. Kelsey and I finally decided that Joan must have come out of the womb middle-aged.

Recently, at Kelsey's and my urging, Joan had colored her long graying hair and cut it into a stylish bob. We'd even managed to get her to use a little makeup. It had perked up her appearance considerably.

"What's up?" I asked Joan. The possibility that her father was still alive hummed in the back of my brain like a trapped hornet looking for a way out. I tried to distract it with a mundane question. "Did you have a good few days off?"

Joan looked down at her hands, then up at me. It was then I noticed how pale and haggard she appeared. I became alarmed.

"Are you all right, Joan?"

She wrung her hands in her lap. "I didn't take the last two days off as vacation, Odelia. We had a family emergency."

"I'm sorry to hear that. I hope it's not your mother?"

"My mother's fine, Odelia. Thank you." She paused, looking down again at her hands. "It's . . . it's my father."

My heart stopped, replaced by the buzzing in my brain. "Your father?" I asked, my words treading on thin ice. "I thought your father had passed away?"

"So had we." She swallowed hard, fighting back tears.

I handed her the tissue box parked next to my computer monitor and got up. "Be right back," I told her.

When I returned, I could see that Joan had been weeping. I handed her the large glass of water I'd retrieved from the office kitchen and resumed my place behind my desk.

"Are you sure you want to talk about it?" I asked her, hoping she did but willing to understand if she'd changed her mind about giving me the details.

She nodded. "Yes. I'm sure. In fact, I'm hoping you can help." She took a drink of water. "You see, Monday night we received a call from the Santa Ana police asking about my father. We told them he was deceased, and they asked if we would come to their station to answer a few questions. They said it was very important. My mother and I went there together on Tuesday. That's when they told us they'd found a man, a dead man, without any identification. They believe he was my father."

"And was it him?" Even as I asked the question, my gut told me the answer.

"Yes," Joan said, dissolving into tears again. "We identified the body."

"Where did they find him?" As soon as I asked the question, I realized I should have asked something more along the lines of *How is that possible?* I hoped Joan didn't pick up on the lack of surprise on my part.

"He was in an abandoned dumpster in an alley." She let out a short sob. "He'd been shot and left there — left there, Odelia, like a piece of garbage!" She took a gulp of water. "The police said he'd been dead over a week."

That was my cue for the question that should have been asked. "How is that possible? I remember going to his funeral."

Joan shrugged her small shoulders until they nearly hit her ears. "I don't know, Odelia. My mother is beside herself."

"I'm sure she is, the poor woman."

Shaking her head slowly, Joan said, "Not because of my father, but because she remarried several years ago. She's worried that she's been living in sin with my stepfather and is going to hell for it. Or that she's a bigamist and going to jail. The police tried to console her about the bigamist part, but God frightens her a lot more than the police. She and my stepfather are looking into the validity of their marriage. They may have to have another ceremony."

"Um, she's not upset about your father showing up dead for a second time?" My family is pretty screwed up, but this seemed odd even by our standards.

"Yes and no," Joan said with frankness. "My mom and dad didn't have the best

98

marriage. Far from it. Although she was upset when he died, or supposedly died, the first time, I think in many ways she felt relieved. She would never have sought a divorce, though I'm sure she would have liked one." Joan's cheeks turned pink. "I probably shouldn't say this about my own mother, but I think she would have been more upset if he'd turned up alive."

"And how do you feel about it?"

Joan dabbed at her eyes with a tissue. "My father wasn't perfect, but we were fairly close, and I missed him terribly after he died. You know that."

I nodded. Alfred's death had hit Joan hard, just as the death of my own father had left me reeling for quite a while.

"But I've had several years to adapt to the situation. Now I feel like I'm grieving all over again." She paused to blow her nose.

"Why are you here today, Joan? You should be home with your mother, not at the office."

"The last few days have nearly driven me insane. My mother hasn't told anyone else in the family about this yet, but I couldn't spend another moment with her worry and drama. And being alone at my apartment is just as bad. I'm either crying or . . . or angry."

"Angry?"

Joan fixed her big brown eyes on my face. "Where in the hell has he been all these years, Odelia?"

Joan Nunez never swore. The fact that she did told me the depth of her feelings and confusion.

It was at this point I decided I should disclose to Joan what I'd learned about her father. I'd made a color photocopy of the photo Clarice had left with me. Pulling it out of my tote bag, I unfolded it and placed it on the desk. I smoothed out the creases and with both hands covering it, pushed it across my desk toward Joan.

"Recognize anyone?" I asked, lifting my hands from the paper.

Joan scanned the photo, then gasped as her hand flew to her mouth in astonishment. I didn't say a word but let her absorb the shock slowly.

"That's my father," she finally said, pointing to the man known to Clarice as Alfonso Nunez. She looked up at me. "Who are these people, and how in the world did you come by this photograph?" Before I could answer, she threw another question at me, this one wrapped in suspicion. "Have you known my father was alive all this time?"

I held up my hands palms out — a defensive move. "No, Joan. I knew nothing about your father until yesterday."

After taking a deep breath, I filled Joan in on what had happened at Hannah's wedding and Clarice's visit and the request to help her find people, including Alfred.

Joan scrutinized the photo while I talked. When I was done, she said, "So all of these people are in hiding?"

"I'm not sure, Joan. I do know that some of them have new identities, but I'm not sure of any of the reasons except for Shirley Pearson's." I paused to get my thoughts in order for my next question. "How about your father? Was he involved in anything illegal?"

Joan looked up from the photo, her wet eyes scrunched in thought. "A few days ago, I would have said absolutely not, but today I'm wondering the same. When he died, my mother received his insurance money. It was a nice tidy sum. The police told us that the insurance company will be investigating for fraud. She might even have to give the money back."

"Does she still have it?"

She shook her head. "She paid off the house with most of it. Got rid of some debts. Stuff like that."

"Joan, when Clarice asked me to look into

the whereabouts of these people, I was going to turn her down. The only reason I agreed was because I recognized your father and wanted to find out what happened to him or even if it was the same man. Now that he's turned up dead, I'm going to turn this over to the police."

"Do you have to?"

Her question surprised me, like a small electrical shock. Joan Nunez was the most by-the-book person I knew.

"There are two homicides here, Joan. Don't you want to know who killed your father? And don't you think the man who did die in that car crash deserves his due? If the crash wasn't an accident, then he was also murdered."

She stood up and walked toward the door. I thought Joan was going to leave, but instead she simply faced the wall, her back to me, like she was serving a time-out. She stayed that way a full minute, obviously thinking about what I'd said. I didn't disturb her thoughts, though it still shocked me that she had to give the situation any second consideration.

Joan finally turned and faced me, both of her hands on the back of the chair she'd vacated. "My father was already dead to me, Odelia. And even though the pain of losing him has been reopened, I'll get over it, as I did the first time. Right now, I'm much more interested in why he disappeared in the first place and where he's been and what he's been doing."

Joan's face was so set and determined it could have been added to Mt. Rushmore. "And yes, I agree with you that the identity of the man who did die in that car crash should be known. However, I need to protect my mother. I'll not have her implicated in any alleged fraud scheme." Her stone face softened into a plea. "Will you help? Please? You're already involved, sort of."

In the years I've known Joan Nunez, she'd never displayed this kind of backbone. She was an excellent paralegal, and her integrity was without question, but she had the reputation of being rather wishy-washy when it came to standing up for herself. Putting my elbows on my desk, I cupped my face in my hands and closed my eyes.

"Odelia," Joan rushed to say. "I'm sorry. Did I say something wrong?"

Ah, there was the real Joan, apologetic even when there was no reason to be.

"Let me think a moment," I told her.

Just as Joan took a seat again, there were two firm knocks on my office door, followed by Steele marching in without waiting for a response.

"One of these days," I said to Steele with a cold glare, "you're going to stalk in here and be embarrassed by what you find."

He scoffed. "I doubt it." He looked at Joan. "No work to do, Nunez?"

"I . . . um . . . ," she stammered. Yep, the real Joan was back.

Instead, I answered Steele. "Joan and I were discussing something."

"Can't this wait until after you finish indexing those documents from Ogle?"

Rolling my eyes, I plucked a document from the printer on the credenza behind me and held it out to Steele. "Here's the updated index to the documents. The highlighted ones are those we received today. They are all printed out and filed in the boxes, ready for review."

Steele looked over the list. His eyes drifted over Joan, then over me, before speaking again. "You're sure these are all of them?"

I turned to my computer screen and checked my office e-mail. "No more have arrived since I updated the index," I reported. "Anything else?"

He seemed annoyed by my efficiency. "I have a conference call at three today. Make sure you update this before my call."

"Don't I always?" Geez, his escalated nastiness was getting on my nerves. Anytime this deal or Lori Ogle was mentioned, it kicked Steele's snarly disposition into overdrive. I couldn't wait for it to be over so he could either pursue the fair Lori or stop thinking about her altogether.

Joan looked uncomfortable. Steele always made her cower. This astounded me since litigation attorneys aren't known for being pussycats, yet Joan was right at home with the attorneys in her department.

"Will you need me on that call?" I asked my boss, praying he'd say he wouldn't.

"Don't think so. At least not at this time."

Steele was stalling. I knew the signs. I wasn't sure if he had come into my office to talk to me about something else or just to break up a suspected coffee klatch, but I knew the document index wasn't his real purpose.

"Anything else?" I asked him a second time.

He looked at Joan again, and so did I. Steele was giving her the sign to leave. I was silently telling her to stay. In spite of her earlier bravado, Joan looked like she wanted to slip onto the floor and dribble out the door like a river of spilled coffee.

While Joan was making up her mind what

to do, Steele cleared his throat and turned to me. "How is that special project coming along?"

I knitted my brows in question. "Special project?"

He blew out air in frustration. "The *special project,* Grey. The one you and I met about yesterday afternoon in the conference room."

The conference room? It took me a moment before I caught on to what he was asking. He was inquiring about my meeting with Dev Frye that he'd crashed. The one about Shirley Pearson's murder. Well, duh.

"Oh, *that,*" I said, trying to sound nonchalant.

"You need any help with *that?*" Steele shifted from one expensive shoe to the other.

"Not at this time. It's well under control," I assured him.

Steele didn't look assured. "Uh-huh. I see."

When I didn't say anything more about it, Steele glanced at Joan one last time and left, leaving the door open. As soon as he was gone, Joan let out a breath of relief, looking for all the world like a rabbit who'd escaped a fox. I got out of my chair and closed the door again.

"Here's what I propose, Joan."

She looked at me with such hopeful expectation, I wondered if she thought I had a magic wand.

"Considering there are now two murders," I began, "possibly more, I'll talk to my friend Dev Frye. He's handling the Pearson murder and can interface with the Santa Ana police about your dad's murder. The police can handle the dirty work like hunting down killers while I look into your father's whereabouts for the past several years."

Joan was visibly relieved. "That sounds good, Odelia. Thank you."

"The thing is," I continued, "the police don't like it when civilians poke around, so I'll have to keep a low profile. That means you can't tell anyone, including your mother. I know Greg will help me."

Joan's face got brighter by the moment.

"But remember, I can't promise anything."

Joan got up and threw her bony arms around my neck. "Thank you, Odelia. When do we start?"

We?

EIGHT

Why is it that while all my friends make fun of, worry about, and caution me on my predilection for finding dead bodies, whenever one pops up they can't wait to jump on the crime-solving bandwagon?

Somehow I'd managed to convince Joan that it would be best for Greg and me to work alone. I pointed out to her that we'd had some experience at this and could go about after-hours snooping without causing too much notice. She, on the other hand, had to help arrange to bury her father and comfort her mother. She'd reluctantly agreed.

After I sent Joan back to her office, I called Greg and filled him in on the latest news. Considering the murder of Alfred Nunez, we agreed that we should only help Joan look into her father's whereabouts for the past several years and leave the rest to the police.

In addition to giving me Alfred's last address, Clarice had given me the addresses for Roslyn Stevens and Scott Johnson, though she'd also informed me both of their places were empty. She hadn't stopped to check on Alfred's place of residence.

The plan was to first go by Alfred's. Then, if there was time, we'd shoot by Roslyn's. Scott's address didn't look too far away from Roslyn's, so we might get lucky and hit a twofer. Whether or not we visited all three depended on traffic and how much time was spent gathering information at Alfred's place. After all, he was our real focus. Finding one person might lead us to another, although now we weren't searching for Alfred Nunez physically but for the life he'd led away from his family. We were starting tonight. Greg, in the meantime, would run names and addresses through a people search engine, though we doubted he'd find much since the names were very generic.

After speaking with Greg, I called Dev and set up a lunch meeting. He offered to come out my way, but instead I suggested we meet at a small Thai restaurant near Fashion Island that was halfway between my office and his. It was a hole-in-the-wall with great food, where I knew there would be no chance of bumping into Steele or anyone else from the office.

I gave Dev a copy of the photo and brought him up to date on everything. While he silently digested the information, I dug into the pad thai I'd dished onto my plate.

"You have a way of getting in touch with Clarice Hollowell?" He started scooping helpings from the serving dishes onto his own plate. "I'd like to ask her some questions."

"No, she said she'd get in touch with me."

He tapped the photo with a finger while he chewed. "Two of these people have been murdered," he said once he'd swallowed the food in his mouth. "Makes you wonder who's next."

"Who knows, maybe the murders aren't even connected." I sucked a large amount of Thai iced tea through my straw.

Dev put down his fork and stared at me, his face a study in skepticism. "You really think that's a possibility?" The question was sarcastic, not a sincere query.

Ignoring Dev's tone, I continued telling him what I knew. "Clarice told me all three went missing before Shirley died. She didn't identify the other people in the photo."

Dev ate on autopilot, shoveling into his mouth the chicken and noodle dishes we'd ordered while his brain went into high gear.

His eyes stayed mostly on the photo, as if one of the people in it might step forward and spill the beans at any moment. I ate slowly, occasionally stopping to sip my beverage, while I waited for him to say something.

Joan had given me the name of the detective in charge of Alfred's murder, and I had also passed that along to Dev. Dev didn't know the man, but right before our food came, Dev had called him and left a message requesting a call back.

Tired of waiting, I broke the silence. "You don't think Clarice killed Shirley, do you? You said you thought it was a man or a strong woman. Clarice Hollowell is neither."

"And I still think so, Odelia. But that doesn't mean Clarice wasn't involved."

"She also said Shirley wasn't seeing anyone at the time of her death, or even shortly before."

"That's the same information Amber Straight gave us."

I pushed the noodles on my plate around with my fork. "Clarice seemed genuinely nervous to me, Dev. Maybe she's concerned that whoever killed Shirley might come after her. She did say she was worried that whatever happened to these missing people might happen to her. I don't think she knew

Alfred Nunez had been killed at that point."

"She still may not know." Dev took a few more bites before speaking. "So, the only thing these people have in common is that they've started their lives over under assumed identities?"

"That's what it sounds like. Clarice also gave me the impression that not all of them are in hiding from the law."

"Mmmm," Dev grunted while chewing and swallowed another bite. "There are lots of reasons why people go into hiding — abusive spouse, debt, fraudulent activities, back child support."

"Oh," I said, remembering something else. "The Santa Ana police said there would be an investigation into insurance fraud because Mr. Nunez's widow collected on his life insurance the first time he died."

Dev wiped his mouth with a napkin. "That's pretty standard procedure in a case like this."

"Standard procedure? Does this happen all the time?"

"Not all the time, no. But it has happened where someone fakes his or her death so that the family can collect the insurance. I'm sure the authorities will be looking into the Nunez family financials at the time of the insurance claim."

I stirred my tea with my straw, watching the yummy concoction swirl in the tall glass as it blended the last of the orange, ivory, and brown ribbons into a creamy, sweet gold.

"Dev," I began, looking up at him. "Is it possible that these folks are part of the federal witness protection program? Maybe they're in hiding because of what they know."

He shook his head. "We checked with the feds as soon as we found out Shirley Pearson's real identity. If Shirley had been one of theirs, they would have been all over it in a heartbeat." Dev poked the photo again. "And people in the federal program don't hobnob like this. They don't know about each other, let alone throw barbecues." He pushed back his plate. "There has to be a reason why a group of people in hiding all know each other. Outside of Shirley Pearson, did Clarice mention knowing any of these people before?"

"No, she only said she'd met Shirley years ago." I thought about Clarice's daughter. "I believe Clarice has a daughter named Jackie. I have no idea where she is now, but Clarice said her daughter knows nothing of her secret life."

"Clarice's daughter lives in France," Dev

announced. "Or at least she used to. Her husband was transferred to the Paris office of his company shortly before we found Hollowell's killer. I also know that Clarice sold the Hollowell home in Corona del Mar about the same time." He finished eating and pushed his plate back. "When I get back to the office, I think I'll see if we still have the daughter's number somewhere. She might know where her mother is or at least pass along to her that we're here to help."

"Yeah, like a call like that from the police would really bring someone like Clarice Hollowell running to the station."

Dev cocked one eye at me, letting me know he didn't appreciate my sarcasm.

The check came. "That goes for you, too," Dev told me as he slapped down a credit card. "If Clarice contacts you, let her know we can help. We just want to ask her some questions. Considering what's happened to Alfred Nunez, it could save her life. As for you, there's no reason for you to be in-volved." He shook a thick index finger my way. "But I know you. Joan Nunez is a close friend, which means wild horses couldn't keep your nose out of it. So all I'm going to say is be careful and contact me immediately if you discover something I should know."

He paused, then tacked on, "Even if it's something you'd rather I not know."

It was then I told Dev a half-truth, which in theory is the same as a half-lie. "I did promise Joan that I'd look into what her father had been doing for the past several years." That was the truth. "But I can do that from the safety of a computer." That was the truth, too. I *could* research from my computer, but I knew, even as I sucked down the last of my Thai iced tea, that I wouldn't.

NINE

Greg was waiting for me when I arrived home after work. He'd already plugged the addresses Clarice had given me into the GPS in his van. I looked at my husband and smiled. He was excited, like a young boy about to go on a treasure hunt. We'd both left work early to get a jump on the evening.

While I changed from my work clothes into a pair of comfortable black knit drawstring capris and a tee shirt, I gave Greg a rundown of my lunch with Dev. I was finished about the time I slipped on some comfy sandals. After grabbing a couple of water bottles, we piled Wainwright into the van and hit the road.

Our first destination was the address for Alfred Nunez. It was on a modest street in the city of Santa Ana. Both sides of the street were lined with older apartment buildings. Some were well maintained, while others were in various stages of neglect.

"Strange," I said to Greg. "You'd think if someone was making a new life for himself, he wouldn't stick so close to his old home. Joan and her mother both live in Costa Mesa. That's almost next door. I know I'd head out of state for sure."

Greg pulled up to the curb across from the address Clarice had given me. It was a two-story pale green building with white trim, one of the better-cared-for buildings on the street. It looked like four or five apartments were on each floor. All of the apartment doors faced the building next door with a small greenbelt and walkway between them.

"Did Nunez speak Spanish?" Greg asked.

"Yes, both of Joan's parents are bilingual, as is Joan."

"Santa Ana is a large city and predominately Latino. It might be a good place to disappear yet stay close enough to keep an eye on things."

"You mean he *wanted* to stay close to his family?" I looked at Greg with surprise.

He shrugged. "Hard to say. But if he didn't care, he could have taken off for any number of cities in California and blended in easily."

"Okay, so tell me why Clarice is still sticking around. According to Dev, her daughter is probably in France. Why would Clarice come back to Orange County when she could live anywhere in the world?"

He shrugged again. "Did she say she was living in Orange County?"

I thought back on my conversation with Clarice Hollowell. "No, only that she was a silent partner in Shirley's business and that she was here a few months ago. That's when she saw me at the bridal shop."

"Then Clarice could be living anywhere in California. She could even live in another state and visit here from time to time."

I groaned. "You're right."

Greg grinned. "And you hate it when I'm right."

My lips raised slightly at his remark. "No, I don't hate it. I just find it inconvenient sometimes, like when I think I have a hot theory."

After tossing me a wink, Greg craned his head back and forth, looking up and down the street. "I don't see any police cars. Did you give Dev this address?"

"No," I answered with a mild attack of guilt. "I didn't give him any of the addresses."

"Nunez is probably a very common name. It might take the police some time to track down this address. Good thing for us."

Greg did a U-turn and pulled up directly in front of the building. He reached behind his seat and pulled out a small box the size of a ream of paper. "Here," he told me, handing me the box. "Take this and go check out the apartment. If anyone asks what you're doing, tell them you have a delivery for Alfonso Nunez. I'll keep the engine running just in case you run into a problem."

"What are they?" I asked, looking at the unmarked box.

"Just some old flyers I was going to toss. There was an error on them."

I started to open the door, but Greg stopped me. "One more thing: put the earpiece to your cell phone in and call my phone right now. Then keep the connection open. I'll be able to hear everything that's going on that way."

My hubby may be one smart cookie, but it was starting to worry me how naturally he was taking to snooping. One nosy Nellie in the family was enough. What would be next, training Wainwright to track?

Following his instructions, I plugged my earpiece into my ear and called Greg's cell phone. As soon as we were hooked up, I climbed out of the van with the box of bogus flyers.

According to the mailbox, apartment number 7 was occupied by a Nunez. That number jived with the apartment number Clarice had given me. A quick glance told me it was located on the second floor. The first apartment at the top of the stairs was number 5. The front door to this apartment was open. I couldn't see anything through the screen, but the spicy smell of cooking filled my nostrils. In turn, my stomach reminded me that we'd left the house without first having supper.

Walking along the narrow upper walkway, I passed apartment 6. The front door and the drapes on the living room window were closed. Next was apartment 7. The drapes were open, the door shut. Tucking the box under one arm, I cupped my hands around my face and tried to look inside the apartment. The living room looked tidy enough. I tried the screen door. It was unlatched, but the front door was locked tight. I jiggled the doorknob but got nowhere.

"What do you want?" a voice asked me.

I turned to my left and saw a young Latina holding a chubby baby. She stood in front of the open door at the top of the stairs, apartment 5, holding the screen door open with her body. She was plump, wearing cutoff jeans and a halter top the color of overcooked peas. Her hair was long and stringy — black hair dyed red, with several inches of roots grown out. Her eyes were heavily made up, her face hard for her age.

"I'm looking for Mr. Nunez." I looked down at the box as if double-checking a name. "Mr. Alfonso Nunez."

The woman looked me up and down. "What's your business?"

My first inclination was to tell the girl whatever it was, it was none of hers, but a little voice in my ear stopped me as if my thoughts had leaked out through my cell phone. "Careful, Odelia," I heard Greg say through the earpiece. "You want her to talk to you. She won't if you piss her off."

I gave the woman a small smile. "I have a delivery for a Mr. Alfonso Nunez. It's some copying he had done but never picked up." I lifted the box as an exhibit to my words.

"You can leave it with me," the woman said, hoisting the baby to her other hip.

"Um . . . he owes $32.95 on the job. I can't leave it unless someone pays for it."

I took a step toward her. The baby giggled and smiled at me. It was a cute little tot with dark straight hair and huge brown eyes, wearing only a diaper.

"Can you pay for it?" I asked the woman, forcing hope into my voice. "I'm sure Mr.

121

Nunez will pay you back when he gets home. Then I can leave it and my boss won't get mad."

"Like hell." She retreated a step, as if I was going to turn out her pockets for the money. "I'm not paying for anybody's shit."

I tried to look disappointed at the news. "Well, can you tell me when Mr. Nunez gets home from work? Maybe I can wait for him."

"Al hasn't been around for a while. Not sure where he's gone."

"Is he friendly with any of the other neighbors? Maybe he told one of them when he'd be back." I thought of Alfred Nunez in residence at the morgue and shuddered, knowing he'd never return to this place.

"Al keeps to himself. Seems nice enough, but he's been here awhile and never says much to anyone." She looked back into her apartment. "I gotta go. My husband will be home soon, and dinner's not ready."

She made no move to go inside, making me think she was worried I'd break into apartment 7 if she turned her back on me. She was right to worry. Had I been able to jimmy the door open, I'd have been inside in a New York minute.

I started for the stairs. When I passed the woman, she backed up into her apartment

122

and let the screen door shut between us.

"Thanks anyway," I told her. "I guess I'll have to come back."

"No luck, I see," Greg said as soon as I was back in the van. "By the way, nice job improvising the money thing."

"Yeah, otherwise she'd want to take the box for sure." I put the flyers down on the floor and buckled up. "His apartment has furniture in it but has an abandoned look, like no one's been home in a while. There were a couple of plants near the front window, both turning brown."

"No sign of disturbance or of anyone going through the place?"

"I could only see the living room and part of the dining area, but it looked neat as a pin."

Greg pulled away from the curb. "Punch up the address for Roslyn Stevens. Let's go see if she's a long-lost cousin."

TEN

Evening rush hour was in full swing as we
made our way out of Santa Ana, but Greg
knew his way to Long Beach, where Roslyn
Stevens lived, via surface streets. His traffic
savvy kept us off the packed freeway. Long
Beach was north of Seal Beach. The plan
was to circle back home after we'd checked
out Roslyn's place. My own personal plan
was to suggest to Greg we pick up dinner at
our favorite Chinese restaurant on the way
home. I didn't think it would be a problem,
especially considering the symphony coming from his growling stomach. I was feeling a bit peckish myself, especially after
smelling the dinner Alfred's neighbor had
been fixing.

Roslyn Stevens lived in a duplex on a
small, quiet street — or at least she *had* lived
there. The place looked even more abandoned than Alfred's apartment. A peek in
the window showed me it was empty except

for a ladder and painting paraphernalia. A drop cloth covered the floor of the living room. Walking around to the back, I found a back door with a window. I cupped my hands around my eyes and pressed my nose against the small window to study the kitchen. It was also empty, except for major appliances, and looked freshly painted. Given the current state of Alfred Nunez, I began to worry that Roslyn was also dead. Hopefully, she'd hit the road before it came down to that.

"You interested in the place?"

I jumped at the sound of the voice and placed a hand over my thumping heart. Turning, I discovered a pudgy, middle-aged African-American man with salt-and-pepper hair. He was dressed in a white tank tee shirt and knee-length blue plaid shorts. On his feet were flip-flops. He stood watching me from the stoop of the other half of the duplex. In his hand was a paper napkin. He finished chewing whatever was in his mouth and swiped at his lips with the napkin while I composed myself. Everyone seemed to be having dinner except me.

"You interested?" he asked again when I remained as silent and thick as a stump. "It's a large two bedroom, one bath. Twelve hundred dollars — first and last due on

125

move-in. No pets."

I moved away from the window. "Actually, I was looking for Roslyn Stevens. Doesn't she live here?"

"Why you asking?" The man stepped off the stoop and took a step toward me.

I didn't think the trick with the flyers would work with this guy. Besides, I'd left them in the van.

"My name is Stevens. I'm working on our family tree. I was given her name and address as a possible relative."

The man laughed. "Yeah, you look a whole lot like Roslyn."

"I know Roslyn is African-American, but that doesn't mean we're not related. Besides, my husband is the Stevens in the family."

As if on cue, I heard Greg call to me. "Sweetheart, you back here?"

A few seconds later, Greg came wheeling down the driveway at the side of the building. The drive ended just past where I was standing at a small detached carport. Wainwright trotted beside him.

When he saw me, Greg beamed. "There you are. Did you find Roslyn Stevens?" He looked up at the man, putting on the most innocent, open face I'd ever seen. "Hello."

In the few years we've been married, I

have marveled at Greg's natural talent for getting into character at the drop of a hat. It was a form of duplicity, yes, but not so much that I was worried. Since he was determined to join me in my nosiness, it often came in handy. I'd noticed that people felt less threatened by a guy in a wheelchair. Although, truth be told, Greg could take on most able-bodied men and win, as long as they weren't running.

I walked over to Greg. "It looks like she might have moved, honey. Sorry."

My husband looked up at the man, who was now studying us — the middle-aged fat woman and the disabled guy with the family pet — trying to make up his mind if we were on the level. He looked in favor of believing us. And why not? To him, we probably looked not only harmless but naïve.

"Do you know where Roslyn moved?" Greg asked the guy.

"Not really." The man took another step closer to us. From his relaxed posture, it looked like he was believing our story.

"Are you the landlord?" Greg petted Wainwright while he talked. Mr. Innocent himself.

The man nodded. "Yes. My wife and I own this building and the one across the street. Around the first, Roslyn stopped by to pay her rent and told us she had to move suddenly — something about a new job, or it could have been a job transfer. She paid through the end of June anyway, even without our asking. We offered to keep the place for her until the end of the month, but she said she was moving permanently."

I shifted my weight. Even though it was early evening, it was still hot outside. I felt like I was melting from the inside out, with only my skin holding my liquid center intact. "What kind of work did Roslyn do?"

"Not real sure, but I know she mostly worked from home. Wife always thought it had something to do with computers."

I prodded a little more. "Did she live here long?"

"About four years. Very good tenant, quiet and polite. We were sorry to lose her."

Greg fidgeted with his wheels, rolling them back and forth while he digested the information. "Did she say if the new job was out of town? I'd really like to meet her."

"Can't say exactly," the man answered. "She and a friend packed up a U-Haul one night and took off."

I wished I had the photo Clarice had given me to show the man, but I'd left it in the van in my bag. As if reading my mind, Greg pulled it from his shirt pocket like a magician pulling a rabbit out of a hat. I could only stare in wonder.

"Was her friend one of these people?" He held the photo out toward the man. "This photo was given to me by another friend — the one who thinks I may have a connection to Roslyn, maybe through marriage or something."

The landlord took the photo and studied it. "Yeah, that's him." He stabbed a finger at a guy standing on the edge of the group — Scott Johnson. "Don't know his name though." He handed the photo back to Greg.

I looked over Greg's shoulder at the photo. Scott Johnson was white, of average height, and slightly built. The top of his head was bald, his remaining hair hanging down gray and stringy like scraggly fringe at the bottom of an old-fashioned lampshade. He stood on the edge of the group with an air of reluctance, his hands jammed into the pockets of his pants. His smile looked forced, a nerd invited by mistake to a party thrown by cool kids.

I looked back up at the landlord. "This was the man who helped Roslyn move?"

He nodded. "Sure was. Saw him here from time to time. More often in the past month or so."

"Was he Roslyn's boyfriend?" asked Greg.

"That's what I thought, even though a lovely woman like Roslyn could have done better, in my opinion." The man chuckled. "But my wife is positive they weren't involved that way. She said they didn't have *chemistry.*" He looked at Greg, shrugging and grinning in sync. "Women, huh?" Greg nodded and laughed, joining him in the manly inside joke.

I didn't think it was funny. I thought the observation was important. "Why did your wife think that?"

The man turned his eyes in my direction and shrugged again, but this time his shoulders moved with confusion rather than mirth.

"Because they never touched," came a voice from behind him.

We all turned in the direction of the landlord's back door to see a tall, thin woman with straightened black hair watching us from the stoop. She studied us with almond-shaped eyes, a wooden spoon in her hand. She turned to her husband. "Gerald, your dinner's getting cold."

Gerald turned back to us. "This is my wife. By the way, we're the Marshalls. That's Amy. My name's Gerald."

"We're the Stevenses. That's my wife

130

Odelia, and I'm Greg."

I took a step forward, but a steely look from the woman stopped me in my tracks. "We're looking for Roslyn Stevens," I said, holding my ground but not advancing. Amy Marshall had obviously graduated from the same school of intimidation as Zee.

"No need for a rerun. I heard everything through the kitchen window."

Greg bravely rolled a foot closer. Wainwright stayed, his butt planted to the ground in the sit position, as he had been ordered. Once given an order, the well-trained animal wouldn't budge until told by one of us he could. It was nice to know someone in our family had some discipline.

"So," Greg began, "you don't think Roslyn and this guy were romantically involved?"

Amy shook her head. "I seriously doubt it. They might have worked together, but they didn't play together."

"What makes you so sure?" Greg ventured.

"Because they never touched," she repeated. When the two men gave her blank stares, Amy looked from Greg to me, settling her stern eyes on mine, searching for someone who might understand her reasoning. More to the point, she was searching for signs of intelligent life. I swallowed, hop-

131

ing I wouldn't disappoint her.

"She means," I said, moving up beside Greg, "that there wasn't a sense of intimacy between them."

Amy nodded, pleased as a teacher when the slow kid wins the spelling bee. "Not once did I see Roslyn and that man touch. Couples do that unless they're on the outs with each other." She tossed her chin in our direction. "I've been watching. You two can't keep your hands off each other. I'd bet a homemade peach cobbler that you've been married less than five years."

I looked down at my hand resting on Greg's shoulder. Without thinking, he'd covered it with one of his. Amy hadn't missed a thing. She'd make a formidable witness if ever called to testify.

"It will be four years this November," Greg answered for the two of us. He flashed her one of his sexy smiles. "Too bad, too, because I love homemade peach cobbler."

Amy melted visibly around the edges, and it wasn't from the heat. Maybe if Greg smiled again, we'd get the cobbler anyway.

"So," I asked, pushing homemade peach cobbler out of my mind, "who do you think this man was?"

"I was never sure." Amy wiped the hand not holding the spoon on her apron. "I asked her once, but Roslyn never said. I'd say he was someone she worked with, maybe even a boss or supervisor. They were comfortable with each other but not overly familiar. And Roslyn definitely deferred to him."

I liked Amy and Gerald Marshall. They seemed like honest and upfront people. But with Amy's uncanny insight, I didn't want to linger lest she see through our bullshit. I gave Greg's shoulder a slight squeeze and removed my hand. "Thank you so much for your time, folks. We should let you get back to your dinner."

Following my lead, Greg rolled closer to Gerald, holding out his right hand. "Thanks a lot. It was a pleasure meeting you both."

Gerald took the offered hand and shook it. "If you catch up with Roslyn, ask her to call us. We still have a security deposit to return to her."

"Will do," Greg assured him. "And if you come across her, please give her this." Greg reached into his pocket and brought out a business card for Ocean Breeze Graphics. It was a bold and iffy move. I wasn't sure I wanted his contact information out there, but if Amy was suspicious about our intentions, at least she'd see our last name really was Stevens.

ELEVEN

"So, what do you think?" I asked Greg as soon as we were seated in the van. Wainwright was hunkered down in the back, busily lapping up water from his portable bowl. Greg and I were sipping from our water bottles.

Greg glanced at me. "I think you should call Ming's and order dinner. We can pick it up on our way home."

"You read my mind, honey, but it's not exactly what I expected you to say."

He favored me with one of his killer smiles. "Sorry, but my stomach interrupted my other thoughts."

Before prodding him further, I called our favorite Chinese restaurant and ordered dinner for pick-up in twenty minutes, about the time I calculated we'd be in that area.

"Okay." I closed my phone. "Your stomach's been taken care of. So, what's your *other* gut telling you?"

"Roslyn's on the run, and that guy helped her get out of Dodge the same time he hit the road. They might even be together."

"Safety in numbers?"

"Could be."

"That was at least two weeks ago. Do you think Alfred and Shirley received a heads-up and ignored the warning, or that Roslyn and Scott were the only ones who received a chance to clear out?"

Greg handed me the photo Gerald had returned to him. "Could be that guy in the photo — that Scott fellow — might have learned something and decided to save Roslyn. Sounds like they hung out together. At least the Marshalls recall seeing him around from time to time."

Greg started up the van and punched up an address on the GPS. "It looks like Scott Johnson's place is fairly close and in the direction we'd be heading anyway. Let's check it out, though I think we'll find it abandoned like the others." He pulled away from the curb.

"What I'd really like to do," I said as the van moved through the streets, "is go through Shirley Pearson's home. But I'm sure the cops have been through it top to bottom."

My husband glanced over at me. "Not to

mention you'd probably never get near it, considering she was a murder victim. It's not like you could just saunter up to it like you did Alfred's place."

The address for Scott Johnson was a small terra-cotta bungalow on a street similar to Roslyn's. However, it didn't look abandoned. Two small kids played on the postage-stamp-sized lawn under the supervision of a young woman. I hopped out of the car and approached her. Greg kept the engine running. In under two minutes, I was back in the van.

"She said they moved in at the beginning of June." I fastened my seat belt. "They rented the place from some management company."

Without a word, Greg got the van rolling again.

I huffed in frustration. "I really want to have a heart-to-heart chat with Clarice, but I have no idea how to reach her."

"Something tells me that once she learns of Alfred's death, she'll show up." Greg cut his eyes from the road to me briefly.

"You think she knows yet? Dev didn't think she did."

"Hard to say. Last she knew, Alfred was missing, and unless she's listed on his contact information, which I doubt, why would anyone tell her?"

Holding up an index finger, I stopped that thought from going further. "Contact information." I paused just long enough to gather my thoughts into a loose bundle. "Alfred Nunez was living a new life. He would hardly have put Joan or her mother down as his contact information. I wonder who *was* listed?"

"Didn't Joan tell you he had no ID when they found him? That's why the police used his fingerprints to find his real identity."

"Yes. And without ID, they wouldn't know his new name or any recent contact information." I paused, remembering lunch with Dev. "I gave Dev Alfred's new name at lunch."

Greg was quiet a minute, then said, "Do you regret giving Dev that information?"

I looked out the window, letting my eyes graze on buildings and cars that whizzed by like a film on fastforward. "No, I don't, Greg. I still believe I did the right thing. It's Dev's job to find the killer, not ours. As it was, I withheld the address in Santa Ana."

"You did do the right thing, Odelia. And I'm sure by now the police have the address. You just gave us a head start before the cops swarmed all over the place."

We pulled into the parking lot of the

Chinese restaurant. I grabbed my wallet and prepared to hop out to claim our food. "Although now, I'm not sure how to find out more about Alfred's secret life. We don't know anything about him other than where he lived. He's still just a guy who faked his death for insurance money, providing he got some of that money. And that apartment didn't look like it belonged to someone with a lot of cash."

"If his wife did share any of that money with him, then it would be evidence of fraudulent intent on both their parts."

I didn't like the sound of that. "Poor Joan. I hope for her sake her mother wasn't involved in her father's disappearance."

I opened the door and put my feet to the pavement. "I'd really like to talk to Clarice again." I looked at the door to the restaurant, then back at Greg. "Sure wish we had some sort of magic lamp to conjure Clarice up when we needed her, but she wouldn't even give me her new identity."

"Clarice is going to have to start trusting you at some point if she wants your help."

I held the van door open, letting the air conditioning blow out into the hot evening air while I waited for him to finish his thought.

"Are we helping Joan find out about her

father," Greg continued, "or are we helping Clarice locate Alfred, Scott, and Roslyn? Seems like we're doing both now."

"We're helping Joan, first and foremost. As for Clarice, we've already located Alfred, for better or worse, but I think we'll need to locate the others to find out more about Alfred — if we find them."

"Maybe we'll get a clue in one of our fortune cookies."

When we arrived home, Wainwright became agitated. As soon as we parked in the garage and opened the van door, he dashed out. He stood at the door to our back yard barking like a he'd seen the devil.

"What is it, boy?" Greg shifted his body from the driver's seat into his wheelchair. I gathered our food and went around the back of the van, meeting Greg and Wainwright at the door. The dog was trying to tell us something, but neither Greg nor I were fluent in golden retriever, though Greg has a better working vocabulary than I do. We both tensed, knowing Wainwright didn't get crazy for no reason. The animal wasn't a drama queen. When he behaved this way, it was for two purposes: one, to warn us; and two, to protect us.

Greg grabbed a hammer from a nearby

workbench. "Stay here." The order was shot in my direction, not Wainwright's. Armed with the dog and the hammer, my husband opened the door leading to our back yard.

As soon as the door was muzzle-wide, Wainwright pushed through, a golden ball of teeth and purpose. Behind him rolled Greg, pushing his wheelchair forward like a war steed into battle. I decided to count to ten, then bring up the rear armed with Mongolian beef, honey-walnut shrimp, and spring rolls.

"Call him off," I heard a masculine and vaguely familiar voice yell before I even reached five. No matter how familiar the voice, had it belonged to a friend, Wainwright wouldn't still be voicing his ferocious displeasure.

I hustled around the corner of the garage until our patio came into full view. The scene nearly caused me to drop the food. Wainwright had trapped the intruder, who'd been caught unawares on his back on our chaise longue, probably in the middle of a nap. The dog had leapt onto the chaise, successfully pinning him in place like a note under a pushpin. Wainwright's muzzle was inches from the man's face. The dog had stopped barking but remained vigilant, a low growl emanating from his gut. Greg, on the other hand, was nearly doubled with laughter, the hammer forgotten in his lap.

"Call him off," the intruder called again. "It's not funny." The tone was commanding yet dotted with flecks of fear. Apparently, Greg didn't agree with him. He thought it damn funny and was too busy laughing to call off our dog.

I deposited the food on our picnic table and grabbed Wainwright by the collar, tugging him off the chaise. "Down, boy." With reluctance, the large animal hopped to the ground but maintained a keen eye on his prey.

Greg stopped laughing long enough to snap his fingers and choke out, "Here, Wainwright." The dog immediately left his post by the chaise and went to his master's side. Greg gave him some pats to calm him down and let him know everything was fine.

My hands were on both of my hips as I faced the trespasser — my half brother, Clark Littlejohn. "What in the hell are you doing here?"

"You've always said I should visit!"

"You couldn't call first?"

"I wanted to surprise you. I was sitting in my car out front, but it was too hot. So I decided to see if I could find some shade back here. I managed to get over the fence."

Clark shot me a small smile of pride. "No small feat for a guy my age, I can tell you that."

I twitched my nose and waited for more explanation. Clark continued, "Guess I fell asleep." He started to stand, then changed his mind, looking with concern at Wainwright, who was sitting next to Greg's wheelchair but still on alert.

"Don't worry," Greg assured him. "Wainwright won't bite unless you attack one of us or we give him a command."

Clark wasn't so sure. "I'd rather not test that theory."

Smiling, I called to the dog. Wainwright trotted over to me and Clark, his long tail wagging happily with the attention. I introduced the two and encouraged Clark to pat Wainwright's large, sturdy head. When Clark's hand moved to scratch the dog behind an ear, Wainwright's tail wagged faster. "See?" I said to Clark. "You're now buds." I held out my arms to my half brother. "Now stand up and give me a hug."

Clark Littlejohn was older than me by about six years. He was my mother's firstborn — a kid she had prior to meeting and marrying my father, a son she conveniently neglected to tell me about. I'm not even sure she ever told my father about him. She sure as hell didn't tell either of us about Grady Littlejohn, the son she had after she disappeared when I was sixteen years old. When my father died, I discovered an old envelope with a clue to my mother's where-abouts. When I followed up on the informa-tion, I'd discovered the existence of my two half brothers and had been reunited with my mother. Like most things involving my family, the reunion had been less of a Hallmark card and more akin to a Hal-loween haunted house.

After Clark and Greg shook hands, we went into the house. Wainwright headed for his water dish, but not until after he'd given Muffin and Seamus the scoop on the stranger.

Unlike me, Greg had remembered to bring in the Chinese food. He plopped it down on the kitchen table. "You're just in time for dinner, Clark."

"Wouldn't be the first time I've caught you two with take-out." He turned to me. "Do you ever cook?"

I had something other than food on my mind. "How's Mom?" I didn't have to ask about Grady; he was dead. "Is that why you're here?"

"Mom's fine," Clark assured me. "Saw her last week." Our mother was now living in a retirement home of her choosing in New Hampshire. "Would you believe she even has a boyfriend? Some old guy named Earle who's pushing ninety."

Greg snorted with laughter while he pulled three dinner plates out of the cupboard. "You two going to end up with more half siblings?"

Clark winked at him. "Never know. Earle's pretty spry with that walker of his. And considering he's one of the few gents on the premises who can chew his own food, he's quite the catch."

I pulled utensils out of a drawer. "Speaking of good-looking old guys, you're looking pretty good yourself, bro. You've dropped your spare tire."

Clark patted his belly, which was now reduced to a small, soft bulge that extended over the waistband of his jeans like a half-inflated balloon. "I stopped eating at the Blue Lobster. Hardly ever eat fried food anymore." He sniffed at the bag on the table. "Not that I couldn't be tempted."

I studied Clark. He was of average height and still thick and solid, even without his previous gut. His hair was also thinner than when I'd last seen him about a year and a half ago. Neither handsome nor plain, he had our mother's eyes and mouth and wasn't half bad-looking for a man of his age. If there was one difference in Clark since we'd last seen each other, it was his overall vibe. He seemed much more relaxed, as if a large concrete block had been lifted from his shoulders. It could be that not having Mom to worry about day in and day out had given him relief.

I started to pull a couple of beers from the fridge, then stopped, remembering that Clark, like my mother, was a recovering alcoholic. Clark noticed my hesitation.

"Don't worry about me, sis. You and Greg help yourself. I don't mind."

"How about some iced tea or lemonade, then?" I peered into the fridge again. "We also have Coke, both diet and regular." I looked up at Clark. "Or coffee. I could make a pot of coffee."

"Diet Coke is perfect."

He held out his hand, and I passed him one. "Glasses are up in that cupboard to your left."

"I prefer the can."

"He sounds like Dev, doesn't he, sweetheart?"

I chuckled. My big brother did remind me of Dev Frye in a lot of ways. "Remember Dev Frye?" I asked Clark. "The Newport Beach cop who called you when I was in

Massachusetts?"

Clark nodded. He popped the top on his soda and drank it down, only coming up for air once. Just like Dev. I handed him another.

"How long you staying, Clark?" Greg pulled take-out containers from the bag. "We could invite Dev over for dinner one night. Get you two law-and-order boys together."

"Not sure."

Greg and I both turned to look at Clark at the same time. Maybe the relaxed look was a façade. I asked with concern, "Things okay with you?"

Clark pulled out a chair from the kitchen table and sat down. "Sure, it's just that I quit my job. I'm not a cop anymore."

Greg rolled in closer to the table. "A cop or the chief of police?"

"Neither."

I was confused, and it was going to take more than Mongolian beef to put me back on track. "But I thought you went back to being chief after you took that leave. Didn't the town want you back?"

"It wasn't the town," Clark explained. "They were happy to get me back, in spite of everything. But my heart just wasn't in it, so I decided to retire from police work."

Greg grabbed his beer bottle and held it out toward Clark. "Then let's toast to you being a man of leisure."

Clark clinked his soda can against Greg's beer bottle. "Thanks, but I'm not exactly that either." He took a swig from his can. "That's why I'm out here. I had a job interview in Phoenix. When it was over, I thought, hell, I don't have any reason to hurry back home, and you guys were just a short drive away."

"It's a seven-hour drive," I pointed out.

"Details, sis." Clark gave me a wide grin. I grinned back, enjoying the way *sis* sounded to my ears. "And you two keep inviting me to visit, so here I am." He paused. "I hope my timing isn't inconvenient."

"No," Greg assured him, beating me to the punch. "You can stay here as long as you like. We're thrilled to have you."

To add my vote, I moved behind Clark, wrapped my arms around his neck, and planted a big kiss on the top of his half-bald dome. I gave his neck another firm squeeze before releasing him and said the first words that came to mind. "Let's eat."

Greg shoveled a fat shrimp into his mouth just as he asked Clark, "So, if you get this job, will you be moving to Phoenix?"

Clark shook his head. "Not unless I want

to. It's a security consultant position. Might entail a lot of travel, but I don't need to be at the corporate office." He bit a spring roll in half. "I'd like to stay close to Mom as long as she's alive. Then I'll probably sell the house and find someplace warm to live. Maybe Florida, maybe here, maybe Arizona. Who knows. I just know it'll be someplace where it doesn't snow."

The three of us feasted while Clark filled us in on the local gossip from Massachusetts. When we were done and our plates were pushed aside, Clark stretched. "That offer of coffee still good, sis?"

"Sure is." I got up, stacked our dirty plates, and carried them to the sink. "Decaf or regular?"

"Probably decaf," he yawned. "Although after that drive, the heat, and this great meal, I doubt the caffeine would keep me awake tonight."

"Make mine iced, sweetheart," Greg chimed in.

Iced coffee sounded great to me, too. I gave Clark a questioning glance.

He shook his head. "Nope, hot and black for me."

I got a pot of decaf coffee going while I rinsed the dishes and put them in the dishwasher. We'd eaten everything but the takeout containers, so there were no left-overs to worry about. Clark went out to his car and brought in his bag, and Greg showed him to our guest room.

We adjourned to the patio to enjoy the coffee. The ocean breeze had cooled things down considerably. Wainwright was snoozing on the patio, Seamus next to him. Muffin, our little social butterfly, was curled up in Clark's lap.

"So," Clark said, stroking the little gray bundle of fur, "find any bodies lately?"

TWELVE

The hand petting Muffin stopped, frozen in mid-scratch. Clark eyed the two of us, his eyes narrowed into a piercing squint, digging for the truth hidden in the folds of our silence. It was his cop face. I remembered it well from our first meeting.

"I meant that as a little joke." Clark's current tone was anything but joking.

Greg and I buried our noses in our iced coffees, not looking at each other or at Clark.

"Real mature, you guys." Clark set Muffin on the ground and leaned forward. "Now tell me what's going on, or do I have to call that detective to find out?"

I put down my glass and frowned at my brother. "Oh, like tattling's any more mature."

"Besides," Greg added, "Dev already knows. He's in charge of the investigation."

"I see. So you two aren't running around

pretending to be Nick and Nora Charles?" Clark took a long drink of coffee. "That's a relief."

Again, Greg and I looked anywhere but at Clark. I don't know about Greg, but I felt like a kid caught cheating in school. Once again, Clark picked up on our lame avoidance ploy. After studying the two of us, he slapped his hand on the table. Wainwright raised his head in alert. Clark's eyes widened, and he held his breath. Finding no real threat, the dog lowered its head again to the ground. Clark resumed breathing.

"Man." Clark shook his head. "It's going to be a long night if I'm always worried about that animal."

"Seriously, Clark," Greg told him with a proud smile. "He's a cream puff unless you try to hurt one of us, or even one of the cats. And now that he sees you're accepted, he'll consider you one of his pack. If someone barged into this house right now, he'd protect you, too."

"That dog saved my life a few years ago," I added with equal pride. "Took a bullet for me."

"Really?" Clark swung his head in Wainwright's direction. On cue, the faithful old dog raised his head and thumped his tail. Clark turned back to me. "Then again, I'd bet if you weren't prowling around where you shouldn't have been, bullets wouldn't have been flying."

I put down my iced coffee and flashed Clark a face of annoyance. "Did you come here to chastise us or to visit? I mean, it's not like you didn't already know I had a certain —"

Clark held up a hand, interrupting me. "I'm sorry, Odelia. You're right." An awkward silence filled the air, but only for a minute before Clark asked, "So, you going to tell me about this latest adventure?"

I wasn't convinced of his sincerity. "You really want to know, or are you going to make fun of us?"

Greg put a hand on my arm. "I don't think Clark was entirely making fun of us, sweetheart. More like he's concerned."

"Greg's right, Odelia. I am concerned. And I do want to know what's happening. Remember, I used to be a cop, and a damn fine one, if I do say so myself."

I looked at Greg, who gave me a nod of encouragement and said, "Tell him. Maybe he has some ideas we haven't thought about."

Greg had a point. Without help from Clarice, it would be tough going to find out more about Alfred Nunez. Maybe Clark's fresh eyes would help. For the next hour I told Clark the entire story, from finding Shirley dead to our striking out with Roslyn Stevens and Scott Johnson. In between, Greg added forgotten tidbits and pulled out the photo. When we were done, Clark leaned back in his chair and closed his eyes, making me wonder if we had bored him into a coma.

"Clark?" I asked tenuously. After his long drive, maybe he'd just dozed off.

"I'm thinking," he replied without opening an eye.

I picked up our empty glasses and cup and took them into the kitchen to let him think in peace. When I returned, Clark's eyes were still shut. I shot a questioning look Greg's way, but he only shrugged in return. I had half a mind to hang a *Do Not Disturb* sign on my brother and go to bed. And I wasn't too far from making that move when Clark cleared his throat and opened his eyes.

"When's the funeral?" he asked, turning my way.

I sat back down at the redwood table. "I have no idea. Joan hasn't said anything."

Clark shook his head slowly. "Not the Nunez funeral, the one for the he/she — what's her name?"

"Shirley Pearson?"

153

"That's the one."

I glanced at Greg. He met my eyes with a half-cocked eyebrow, both of us sensing that Clark was onto something. "I don't know," I told him. "Why?"

"This Clarice woman may not know yet that Nunez is dead, but she does know that Pearson is dead. If they were such good friends as she claims, she'll probably be at the funeral." Clark got up from his bench and stretched, reaching his arms toward the patio cover in a goal-calling gesture. He grunted like an old bull as he moved. "In fact, you might find several other interesting folks at the funeral." He twisted his torso and I heard several crackles and pops.

"You need some ibuprofen?" I asked with concern.

"Got it covered, sis, but thanks. That drive was a bitch on this old body."

Instead of sitting down, Clark squatted next to Wainwright and scratched him behind his ears. The dog went into a state of bliss. So much for being afraid of our watchdog.

"Funerals," Clark told us, standing up straight with a groan or two, "tend to bring out all the nut jobs, along with the usual mourners. Wouldn't surprise me if you saw a few others from that photo at the service."

Greg nodded his head in agreement. "That's a great idea, Clark." He turned to me. "You think you can find out anything about the funeral, Odelia?"

I held up an index finger. "I have an idea. Sit tight, I'll be right back."

Heading into our home office and my waiting computer, I did a search for Rambling Rose and located its website. It was sweet and girly, mostly done in pinks and greens, the text portions printed on an antique lace background bordered by a trellis festooned with blooming roses. On the home page, someone had posted a photo of Shirley Pearson and a short notice of her death. Along with it was another notice assuring clients that Rambling Rose would be fulfilling its existing commitments. Was Amber Straight going to take over the booked weddings? Or maybe Clarice would. She did say she was a silent partner. I read all the information again and checked each page link, but I didn't see anything about a memorial or funeral service. I didn't know where Shirley lived, but the office for Rambling Rose was in Corona del Mar.

Corona del Mar — a small seaside village located in the southern part of Newport Beach. It was the same area in which Clarice and John Hollowell had their home back when I was looking into Sophie London's death. Maybe Clarice was still living in the area, even though she'd sold the house.

If an obituary had been published, it was probably in the *Orange County Register*. I switched over to the newspaper's website. It took some hunting to find recent obituaries, but there it was, a short paragraph without a photo dedicated to information on Shirley Pearson's death. From it, readers learned that Shirley was the owner of Rambling Rose and that she had died last Saturday at the age of thirty-seven. Tidbits about being murdered, her past bank heist, and the fact that she began life as a he rather than a she were conveniently left out. However, it did contain information about an upcoming memorial service on Saturday morning at ten o'clock, the day after tomorrow, and requested that in lieu of flowers, donations be made to the AIDS Services Foundation of Orange County. Information in hand, I returned to the guys.

"Damn." Greg knitted his brows. "I have to be at the shop all day this Saturday."

"There's no way you can get away for a few hours in the morning?" I asked him.

"None. I'm meeting a new client first thing, and we're working on a special order for delivery Monday morning. And Chris is

156

out of town until Monday." Chris Fowler was Greg's right-hand man at the shop. He'd been sent off to Mountain Breeze Graphics, Greg's shop in Denver, to work with Greg's partner, Boomer, on installing and training the staff on new equipment.

"I'll go with you."

I turned to find Clark scratching his back on a post like an old bear.

"If you two don't mind," he continued, "I could stick around and go to the service with Odelia."

Greg gave Clark a short grunt of decision — one bear talking to another. "I think that's an outstanding idea, Clark. Thanks."

"What about me? Don't I get a say in this?"

"No," the two growled in unison.

"I'll bet Zee will want to go. After all, she knew Shirley. She can go with me."

Greg stroked my arm. "Whether Zee goes with you or not, I'd feel better if you took Clark along. Considering there are now two murders, there's no telling who will show up at that funeral."

"Greg's right. Think of me as just another pair of eyes."

As much as I claimed that I didn't need a babysitter at Shirley's memorial service, inside I was glad Clark would be by my side.

■ ■ ■ ■

The next morning, Joan Nunez found her way to my office. I had just called Zee and given her the info about the memorial service for Shirley. As I expected, she did want to go. Since it was in Corona del Mar, I told her Clark and I would pick her up on Saturday morning. Zee was surprised and excited to meet Clark, having heard about him when Greg and I had returned home from Massachusetts.

The visit from Joan didn't surprise me. I knew she'd be eager to see if I'd learned anything about her father during the previous evening's fact-finding mission. Unfortunately, I'd learned butkis. After she closed my door and took a seat in the visitor's chair, I told Joan so. When I gave her the news, the sight of her forlorn face about broke my heart.

"I'm sorry, Joan. I only came across one neighbor, and she wasn't very forthcoming with information. She only said she hadn't seen him in a while and that he appeared nice but kept to himself. From what I saw of his apartment, it looked liked he hadn't been home for some time. But that doesn't mean I'm not still trying." I also knew that by now the police would be all over that apartment, and the young woman with the baby would be telling them all about the nosy woman with the flyers.

My office phone rang. The display told me it was Steele. I ignored it and returned my attention to Joan.

"How's your mom doing?"

"She and my stepdad are having some problems. He wants to drive to Las Vegas this weekend and get quickly remarried."

"And she doesn't? Seems like after what you told me about her worrying about living in sin, she'd be eager to do that."

"You'd think so, wouldn't you?"

Joan wrapped her arms across her thin chest in a self-hug. Dark circles cupped her eyes like two ashy hammocks.

"My mother is now afraid that if she's found guilty of fraud, she'll drag my stepfather into it legally if they remarry. If their marriage isn't valid, she thinks he might be able to stay clear of any problems."

"Has she consulted a lawyer?"

Joan looked up at me with the eyes of an expectant waif, like an orphan from a Charles Dickens novel looking for food and a bed.

"Do you think, Odelia, that Mike Steele might talk to her?"

"Steele?" I had been leaning forward in my chair, but her request pushed me back with surprise. "Of all the attorneys in this office, you want to ask *Steele* for help?"

She shrugged a *why not* my way. "He's the best. You've said so yourself."

"He is, but you know yourself that empathy is not his strong suit." I shook off the surprise. "Why not ask one of the litigators? Someone like Carl Yates, who has a heart instead of a block of ice in his chest. Or maybe Marc Boer? You work closely with both of them. They're almost like family to you."

Joan unwrapped her arms and leaned forward, fixing me with a determined eye. "Carl and Marc are lovely people, Odelia, and excellent attorneys. But I don't want kind and nice. I want someone tough and brutal. Someone who'll tell us the truth without any sugarcoating."

"Well, you'd certainly get that with Steele."

"So you'll ask him if he'll help, or at least talk to us about the insurance thing?"

As if summoned from the underworld, Steele knocked and swung open the door to my office. "When I call you, Grey, I expect you to pick up the phone, *especially* if you're in the middle of girl-chat." He

160

flashed his eyes to Joan. She wrapped her arms around herself again as if her limbs were made of Kevlar.

"Do you mind, Steele?" I scowled in his direction. "We're talking about something important here."

He stepped past Joan and placed his hands, palms down, on my desk. "If you two ladies aren't talking about my deal, then it's not important. Got that?"

I turned to Joan, who'd shrunk in her seat in an attempt to disappear. "Sure this is what you want?"

Without looking at Steele, Joan shook her head up and down in short, fast staccato nods like spiked heels hitting pavement.

When Steele glanced her way, she froze. "As I asked yesterday, Nunez, don't you have any work to do?"

Joan shifted her big brown eyes to me. "Maybe we should do this another time?" She got up to leave.

"No," I said to her. "Stay where you are. It's now or never, Joan. If this is what you want, best to face it head-on." I looked up at Steele, who was glowering down at me, expecting me to jump at his command. "Joan has a problem, Steele, and she needs your help." Before he could say anything snarky, I added, "It's a legal problem."

At the mention of a legal problem, Steele's eyes sparkled with such interest, I half expected him to lick his chops. Encouraged, I threw more motivation into the pot. "And it may have something to do with Shirley Pearson's murder."

Steele pivoted his body fully toward Joan. His eyes went wide, his brows shooting upward with eagerness. His excitement buzzed like a loose electrical wire. "Really?" He studied Joan like a specimen under a microscope until she visibly squirmed.

"Joan, Steele knows about Shirley Pearson. He was in part of the meeting I had with Detective Frye, but he doesn't know about your dad."

"Your father?" A look of confusion replaced Steele's mad-scientist zeal. "But I thought your father passed away several years ago."

"He did," Joan squeaked out, not looking up at Steele. Instead, she looked at me, hoping for me to throw her a lifeline.

"It's a complicated story, Steele," I said, taking some of the pressure off my pal. "But mostly, I think Joan needs your advice on a possible insurance fraud situation."

Steele looked from Joan to me and back at Joan, his mind keenly zeroing in on and weighing the topic. "You, Nunez? Possible

162

insurance fraud?"

"Not Joan," I added. "Her mother. Seems her father didn't die after all and was recently found murdered. Now her mother is being investigated for insurance fraud on the money she collected after his first death."

"Damn!" Steele was seldom at a loss for words, but this definitely surprised him, though I wished he'd come out with something a bit more sympathetic and appropriate for Joan's sake. On second thought, I guess his enthusiasm was better than his usual snide remarks.

I turned my attention to Joan and jerked a thumb in Steele's direction. "Are you sure you want this clown involved?"

"Clown?" Steele interrupted his astonishment to raise a brow my way. "Remind me to have Jill add that to my résumé."

Joan raised her head and looked at Steele — really seriously considered him — as if seeing him for the first time. "Yes, I do. That's if *you* want to help, Mr. Steele."

In spite of his displeasure at being tagged with a circus moniker, I could tell Steele was near wetting himself with legal exhilaration.

"Sure," he told Joan. "As long as you drop the Mr. and as long as it doesn't interfere with this deal Grey and I are working on." He turned to me. "And that goes for both of us."

"No problem," I assured him.

Steele tossed me a look that screamed he didn't believe me. Sticking his hands back into the pockets of his fifteen-hundred-dollar suit, he leaned against my bookcase and addressed Joan. "So, Nunez, tell me what's going on, and how is this linked to Grey's latest murder?"

After Joan gave Steele a synopsis of what was going on with her mother, she had to leave. Jill had buzzed my phone to let us know that Marc Boer was looking for Joan and needed her.

"Glad to see someone still works around here," Steele quipped after she left my office.

Before Joan left, Steele asked if her mother could come in the next day, Saturday, around ten, saying they could meet more privately at that time. Joan had nearly kissed the hem of his pants in gratitude.

"It looks like there will be no leisurely Saturday for either of us." I shuffled the papers on my desk to find my way back to where I'd left off.

Steele took the seat Joan had vacated. "Why, Grey, you coming in to finally get some work done?"

I squinted at him. He knew damn well I was on top of everything, especially his deal of the moment. "No. Tomorrow at ten, I will be at Shirley Pearson's memorial service, along with Zee and Clark Littlejohn."

I'm not sure which part of my comment snagged his attention more, the part about Shirley's memorial or the part about my half brother being in town. Steele seemed torn about which to ask about first.

"Your brother's in town?" Curiosity about Clark won.

"Yep, showed up unannounced last night." I looked up from the clutter on my desk. "Seems he's retired from being a cop. He was interviewing for a consulting job in Phoenix and decided to pop on over."

"Will I get to meet him while he's here?"

"Not sure how long he's staying, but Greg and I were talking this morning about having a few folks over on Sunday afternoon for a barbecue. I'll be e-mailing details out tonight."

"Great. I'll bring the beer."

"Uh-huh. Are you being nice, or is it that you don't like our usual Sam Adams?"

Steele winked at me. "A bit of both."

He settled back in the chair as if he were the one with no work to do. "So have you really not found out anything about Joan's father, or are you keeping it to yourself to save her feelings?"

"I got nuthin'. Alfred Nunez lived in a modest apartment in Santa Ana and hung out with some other dead people. That's all I know."

"You think Joan's mother knew about his disappearance?"

"You'll need to ask her that tomorrow, Counselor."

Steele chuckled. "I intend to, but I want to know your opinion. What's your Spidey sense telling you?"

I put down the papers in my hand and sat back in my chair to give it some thought. "Hard to tell. I'm sure Joan knew nothing about it, and I'm leaning toward her mother not knowing either. Joan's mother is a lot like Joan, a real straight arrow. But Joan told me that her parents' marriage wasn't the best and Joan's mother, a devout Catholic, would never have divorced Alfred. Maybe they came to a mutual agreement to go their separate ways. Maybe not. Maybe it was all Alfred's idea."

Steele soaked in my middle-of-the-road opinion and considered it. "So why the funeral tomorrow?"

"It's actually just a memorial service. Not

166

sure the body's been released by the police yet. Going was Clark's idea, and a good one. I'm hoping to see some of the other folks in the photograph there — at least Clarice. Somebody had to arrange the service. I want to see who did and talk to them. Too many people in that photograph have flown the coop or died for it to be a coincidence."

Steele stood up to go. "Just be careful, Grey. It's very likely the killer will be there, too. If you seem too nosy, you might make the hit list."

"Is that a warning or wishful thinking?"

He opened my door. "Whichever it is, don't let anything happen to you until after this deal with Ogle closes. Got that?"

I threw him a salute. "Yes, sir!"

"That's more like it."

THIRTEEN

"Are you sure you have the right address?" Clark asked as we drove up and down Pacific Coast Highway in search of the location for the memorial service. "Maybe you jotted the numbers down wrong."

My nose twitched of its own accord. "I didn't jot down the numbers at all, I printed it out, so it's exactly as it was in the newspaper."

"Maybe you're reading it wrong," came Zee's voice from the back seat of Clark's rental car. "I keep telling you to get reading glasses."

Now my nose was vibrating with annoyance like a tuning fork. "I'm reading it just fine, thank you very much."

"Even if you are reading it wrong," Clark added, "I don't see any churches or funeral homes anywhere. In fact, no place where a memorial service would be held. Didn't the obit give you the name of the place?"

"Nope, just the address."

Clark was right. We were cruising the stretch of PCH just north of the touristy section of Laguna Beach, where the art galleries, high-end shops, and expensive hotels were located. In this section, the highway was lined with small everyday businesses and more budget-minded hotels. Not that it still wasn't lovely, just not as snooty. Nowhere along the street did I see any building suitable for housing a memorial service.

From the car, I tried to read the numbers on the buildings. Some I could see; some seemed nonexistent. "Maybe it's not at a church or a funeral home."

"If it's along here, it won't be."

"Steele lives down here." I turned to Clark. "That's my boss. He has a condo right on the beach a little farther down."

"Well, if all else fails, we can pop in for coffee."

I laughed. "Not sure Steele is the sort you can pop in on." I glanced at my watch. It was quarter to ten. "Besides, he had a meeting this morning at the office."

"On a Saturday?"

"My husband's in the office this morning, too," added Zee. "He's also an attorney."

Clark snorted. "Almost as bad as being a cop."

I returned to studying the numbers on the buildings. "We've gone too far again, Clark. Make a U-ey when you can, and let's go back. It should be on our right. On my side."

"But we're in the vicinity, right?" Clark's voice was cloaked in barely restrained frustration.

"Yes."

It was quite a stretch before Clark found a legal place to make a U-turn so we could go back for another pass. When we approached the addresses similar to that on my notes, I told him to slow down.

"Damn it, Odelia." Clark huffed and puffed. "It's a Saturday in June in a beach town. If I slowed down any more, we'd be parked."

"That's it!"

"You see it?" Hope swelled Zee's question like bad water retention.

"No," I clarified. "What I meant is, we should park. We know it's somewhere on this block, so we'll park and walk. There's no way we can miss it that way."

Up ahead, I saw someone pulling out of a parking spot. I patted Clark's arm. "There, Clark." I pointed. "There's a spot now. Right where that convertible is pulling out."

Fortunately, the two cars ahead of us didn't want the spot. Clark pulled in.

"Maybe you two should stay here and I'll hoof it solo and look for the numbers. No sense all of us getting hot and sweaty."

He had a point, but it hardly seemed fair. "That's okay, Clark, it's only on the next block."

Zee tapped my shoulder from the back seat. "He's being a gentleman, Odelia. Let him. It's okay by me."

Clark chuckled as he turned off the engine but left the AC on. "I'll wave if I find it. Just remember to pull out the car key and bring it with you."

Clark wasn't gone long before I saw him signaling us from the next block, indicating he'd found our destination. As instructed, I turned off the power and pulled the key out of the ignition before climbing out of the car.

It was warm, but it was still early in the day and we were close enough to the ocean to catch a lovely sea breeze. The weather man had promised temperatures in the mid-nineties by midday. Zee and I stepped lively along the sidewalk to where Clark stood in front of several storefronts and a bar. Even with the breeze, I could feel dampness gathering in my armpits, light seepage promising to be lakes in no time. Most of the people we passed on the street were

171

dressed in shorts and tank tops. Many of the women wore bikini tops with their shorts. In keeping with usual memorial service protocol, Zee and I were both wearing conservative dresses with heels.

When we reached Clark, I handed him his key. Looking around, I didn't see anything promising a staid and respectful memorial service. "Did you find it?" I asked. "Or did you decide to take us out for brunch instead?"

Without speaking, Clark held out the paper with the address on it, then pointed to some numbers above a garish, bright purple-lacquered closed door. They matched. A large sign proclaimed the place as Billie's Holiday. I showed the match to Zee.

She fanned her face. "Are you kidding?" She kept fanning.

My shoulders sagged. "I guess the address in the paper was wrong. Probably a typo. Sorry, guys."

"No, ladies," Clark told us with an odd but amused look on his face. "This is the right place. I poked my head in and asked someone. The memorial service is about to begin."

"Here?" I didn't believe him.

"Here," he assured us.

Besides the large sign proclaiming the place's name, there was an even larger sign claiming Billie's to have the "Best Drag Revue in Orange County" every Saturday evening. Two shows — nine o'clock and eleven o'clock. Knowing Orange County, it was probably the only drag queen revue in the county. Another sign to the left of the door announced drag queen bingo every Monday night at eight o'clock. I was a little worried about the type of business Billie's Holiday conducted the rest of the week. Nowhere did it claim to be available for memorial services.

When Clark pulled open the door, I noticed a sign printed in large block letters stuck to the front. It announced that the club would be closed until one o'clock for a private party. *Party?* Zee and I looked at each other, but neither moved to enter.

"You first, Odelia," Zee finally said. "By all means."

Squaring my shoulders, I stepped inside. Considering some of the places I'd been while pursuing witnesses and information, this should be a piece o' cake.

A welcome blast of AC greeted me as I stepped down the rabbit hole.

Also greeting me was a slim man with skin the color of caramel, wearing eyeliner and a light blue caftan. He had delicate features and short black hair tipped the color of a Creamsicle. "You here for the memorial?" he asked in a respectful whisper.

"Yes." I accompanied my own whisper with a nod, just in case he had any doubts. Behind me the door shut, closing off the light from outside. I glanced over my shoulder to make sure Clark and Zee hadn't abandoned me.

"You're just in time," the man said with a sad, small smile. "My name's Corey. Follow me."

Like a trio of ducklings, the three of us followed Corey into the club, which was much larger on the inside than it appeared outside. A long wooden bar with a lineup of empty stools ran along the left side. Behind the bar was the requisite mirror and colorful bottles of booze lined up on shelves, one behind the other, like fans at a sporting event. Half the length of the bar was set out with platters of food covered in plastic wrap and chafing dishes being kept warm with Sterno.

Across the way, on the other side of the room, was a low stage, its sparkly silver curtain pulled back on either side to reveal a thick backdrop. Corey blazed a trail through the valley of tables and chairs, a napkin dispenser and set of salt and pepper shakers on each, to the aisle between the tables and the bar. From there, he headed for a large open door on the far side of the place. The lights inside the club were turned up, exposing the scarred wood of the tables, the worn vinyl on the bar stools, and the less than glamorous stage. In a dark bar with the right lighting, it probably looked spectacular.

"Is this a restaurant or a nightclub?" I whispered, taking a couple of quick steps to get closer to our guide.

"Both," he whispered back. "We usually open on the weekends for lunch at noon. Best burgers in the area. During the week, we don't open until four thirty."

On the other side of the door that was our destination was a separate room, still good-sized though only about half the size of the restaurant. It was probably a space they rented out for private parties and meetings. Inside, metal folding chairs were lined up with their backs to us, facing a makeshift altar on which stood an easel holding an enlarged photograph of Shirley Pearson. Next to the photograph were several gorgeous baskets of flowers. Flanking it all were two tall candelabras finished off with lit white tapers, standing like guards to an

175

ancient tomb. Nearly all the seats were full, and many people stood along the walls. Corey led us to the back row on the left side, where a couple of empty chairs dotted the row like missing teeth. Two men, their eyes wet and hands clasped, scooted down, condensing the empties to make room for the three of us to sit together.

The photo of Shirley was a glamour shot or possibly a professional headshot. She looked out on the attendees like royalty waiting for the crowd to hush so she could impart words of wisdom to her subjects. From unseen speakers, a soft instrumental piece played.

We were barely seated when the music stopped and a tall, slender man dressed in a black shirt, shiny black tie, and black pants took the stage. He looked to be pulling forty rather than pushing it. His dark hair was cropped close to his head, as was his beard. His angular face sagged with grief. He introduced himself as Marvin Gunn, the owner of Billie's Holiday and longtime friend of Shirley Pearson's. He thanked us all for coming.

Gunn talked with emotion, saying the things usually said at a memorial service for a loved one. He told the gathering how he'd first met the then-Doug Pearson shortly after Doug had arrived in Los Angeles as a very young man, confused and alone, seeking a new life and to be accepted as himself. Next to me, the two men who'd moved to accommodate us nodded in understanding and clutched each other's hands. As tears welled in his eyes, Gunn continued, describing how Doug had blossomed after becoming Shirley. How she'd been a natural onstage and an astute business woman offstage, even starting her own successful event planning business.

I craned my neck this way and that until I thought it would snap. Being short and being in the back row, I couldn't make out the faces of any mourners except those seated in my row. All I could see was a lake of heads of various heights, colors, and genders, and even the genders were hazy in many cases. If Clarice was here, I wouldn't know until the service was over and people left their seats. From the back, none of the people I could see looked like Clarice. Three mourners wore straw hats. When the service was over, they would be my first targets.

As Gunn continued to speak, I studied him, getting a sense of familiarity. I'd left my large, bulky tote bag at home, opting instead for a smaller shoulder bag. It currently sat on my lap. From it, I discretely removed the photo and looked from it to the altar several times. Standing in the back of the group in the photo was a man who looked sort of like Marvin Gunn, though I wasn't positive. The man in the photo didn't have a beard, and his hair was longer. He was standing almost directly behind Shirley Pearson, who was sitting next to Clarice.

Was Marvin Gunn also running from something in his past? Was it a criminal act, like Shirley, or something else? Or maybe he wasn't a runner at all. For all I knew, Marvin Gunn always was his real name, and he just happened to know the same people.

I scanned the photo again. There were a couple of other unidentified people in it, making me wonder if they'd be here today to say goodbye to Shirley. I focused on the unknown faces, hoping to burn them into my memory. It wasn't as if I could go around the service holding the photo up against people's faces for comparison.

To my left, Clark gently poked me. When I glanced his way, he bent close to my ear and whispered, "There's a cop here. I'm sure of it." He directed my gaze over his left shoulder.

Crap!

Standing against the back wall was Dev Frye. He was just a few feet away, wedged into the corner, trying to look inconspicuous. But between his bulk and his conservative suit in a sea of colorful caftans and trendy attire, he was failing big time. He was looking straight at me. He didn't look pleased. I gave him a small smile and finger wave before turning my head back toward the altar. After all, it was a free country, and I did know Shirley — sort of. Why shouldn't I be here?

"That's not just a cop," I whispered to Clark. "That's Dev."

Clark didn't glance back but looked straight ahead, a smart-ass grin plastered to his face. "I like the man already," he whispered from the corner of his mouth.

When he was done, Marvin Gunn invited people from the audience to come up and say a few words about Shirley. At first, the crowd remained self-conscious and silent until one young man got up and talked about how Shirley helped him find a job and a place to live. Then another man stood and praised her generosity. A woman, beset with tears, told the crowd how Shirley had helped her family get through her brother's death from AIDS. One after another, people somberly filed up to the altar to sing Shirley Pearson's praises, making her sound more like a saint than an armed bank robber.

179

When people were finished, Marvin Gunn returned to the altar. In closing, he invited the gathering to stay for refreshments. His last action was to call a man from the front row up to the altar, introducing him as a pastor from a local church. The pastor invited us all to bow our heads in prayer.

Not that I wanted to tick off God or anything — I need every advantage in my corner — but I couldn't help but raise my head while everyone else's was bowed to survey the crowd. And I was glad I did, because one of the ladies wearing a straw hat was trying to sneak out.

I wasn't the only one who noticed. From the back of the room, Dev Fry was dividing his time between watching me and watching the woman make her getaway.

FOURTEEN

The woman had been seated on a far aisle seat. As she tiptoed out, I stood as quietly as possible, which caused Zee to open her eyes and turn her bowed head my way. Zee didn't approve of people sneaking out during prayers of any kind, and the look she gave me told me so. I pretended I didn't see it and turned to edge pass Clark, who had the aisle seat on our side. For a brief moment, he blocked me with his knees. Then, seeing my quarry, he moved his legs to let me pass. I felt sure he wanted to get up and follow, too, but there was no sense spooking the woman with a mass exodus. As it was, I was going to have Dev tailing my every move, and Clark knew it.

I still wasn't sure if it was Clarice Hollowell or if she'd noticed me yet. The woman had her head down, the hat tilted to cover her face. But the slim build was the same, and I was sure it was the same dress she'd worn the day she stopped by my home. Fortunately, there was only one exit from the room, and we were going to reach it about the same time.

Glancing at Dev, I saw that he was watching me like a hawk. He was really screwing up my plans. I needed to ask Clarice some questions, but she would never talk while he was there. And I would never get a chance to ask her anything if Dev swooped in and nabbed her for police questioning.

Good thing for all of us, the pastor was long-winded. Most of the mourners kept their heads down while the quiet and desperate race for the door went on behind them.

The woman was scurrying, moving fast and quietly on wedged espadrilles. She made it to the door just before me. Not moving from his corner, Dev never took his eyes off us. He was letting me do his legwork — waiting until I tackled her before he sauntered in and took charge. It annoyed me, but I was too occupied in my pursuit to shoot him a look full of daggers.

Out in the bar area, waiters in white shirts and black pants were removing the plastic wrap and readying the food for the mourners. I wanted to call out to the woman as she scooted toward the front door and her getaway but knew my voice would carry back into the quiet memorial service. Instead, I picked up my pace, my heels sounding out a choppy Morse code across the hard club floor. So much for not disturbing the service.

"Pssst," I called to Clarice through my teeth. "Hold up." She didn't stop.

Determined to catch up to her before she made it out the front door, I briefly entertained the thought of a tackle. Instead, with one last effort, I put some kick into my step, thankful the maze of tables was slowing her down. Just as she reached the door, I got a hand on her arm and stopped her.

"I need to talk to you."

She spun around, her head still down so I couldn't see her face. With a sinking feeling in my gut, I grabbed the straw hat and snatched it from her head.

"Hey!" A head shot up, eyes frightened and indignant at the same time. It wasn't Clarice. It wasn't even a she. Under the hat was a slight young man wearing makeup and lipstick.

"I'm sorry." I handed the hat back. "I thought you were someone else."

"You Odelia Grey?" my prey asked in a forced breathy voice.

Behind me, I heard the service breaking

183

up and people filing into the restaurant.

"Yes, I am."

"This is for you." He opened his bag, pulled out a slip of paper, and handed it to me.

"Hey, Betty," a man called from the bar area. "This woman bothering you?"

"No, Stan," the guy in the Clarice costume called back. "We're good."

"Everything okay here?" came another voice. I didn't have to turn around to know that Dev Fry would be behind me. Betty started to head out the door, but Dev stuck out a hand to detain him. "Hold on a second, please." He discreetly flashed Betty his badge.

"I didn't do anything wrong," Betty protested, his Adam's apple bobbing like a trapped mouse in a snake's belly. Dev guided Betty away from the door to a nearby table, depositing his keister on a chair.

Ignoring both of them, I opened the note to read three words written in a tight hand: *Odelia, you're fired. — C.*

Fired?

People not staying for the reception were slipping by me and out the door, murmuring various subdued forms of "excuse me" as they passed. I stood rooted to the floor, staring at the note in my hand, a confused island in an eclectic sea of mourners, until a strong hand gripped my arm and dragged me to the side and out of the way. I looked up to see the hand belonged to Clark. Next to him was a concerned Zee. I passed the note to Clark.

After reading the note, Clark handed it off to Dev. "By the way, I'm Clark Littlejohn."

The announcement caught Dev by surprise. "Odelia's brother?"

"Yep, one and the same. I understand you're Detective Dev Frye." Clark stuck out his hand. Dev took it and gave it a strong shake, his other brawny hand on Betty's shoulder like a paperweight.

"Dammit," I said to no one in particular, "I should have known Clarice wouldn't have worn the same dress twice in a month, let alone in the same week." I wanted to kick myself for taking the bait.

"Odelia, are you okay?" The question came from Zee.

"She fired me, Zee."

"Who fired you?"

It was then I realized I hadn't told Zee anything about the past few days' events — and with good reason. She was still reeling from her daughter's wedding being a murder scene, and I had wanted to keep her out of the peripheral problems.

"Never mind, Zee. It's just crazy talk."

Zee moved directly in front of me, one hand on her hip, the other clutching her purse. "I'm far from stupid, Odelia. I knew you didn't come here just to say goodbye to Shirley Pearson."

"You're right, but let me fill you in later." She looked at me, her dark face full of doubt. "I promise," I tacked on quickly.

"I'm going to hold you to that." The hand once on her hip was now pointing a finger at me.

A waiter came by with a tray of champagne flutes filled with orange liquid. "Mimosa?"

I took one. Zee, who hardly ever drank alcohol, declined. Clark didn't drink. And Dev was on duty. Before the waiter could get away, I kicked back the sweet and bubbly concoction, replaced the empty glass on the tray, and scooped up a second one as backup.

Zee eyed me as if I were one of her kids caught in a suspicious act.

"What?" I looked at the drink in my hand, then back at her. "They're small."

"If you're going to guzzle like that," Zee told me with disapproval, "I'm going to get you some food."

"Swell," I answered, my eyes not on her but on Betty.

Zee left, and I took the chair next to him. Dev was standing like a skyscraper over the tiny cross-dresser, questioning him but getting nowhere. Clark stood nearby, his trained eyes surveying the milling crowd for anything out of the ordinary. Two cops hovering over the person I wanted to question were two cops too many, even if one was supposedly retired.

"When did Clarice give you that note?" I asked Betty.

"Like I told this . . . this *brute*," he shot his eyes up at Dev, "my name is Betty Rumble, and that's all you're getting from me." He crossed his arms over his flat chest like a petulant child.

Betty Rumble? My eyes did a quick scan of the man in drag next to me. He wasn't wearing a wig. Under the hat, his hair was blond, short, and spiked. He had great cheekbones and knew how to wield both blush and eye shadow to his advantage. But even by female standards, he was pretty skimpy in the bulk department. He didn't look like he could rumble with Muffin, let alone go a few rounds with Wilma Flintstone.

I took a drink from my mimosa. "Look,

Betty," I started again, infusing my voice with softness, helped no doubt by the booze, "I know you didn't do anything wrong, but I need to talk to Clarice. Where is she?"

He uncrossed his arms — a good sign. "Look, if I tell you, will you let me go?" He didn't look up at Dev, just at me. When Dev squeezed the hand on his shoulder, Betty jerked it from his grasp. "I really have to get home. It's an emergency." He sounded genuinely flustered.

I looked up at Dev. He nodded, then added, "As long as we know how to reach you."

"Yes, Betty," I confirmed. "You can go. We also need to know how to reach Clarice Hollowell."

"Hollowell?" Betty looked surprised. "You mean Clarice Thomas, don't you?"

"Yes," I said quickly, trying not to look surprised. "Hollowell was her married name." I didn't look up at Dev. I didn't have to. I knew he was listening and taking mental notes. A quick scamper through my memory reminded me that Clarice's maiden name had been Thomas. It sounded as if she'd gone back to using it. It was a common name, and no one would question her use of it.

"Clarice came in here last night," Betty began. "I wait tables Friday nights and weekends." Betty crossed his slim legs and leaned forward. He seemed jumpy and eager to say his piece and leave. "She told me she'd pay me to wear her clothes and come here today and give you that note."

"But you almost left without giving it to me," I pointed out.

"I know. I'm sorry," he said in a hurry. "But I got a text telling me to come home right away."

"What's the rush?" Dev asked.

"Tiffany — that's my dog — she's having puppies. Right now," he emphasized. "Please, I have to get home."

When we didn't say anything, Betty dug a phone out of his purse and showed it to me. There on the screen was a text message: PUPPIES COMING. He also flashed it at Dev.

"Anything wrong, Betty?"

Marvin Gunn had stepped up to our table. Behind him was Zee, holding two small plates of finger foods. I also saw that other people, while keeping their distance, were watching us and straining to listen while they munched snacks and drank their mimosas. We may not have been onstage, but we were definitely the entertainment.

"I . . ." Betty looked from me to Dev, then

189

whined, "Tiffany's having her puppies, Marv, but they won't let me go."

I started to say something, but a look from Dev stopped me. He showed Marvin Gunn his credentials. "I just wanted to ask Betty a few questions in connection with the murder of Shirley Pearson."

"Shirley?" Betty turned pale. "But I thought this was about Clarice? I don't know anything about what happened to poor Shirley!" With each word, Betty's voice got noticeably higher.

Several tables of people near us went silent, and soon we elevated from a casual floor show to an entire roadside attraction.

"Do you have to do this here, Detective?" Gunn moved closer to the table and shot his eyes over the watching crowd.

"You have a point, Mr. Gunn." Dev placed his hand back on Betty's shoulder. "We can take Ms. Rumble here to the station. That way you and your guests can continue in peace."

Betty fluttered a delicate hand. He looked about to have an old-fashioned attack of the vapors. "All I know is Clarice paid me a hundred dollars to wear her clothes today and give that note to someone named Odelia. I figured, why not? I was coming to the service anyway." His big eyes begged

Dev to believe him. "That's all I know, honest."

Clarice was that sure I'd be here. I didn't like the fact she had me so pegged. "But what if I hadn't come to the service?"

"Then I was simply to come and pay my respects. I got the money either way."

Dev tossed his small notebook and a pen on the table in front of Betty. "Jot down a number and address where you can be reached, just in case." Betty snatched up the notebook and started writing as if time on a pop quiz were running out.

"What about you?" Dev asked Marvin Gunn. "What can you tell me about Clarice Hollowell? She might be going by the name Clarice Thomas."

Gunn shrugged. "I've seen her in here, mostly with Shirley. They were close friends and business partners, but that's all I know about her."

"You don't know how to reach her?"

"Sorry, Detective. I didn't even remember her last name until you just said it."

Dev didn't give up. "How about the name Alfonso or Alfred Nunez? That mean anything to you?"

Gunn thought a minute, then shook his head. "Sorry, not a clue. Should I know it?"

"He might have hung around the two of them."

"Look, Detective." Gunn leaned in and lowered his voice. "After Shirley stopped performing here and became a fancy event planner, she started traveling in a different circle. She and that Clarice woman came in once in a while for drinks or a bite to eat. Rambling Rose is just up the street. It was convenient for them. But that's it."

"But I thought you and Shirley were tight." Dev never took his eyes off Gunn's face nor his hand off Betty's shoulder.

"We were," Gunn explained, "once upon a time. When she died, all her new friends disappeared. Giving her this service was the least we could do."

I remained quiet — not an easy thing. I was antsy to question Marvin Gunn about his knowledge of not just Shirley and Clarice but of Scott Johnson and Roslyn Stevens. I hadn't told Dev about what Greg and I had learned Thursday night, and I didn't know if he recognized Marvin Gunn from the photo. Geez, even I wasn't sure it was him. The face was similar but not quite the same, though it was difficult to tell with the beard.

Dev took his hand from Betty's shoulder. "You can go."

Betty got up to leave but Dev stopped

him, holding out his hand. "The notebook."

Betty closed it and handed both it and the pen back to Dev, then skedaddled out the door as fast as his espadrilles could carry him.

Zee approached the table and placed a small plate of food in front of me. Without a word, she picked up my half-empty mimosa glass and drank it down in one gulp.

Dev was about to say something to Gunn when Betty raced back in, slightly flushed. "Marv, I'll need tonight off. Tiffany and all, you know."

FIFTEEN

Dev popped a whole stuffed mushroom in his mouth and chewed, his thoughts a million miles away. Without losing a step, he popped another into his face.

"How many did you grab on the way out?" I asked.

"Just a couple. Too bad we couldn't stay. These are great. Wouldn't mind a few more." He popped in the third and final, then looked around for a napkin. That, he'd forgotten to grab. We stopped several yards away from the entrance to Billie's Holiday while Dev tried to figure out what to do with his greasy fingers.

"Oh, for heaven's sake," huffed Zee. "Here." From her purse she produced a couple of tissues from a travel-size pack and handed them to the large, oily detective. Zee wasn't happy, but it had nothing to do with Dev grabbing the stuffed mushrooms from the buffet on our way out the door.

"Never!" she said, walking off ahead of us toward the car. "*Never* have I been asked to leave a funeral. Or anywhere else, I might add."

"Technically," I offered, trying to be helpful, "it wasn't a funeral, Zee. It was a memorial service. The body hasn't been buried yet."

She did an about-face and glared at me.

I turned to Dev. "Am I right or am I right?"

"Odelia's right. It was a memorial service."

Zee narrowed her eyes until they were no more than dark, furious slits. "I don't care what it was technically. We were still asked to leave, as if we were a bunch of hooligans."

"Oh, come on, Zee," I told her. "It's not like we were dancing on tables or throwing punches." She rolled her eyes at me. "And," I continued, "it was really Dev who was asked to leave."

Dev tossed the dirty tissue into a nearby trash can planted on the sidewalk. "No, I'm pretty sure we were all asked to leave. Though if we're getting technical, I was there on a murder investigation. I didn't have to do a damn thing Gunn asked. I left because it would have been counterproductive to stay."

I shrugged. "Let's face it, it could have happened to anyone."

Both Dev and Zee came to a halt on the sidewalk and stared at me like I was a giant mouse asking for directions to Disneyland. Looking down at my shoes, I noticed meatball gravy oozing from the peek-a-boo toe of one. It was squishy and totally clashed with the large pale orange abstract of mimosa staining the front of my linen dress.

Right after Gunn had granted the new doggie daddy leave to take the night off, he'd given Dev a gracious smile and turned him away from the prying eyes of the crowd as if they were two old friends consoling each other. Gunn's real purpose was to ask if there might be a more appropriate time for Dev to be asking his questions. As discreetly as possible, I had scooted my chair closer to them.

"This is a murder investigation, Mr. Gunn," Dev explained again. "What better time than when all of Ms. Pearson's friends are gathered?"

"It's disrespectful, Detective."

"I find murder the ultimate disrespect, Mr. Gunn. Don't you?" Dev looked back around the room. "And we believe Ms. Pearson was killed by someone she knew quite well. Possibly someone in this very room." Dev put some distance between Gunn and himself. "Speaking of which, may I ask what you were doing last Saturday evening?"

"It happened at my daughter's wedding reception," Zee added, as if that might jar Gunn's memory. Instead, he looked at her as if she were an annoying fly.

When the mimosa man came by again, I took another glass. This time, Zee took one of her own. I asked the waiter if he could bring us two Cokes, diet or otherwise, one each for Clark and Dev. Then I noticed Clark wasn't around. I stood up and scanned the room but didn't see him. I sat down again, thinking he must have gone to the men's room.

Gunn looked surprised by Dev's question. "Why, I was here, as I am every Saturday night. The revue is our biggest night. I'm always here on Saturday evening, and I personally close the place at 2 a.m. Sunday morning."

I couldn't help but chuckle. "Detective Frye doesn't exactly hang out in gay bars."

Again, Gunn was surprised. "Billie's Holiday isn't a gay bar. Most of our clientele is straight, especially for the drag revue and Monday night bingo." He gave us all a smug look. "You folks don't get out much, do you?"

Ignoring the dig, Dev plodded on. "You have anyone who can vouch for you last Saturday?"

Gunn looked around the room and smiled. "Ask almost anyone here in drag."

About the time Gunn took his leave, the sodas arrived. Dev pulled the straw out of one and drank down half of it, followed by downing a flaky phyllo dough triangle stuffed with cheese from one of the plates Zee had fetched. He ate and drank in silence and watched the crowd, the wheels in his skull working in sync with his chewing.

Seeing the small plates on our table were nearly empty, Zee started to get up for a refill. I stopped her. "I'll go. I need to stretch my legs and see where Clark's at."

"Snag some of the tiny meatballs while you're at it," Zee requested. "There was a big crowd around them before."

"And more stuffed mushrooms," Dev called, still not taking his eyes off the crowd.

Even though the crowd had thinned some, it was still healthy in number. People were hanging around, talking and laughing. Some were hugging. Nowhere did I see Clark. I worked my way to the bar and the food, hoping the meatballs and mushrooms were still in good supply. I grabbed two of the small plates and filled one with carrots and celery, some cheese cubes and crackers. On the other I piled a few of the phyllo pastries and several mushrooms. A man watched me fill my plate. In an exaggerated gesture, his disapproving eyes scanned my plus-sized body like an MRI.

"I'm eating for four," I explained, treating him to a gooey, sweet smile.

I moved on to attack the meatballs. They were arranged neatly in their chafing dish, each speared through with fancy toothpicks like tiny gravy-coated lollipops. I plucked out several and added them to the plate with the other hot foods.

Across from me, a man was adding a few meatballs to his own plate. He looked vaguely familiar. I stalled, pretending to be picky about which gob of meat I chose while trying to place him. He was middle-aged and kind of nerdy, like a junior college math teacher. He wore wire-framed glasses and his head was mostly bald. What hair he had left was gray and trimmed close to his head in a ring.

"They look delicious, don't they?" I asked, striking up a conversation.

He glanced up as he put two on his plate

but didn't say anything. He took a step sideways to consider the next tray of food.

"A friend of mine is addicted to the mushrooms." I held out my plate, showing off the small pile I'd made for Dev.

He sighed and concentrated on his food, clearly blowing me off. Either he thought I was trying to pick him up or a silly woman starved for chitchat. I had my suspicion as to his identity, and my knees nearly knocked in anticipation. The hair was different, but the build and face were the same. I hadn't seen him in the crowd of mourners in the service, but he could have arrived after or simply blended in with the crowd. He had the kind of face and nondescript appearance that wouldn't stand out even if he were alone in a room. Some people were like that. Even when they showed up, others had trouble remembering they were ever there. It was the perfect persona for someone trying to hide in plain sight.

I held out the meatball still suspended in my hand. "Do you think they make these with ground turkey, ground beef, or a blend?"

This time the man looked up at me with undisguised disgust. Getting a full-on look at his face gave my notion legs to stand on. I was talking meatballs with Scott Johnson.

I'd bet my next mimosa on it.

"I don't want to appear rude," he said to me in a quiet voice, "but I'd like to be left alone."

"I'm sorry," I told him, putting the meatball on my plate. "How insensitive of me." I pretended to leave the buffet, then turned around and stood in front of him again. "One last question, if you'll permit me?"

He looked up, making no attempt to hide a look of barely reined impatience. "What else?"

I leaned slightly forward, my boobs dangerously close to the meatballs. I motioned for him to lean forward, too, so we could have a private word. Surprisingly, he did so.

"Tell me, Scott," I whispered. "Where have you stashed Roslyn Stevens?"

Scott Johnson jerked back quickly like I'd spit in his face.

"And what are you running from?" I tacked on.

"Who the hell are you?" He'd leaned forward again, his hushed words sounding like the first complaints of a tea kettle.

I'd expected my questions to elicit some sort of fear, but I saw none in his medium-brown eyes, only surprise and anger — and emptiness. His eyes were a cold dead zone that made me pull back on my side of the serving tray.

A woman came up next to me and surveyed the mushrooms. "Don't bother," Scott snapped at her. "They're awful."

She looked shocked by his words, having probably already eaten some and found them delicious, but the edge in his voice turned her away.

Scott turned his attention back to me. "Who are you?" he asked again, this time coating his question with menace.

"Who I am doesn't matter, Scott. What matters is that huge, bulky homicide cop over there." Without taking my eyes from Scott Johnson's face, I pointed in the general direction of Dev Frye. "Besides Shirley Pearson, he's asking people about some other folks you know, like Clarice Thomas and Alfonso Nunez."

His eyes never left mine, but instead of widening with surprise, they narrowed until they almost joined to make one horizontal abyss.

"I'll bet he'd also be interested in asking you about Scott Joyce."

The chafing dish of meatballs flew at me so unexpectedly I barely had time to jump back. It landed on the floor with a crash, dousing my ankles and feet with warm gravy. Instead of apologizing for the mishap,

Scott took off toward the back of the room and disappeared down a corridor marked with an exit sign.

Heedless of the stares from the crowd, I took off after him. I didn't get far. Actually, I didn't get more than one single step before my foot hit a puddle of gravy and I went down like a pudgy cat surprise testing a Slip 'n Slide — howl and all. On the way down, I grasped at the nearest thing to me — a waiter carrying a tray of mimosas. I took him to the floor with me. The two of us wallowed in gravy and booze while mourners snapped off photos with their phones like a bunch of tourists.

Marvin Gunn was not amused. He rushed over, reaching me about the same time as Dev and Zee.

"Enough!" Gunn bellowed. One of his feet skidded on a meatball, and he went down on his backside.

Zee grabbed napkins from the buffet and did her best to dry me off. "What on earth is going on, Odelia?"

Dev was more solicitous. "You okay?" he asked. He looked toward the exit. "Who was that you were talking to?"

"Scott Johnson," I whispered.

Dev took off for the corridor. When he returned a couple of minutes later, Gunn, the waiter, and I were back on our feet. Dev shook his head, letting me know he'd come up empty in his late pursuit.

Gunn, his face red and puffy with rage, stomped up to Dev. Even though Marvin Gunn was tall, he still had to look up. "I want you and these lunatics out of here, Detective. Right now!"

That's how we ended up on the sidewalk, me with gravy in my shoes.

We were just a few feet from Clark's rental car when Dev asked, "Are you sure it was Johnson who threw the meatballs at you, Odelia?"

My eyes moved from my shoes up to Dev, but it wasn't Scott Johnson who was on my mind. "Has anyone seen Clark?"

The two of them looked around as if he'd materialize from one of the nearby shops. Like me, they'd completely forgotten he was with us.

"You two stay here," Dev ordered. "I'll go back in and get him."

As soon as Dev headed down the street, Zee cornered me. She grabbed my arm, and not too gently. "What is this about, Odelia?"

Since Clark had the car keys, we had no choice but to stand on the sidewalk in the heat. I steered Zee out of the sun, taking refuge under an awning that stretched across several storefronts. Leaning against the brick wall between a nail shop and a dry cleaners, I brought her up to date on everything.

"So the Clarice you were talking about in the bar was the same one you met when Sophie died?"

I nodded. "Yes."

"And she wants you to find her missing friends?" Zee took out another tissue and touched it to her damp forehead.

"Did," I corrected. "She fired me. That's what was on the note Betty Rumble gave me. It was a note from Clarice saying I was fired." Remembering I had stashed the note in my bag, I dug it out and handed it to Zee.

After reading it, Zee handed it back. I returned the note to my purse and said, "I want to talk to her. Maybe I can change her mind."

Forget a wooden coat hanger, Zee looked like she wanted to smack me in the head with a shovel. "You are joking, aren't you?"

"No, Zee, I'm not. I demand to know why she changed her mind. Fired? No one fires me without good reason. In fact, I've only been fired once in my life, and that was when I was twenty and working at a greasy spoon. My boss grabbed my ass, and I decked him."

I paused a moment to corral my thoughts, sensing they were about to jump the track. "And I want to know who killed Alfred Nunez. That's the least I can do for Joan."

Pointing back down the street in the direction of Billie's Holiday, I added, "And after the way Scott Johnson spooked, I damn well want to know what has happened to Roslyn Stevens. There was something not right about him, Zee. I could almost smell it. Like milk on the verge of turning sour."

Grabbing both of my upper arms, Zee gently shook me. "Get a grip, Odelia," she ordered. "First of all, it's not like you were fired from a real job. Secondly, Dev Frye is working the murder case, not you. Fill him in on everything, and then let it be. He's a trained professional with lots of other trained professionals at his disposal."

As if on cue, we spotted Dev coming out of the bar, heading toward us. He was alone. When he saw us, he shrugged. He hadn't found Clark. Then we heard someone call to us. Zee and I turned toward the sound to see Clark across the street. He waved to us as he waited for a break in traffic to cross. What in the hell was he doing over there, sightseeing?

A dark car moving south in the traffic

passed Clark, then swung out of the line of cars, making an illegal U-turn in front of Billie's Holiday. Northbound traffic came to a screeching halt. Clark yelled and ran toward us across the four-lane highway, dodging cars and waving his arms. The sound of more screeching brakes and tires filled the air as cars did their best to avoid hitting him and each other.

I couldn't hear what Clark was yelling over the traffic, but I felt like one of the cars had hit me head-on. Zee and I fell to the ground together behind the rental car, brought down as easily as peewee football players tackled by a professional linebacker.

I had no trouble hearing the bullets. They hit the wall behind us with a crack that nearly split my eardrums. One hit the back window of Clark's car. Bits of brick and glass showered down on Zee and me as we lay under the bulk of Dev Frye.

SIXTEEN

"There's no barbecue today, Steele. Didn't you get the e-mail from Greg?"

Mike Steele was standing in my kitchen Sunday afternoon wearing cargo shorts, top-siders, and a blue knit shirt with an alligator on the breast. He looked different in his casual clothes — more human, less cocky. On the counter next to him were two six-packs of fancy beer and a bakery box. Hanging from one of his arms was a fabric grocery bag.

"Of course I did," he told me. His mouth played with the idea of smiling, then gave it up, settling for the safer and more noncommittal straight line. "Doesn't mean I paid any attention to it."

Greg had coaxed me from the bedroom, saying I had company. Steele being here today did not constitute company. It smacked of an invasion. "I'm not in the mood for your shenanigans, Steele, so get your butt back in your Porsche and hit the road."

Wainwright stood in front of Steele, wagging his tail enthusiastically. He loved Steele, proving once and for all even the most astute animal can be snookered. Clark, leaning on the kitchen counter, also looked taken in by Steele's uncharacteristic kindness.

"See," Steele said, indicating the dog, "Wainwright wants me to stay. Besides, I brought a bribe — for both of you."

I placed a hand on a hip and rolled my eyes. "You think overpriced beer is going to bribe me?"

"Nah, that's for Greg. For you, I brought cheesecake. New York style, just the way you like it, with fresh strawberries on top." He looked down at Wainwright and made a clucking noise. "And for you, Wainwright, I brought steak — top of the line, wrapped in bacon."

"You brought our dog filets wrapped in bacon?"

Steele let his eyes drift from Wainwright up to my face, still not sure it was appropriate to smile or not. He was walking on egg shells around me, like I was a bomb that could detonate just by a misguided look. And I was.

"I brought the steaks for all of us, Grey."

I was starving. The last thing I remember eating was a phyllo triangle at the memorial service the day before. But hungry or not, thinking about food made my gut lurch. What I wanted was to be left alone.

The barbecue had been cancelled yesterday afternoon — after the Newport Beach cops had questioned me, Zee, Clark, and even Dev, one of their own, about the shooting until we all thought we'd go mad. Cancelled, right after Seth and Greg arrived on the scene, and Seth told me I couldn't play with my best friend anymore. Right after Zee looked me in the eye and said enough was enough: I had to choose between murder and her friendship.

After we'd returned home, Greg had convinced me to take a hot shower. When I refused food, he held me while I cried myself to sleep. Beyond that, Greg and Clark were both at a loss about how to console me. Zee was right. I had to choose. I'd nearly gotten my best friend and Dev killed. And what if Clark had been standing with us instead of across the street? I'd killed someone once. I didn't want the blood of people I loved also on my hands.

As Clark reported to the police, while he was waiting for the traffic to break so he could join us on our side of the street, he'd noticed a black BMW roll by and saw the passenger holding a gun. After the car made its hasty U-turn, Clark quickly realized a drive-by was in progress and assumed Dev was the target. But the shooter had waited until he passed Dev before he took aim. Dev also saw the gun and made a leap for Zee and me, knocking us out of the way of the flying bullets. Three shots had been fired — three too many — before the car sped away. Dev and Clark had saved our lives.

When we fell, the side of my face hit the pavement, giving me a nasty scrape across most of my right cheek. Zee had broken her wrist. It wasn't a bad break, and it certainly was better than the alternative, but had it not been for me and my nosiness, she wouldn't have been put in such danger. None of us would have been.

I sniffed back the tears beginning to form and stuck my jaw out at Steele. "Maybe we've already eaten."

"I told him we hadn't, sweetheart." From behind me, Greg rolled up.

Steele stepped forward and put his hands on my upper arms, just below the shoulders, just as Zee had done moments before the shots were fired. I didn't look up at him. Instead, I studied the floor between us.

"After I heard on the news about the shooting, I wanted to see for myself how you were doing. I called Greg this morning to check on you."

And it had been on the news — all over the news. Drive-by shootings never happened in Corona del Mar. It had been a first for the sleepy, upscale beach village. I'm sure when the police first got the call, they'd thought it a hoax, an early Halloween prank, or late April Fool's joke.

"You mean, you wanted to make sure I was able to go to the office tomorrow and work on your precious deal."

Steele gently squeezed my arms. His hands were warm through the short sleeves of my tee shirt. "Take tomorrow off, Grey. I insist on it."

"Tell you what, Steele. I'm gonna take you up on that offer." I disengaged myself from his clutches and went into the kitchen. Nudging Clark out of the way, I opened a drawer and pulled out a fork. "In the meantime, you and the boys here fire up the grill. Stuff yourselves silly on steaks and wash it down with beer. I don't care." Picking up the bakery box, I headed back to our bedroom, fork held aloft like a lance.

"No, you don't, Odelia." With speed and moves usually reserved for the basketball court, Greg rolled between me and the doorway to our master suite, blocking my way. "You are not running away from this. And you are not eating that cheesecake. You can have some after you've had something healthy to eat."

Oh no, he did not just say that to me. Tell me, dear God, he didn't. I stared at my husband, my eyes wide with rage. "I'm not five years old, Greg. Get out of my way or you'll be wearing the cheesecake as a hat."

He didn't back down. "I'd rather be wearing it than you eating it. In the condition you're in, it will make you sick. You know that. Stress eating always does a number on you, emotionally and physically."

He had a point, but I didn't want to hear it. "I just lost my best friend. I'm already sick, so what's the difference?"

Greg put his hands on the bakery box and gently attempted to tug it out of my grip. I resisted. He pulled harder, never taking his eyes off of mine. This time, I let him have it. I started crying.

Clark came over and took the box from Greg. Being a smart and cautious man, he also removed the fork from my hand, taking them both back to the kitchen.

"Would you like to join me outside?" I heard Clark ask Steele.

I didn't hear Steele's answer but heard footsteps and the back slider open, then close.

"I need to pee."

Greg moved out of my way so I could go into our bathroom. When I came out, he was positioned by our bed. The door separating the bedroom area from the rest of the house was closed.

"Sit down, sweetheart," he said, patting the comforter. Both cats were already there, curled up in a beige and gray ball, the colors the only suggestion of where one cat left off and the other began. Wainwright was probably outside playing host to our guests. I took a seat on the edge of our California king bed close to Greg's wheelchair. He took both my hands in his.

"I know you're breaking apart over this thing with Zee, sweetheart, but it's going to turn out fine. You'll see."

I started weeping, my chin down, nearly resting on my chest. "But I've lost her, Greg. My stupidity cost me my dearest friend."

"And *I* almost lost *you*." Cupping my chin in his hand, Greg raised it up so he could look into my face. His words and gesture were gentle, but his eyes were hard. Their usual twinkly blue had turned dark — an ocean warning of an approaching storm. "How do you think *I* feel? Or how Seth feels? He nearly lost Zee. We all had a very big scare."

"I'm so sorry to put you through this, Greg." My tears started flowing again. His fingers swiped at them like a windshield wiper. "I won't ever do it again. I'm through with it — these dumb-ass investigations, murders, finding people — it's all over."

Greg's fingers paused against my cheek. "No, it's not, Odelia."

"Yes, it is." I punctuated my words by smacking my right fist down on the comforter.

"If you don't want to do it anymore, then don't." He fixed his stormy eyes on mine again. "But this won't be over until I find the bastards who took a shot at you."

As if he said things like that every day, Greg casually reached over, plucked a couple of tissues from the box we keep on the nightstand, and started dabbing at my tears and snotty nose.

"No, Greg."

"Yes, Odelia. We're finishing what we started. We're going to find out what happened to Joan's dad and to Roslyn Stevens, especially since you say that Scott guy is so creepy." He took my hands again and leaned

215

forward, planting a sweet kiss on my mouth to seal the deal. "And when I find the assholes who shot at you, I'm going to beat them till they're raw."

Speechless, I stared at my husband. I've always known that I married a very nice guy, and I've always known he's no milquetoast. But this?

"But . . ."

"I could have just done this without telling you, but as I've told you many times, we're in this together, and that means being totally honest."

Greg gave me another short kiss and handed me a couple more tissues. "Why don't you splash some water on your face and join us on the patio." He winked at me, his eyes back to their sparkling blue, the storm clouds gone for now. "You eat some steak and veggies, then you can have some cheesecake."

He started for the door, then swiveled back around to face me. "Just so you know, Clark is totally in on this. He'll be staying until it's over. It'll be convenient having an ex-cop around." He started again for the door and again turned back to me. "By the way, I gave Willie a shitload of names to run through his magic all-knowing databases for us. He said it might take a day or so."

"You called *Willie?*"

Willie had resources, both computer and manpower, the cops could only dream about. He called from time to time to see how we were doing and occasionally made a surprise appearance, but we had no idea of his whereabouts — where he lived in general or at any given moment. We only had a number in case we needed to reach him. In spite of our calls going through various channels, our messages reached Willie with surprising speed.

"Actually, he called me last night after you fell asleep. He wanted to see how you were doing. He and Sybil send their love."

"He knew about the shooting already?"

Greg grinned. "He knew about the shooting, Shirley, your hunt for Clarice's friends — everything. But then, why are you surprised?"

I stood up and started looking around the room with alarm, my previous concerns replaced for the time being with a new one. I started with looking under the lampshade of the bedside lamp. "You don't think he has our home bugged, do you?"

"I have no idea, but I would certainly hope not, especially the bedroom."

For the first time in twenty-four hours, a smile tried to creep across my face. I let it have a brief fling, then banished it behind my other worries.

"Probably," Greg added, "one of his lackeys keeps an eye on us. That or Dev sought him out, knowing he can help faster than police bureaucracy."

Greg and Clark and now Willie were moving forward. Whatever was going to happen, it was going to happen with me or without me. Greg was right: we needed to finish this thing.

"I have one request, Greg."

"What is it, sweetheart?"

"I know from the set of your jaw I won't be able to talk you out of this, and probably not Clark either, but don't get Steele involved in hunting down the shooters, no matter how much he wants to be. We can't ethically compromise him."

Greg smiled. "Clark and I discussed that right after Steele called today. His job will be to help Joan and her family, nothing more. If we have to, we'll make him understand that."

I wasn't sure what that last sentence meant exactly, having undertones of thugs, guns, and cannolis, but I hoped they would remember to shoot some video if the moment arose.

I took a long look at my husband sitting

so determined and sure of himself in his wheelchair. He never, ever let being physically handicapped stop him from doing whatever he wanted to do — what he felt he had to do. I, on the other hand, was far more crippled by my emotional injuries and insecurities. A part of me wanted to lock Greg in a closet to keep him secluded and safe until Dev and the other cops solved everything. Another part of me wanted to swoon and call out "My hero!" in girly delight.

The last thing I wanted was to be a proud widow.

SEVENTEEN

"Do Dev and his crew have any idea who the shooter might be?" Steele shoveled a bite of medium-rare steak into his mouth, chewed, and swallowed, waiting for an answer to his question.

Greg shook his head. "None, yet. By the way, Mike, the steak is fantastic. Thanks for bringing it."

Steele raised his beer in salute to Greg's praise. "There's a butcher in Laguna Beach I use for my meat. A *real* butcher."

"Yes, thank you, Steele." I turned toward my boss and gave him a weak smile. He really was concerned for my welfare, and I had behaved abominably. "Thanks for everything. And I'm sorry for being such a bitch toward you earlier."

"No problem, Grey. It's not like I haven't given you reason in the past to believe the worst of me." He laughed just as he brought the beer back to his mouth for another drink. "And it's not like I won't give you similar reasons in the future."

I cut a bite-sized piece of meat. "Somehow, I find that oddly comforting. Kind of like the circle of life continuing in spite of near tragedy — like something I can count on to stay the same."

Everyone around the table laughed heartily, including Steele.

The good food and the beer were doing wonders for my state of mind. Still feeling like I'd been run down by an out-of-control bus, at least my blood sugar was back to normal, and a sense of safety and well-being was slowly creeping over me — something a load of cheesecake would not have done for my body. My darling husband had been correct, as usual.

In addition to the steak, Greg had added some eggplant and zucchini brushed with olive oil and sprinkled with garlic salt to the grill. To round out the meal, Clark had tossed together a salad and thrown some potatoes into the microwave. Steele helped with the salad and set the table. They wouldn't let me do a thing.

Being in shock after the shooting and Zee's ultimatum, I hadn't had a chance to ask Clark any questions about the incident. I only knew what I'd learned from his report. Steele's question jarred another that had been hiding in the back of my mind. I asked Clark, "Did you see the license plate or anything that might identify the car?"

"Actually, I did." Clark took a drink of his iced tea. "I got a partial plate, but just the first digit and couple of letters. It was a black, late-model BMW coupe. Almost new, from the looks of it."

Steele scowled at his next bite as if the meat were withholding information. "Those cars are a dime a dozen in Orange County, especially in that area. Every asshole's got one. That or a black Mercedes."

I cocked an eyebrow. "Not a Porsche?"

Steele didn't miss a beat. "Every third asshole has one of those."

Clark gave Steele a half grin. "So I've noticed. Hardly see any pickup trucks around here. Not like back home. In Holmsbury, a fancy car would be out of place."

Greg shook his fork in Clark's direction, a piece of steak speared to the end. "Dev and his people will track it down."

"Yes," Clark agreed. "They'll find the car but not the people driving it. My money's on it being stolen. Dev agrees with me."

"By the way," I asked Clark. "What were you doing across the street, anyway? We thought you were in the club all that time."

"I got a call on my cell and went outside to take it. I was on my way back in when that kid — you know, the one dressed as Clarice — came running out."

"You mean Betty Rumble?" I stuck my fork into a piece of lettuce and waited for Clark's response.

"Yeah, him. He seemed squirrelly, so I decided to follow him. He climbed into a beat-up silver Honda parked on the south side of the highway on a short side street and took off. Kept yelling into his phone all the way to the car that he was on his way."

"Betty Rumble?" Steele stopped eating and looked at me in disbelief.

"A drag queen at the service for Shirley Pearson," I explained. I turned my attention back to Clark. "Betty's dog was having puppies. That's why he left the service. He received a text about it."

"Anyway, I was on my way back to the club when I saw you and Zee waiting by my rental car."

Greg shook his fork again for emphasis. This time, a small chunk of eggplant was aimed at Clark. "Dev told me they never found the guy who dumped the food and ran. He took off through the kitchen and out a back door."

"Yeah," Clark added. "That Marvin Gunn

guy claims he doesn't know any Scott Johnson or Scott Joyce. Seems he doesn't know a lot of people we think he should."

Steele listened to everything, sucking up the information along with his beer.

I stopped eating. "But the photo."

The three men turned their heads my way in a nearly choreographed move — beverages and forks held aloft as if frozen in time.

"The photo Clarice gave me of her friends," I explained. "Scott is in it, and so is Marvin Gunn." I paused to recall his face. "At least I think it's Gunn."

Getting up, I went looking for my purse. I found it on our dresser and retrieved the photo from it. In all the hubbub surrounding the shooting, I had forgotten to mention it to Dev.

When I returned to the table, I handed the photo to Clark. "Doesn't that look like Marvin Gunn?" I pointed to the guy in the back behind Clarice and Shirley.

Clark glanced at the photo, then went into the house. He came back out toting his reading glasses. Putting them on, he studied the photo as if looking for treasure.

"Hard to say, sis, with Gunn having a beard. It does look like him, but in some ways it doesn't." He covered the lower part of Gunn's face with a finger, trying to focus

224

on the upper half of his face. "But it's certainly worth checking out. Seems too much of a coinkydink for all these people to be at Marvin Gunn's bar with this look-alike in the photo."

"Coinkydink," I repeated. "Dev uses that word when he's being sarcastic."

Clark put the photo down. "What can I say? It's part of our police academy training — official police jargon."

I resumed my place at the table next to Greg. "After meeting Scott Johnson, I'm really starting to worry about Roslyn Stevens. He really did seem unhinged."

Steele craned his head to look at Scott's picture, following up with a shrug. "I would think if you were in hiding and were out in public, you'd look suspicious and frightened, too. Especially if you were at the service for a friend who was murdered and were worried you were next."

Clark ran a hand over his stubbly face and continued studying the photo. "Maybe, but Odelia might be on target. Even in the photo, surrounded by his supposed friends, this guy Scott looks hinky."

"Hinky enough to kill Joan's father *and* Shirley?" I asked. "He hardly looks the type to send all those people into a panic."

"You never know. Though it would help

225

to find out what all those people are hiding from in the first place."

Steele pushed his plate back. "Anyone looking into that?"

I fielded the question. "I know Dev is trying to track down people who knew Roslyn Beckworth before she became Roslyn Stevens. He told me she used to attend and work at the University of Chicago, then simply disappeared."

"Clark and I made a call this afternoon to start our own search," Greg added.

Steele studied Greg with an inquisitive and eager eye. "That call wasn't to that special friend of Grey's, was it?"

Before Greg could think of a fib, Clark threw out his own explanation. "We called a buddy of mine. He's a whiz at finding out anything on anyone."

Although Steele is a straight arrow when it comes to the law, he has a fascination with my friendship with Willie. Steele's almost in awe of the man, like a pimply teen obsessed with a rock star. So far, the two of them had not crossed paths except briefly by phone, and I wanted to keep it that way.

"Well," Steele said, disappointment swelling his voice, "if Clark's friend doesn't work out, Grey here can rub a magic lamp and get you Superfelon."

Eager to change the subject, I started to get up. "Anyone want coffee?"

"Sit, Odelia," Greg ordered. "I'll make coffee, and Clark will clear and get the dessert." Steele made a move to help, but Greg stopped him. "We've got this, Steele."

"Yeah," I said to Steele. "You can fill me in on what's happening with Joan and her mother."

"You know that's privileged information, Grey. She's a client."

"And I'm your paralegal. Spill."

He played with the salt and pepper shakers in the middle of the table. "All I'm going to tell you is that it looks like we might be able to convince the insurance company that Joan's mother knew nothing about her husband's faked death."

"Do you believe she had nothing to do with it?"

"I believe there's a very good chance she didn't. Nor did Joan." Steele released the shakers and turned to look at me. "Like you said, Joan's mother appears to be a lot like Joan — a very conservative and decent woman. I didn't get any sense of duplicity, but I definitely got a clear understanding that his disappearance, dead or not, was the best thing that could have happened to her."

"Joan told me her parents didn't have a

good marriage, but that her mother would never get a divorce."

"Exactly. But an insurance company hell-bent on getting their money back might read that relief as a motive for fraud." He ran a hand through his hair. "But we're going to do our best to see that they don't make that assumption stick."

"What about Joan's stepdad? Joan's mother is afraid to remarry him in case he might be drawn into it."

"We can prove they didn't meet until two years after Alfred disappeared, so he's in the clear as far as the fraud is concerned."

"Thanks, Steele. I'm sure Joan is very appreciative of your help."

"Don't thank me yet, Grey. I haven't gotten her mother out of trouble yet."

There was a pause, so I decided to fill it by tweaking Steele's nose. "So how's everything going with Lori Ogle?"

Steele shrugged. "The deal's on track, but you know that."

"How about with Lori herself?" I pressed. "I understand she's quite beautiful."

Another noncommittal shrug. "She's okay, if you like that sort."

"That sort?"

"You know, an arrogant, overachieving know-it-all."

"Gee, sounds like someone else we know, doesn't it?"

Steele turned to me with suspicion. "Why all the questions about Ogle?"

"Just making conversation. I heard she was lovely and quite accomplished. Just wondering what your take on her was."

Finished with clearing the table, Clark brought out a stack of dessert dishes and forks. Greg followed with the cheesecake and a pie server. He placed the cheesecake in front of me and handed me the server, presented over his forearm like a fine sword. "Your only job, sweetheart, is to serve the dessert."

"So," Steele started when I handed him a piece of cheesecake, "you coming in tomorrow or not?"

I stopped slicing. "Why? You reneging on your offer?"

"Not at all. I just want to know what your plans are."

I completed the cut, scooped out a slice of cheesecake, and plopped it on a plate. Picking it up, I handed it to Clark. "I was thinking I would stay home tomorrow and run some errands. You know, do stuff to pull myself back together."

Steele swallowed his first bite of dessert. "Good idea. Put your feet up. Go to the beach. Read a book."

"Sounds good to me, sweetheart," Greg agreed as I handed him his dessert. Clark, his mouth full of cheesecake, nodded in agreement.

"Tomorrow night, I thought I might go out. Something fun and different."

Greg gave me a curious look. "Can I come?"

I scooped a small piece of cheesecake onto my own plate and put the pie server down. "Looks fabulous, Steele. Thanks." Wielding my fork, I prepared to dig into the smooth and yummy desert. "You sure know the way to my heart."

I stuffed my mouth and chewed, again realizing Greg had been right to take the cheesecake away from me earlier. It was so rich and I was so distraught, halfway through I would have been sicker than a seventy-year-old on a Tilt-A-Whirl.

"Is this the best cheesecake or what?" I turned to Steele. "Where did you get it? It's authentic New York style, just the way I like it."

Around me, the table went quiet.

I washed the cheesecake down with a sip of decaf coffee and looked at the men. "What?"

Greg and Steele were exchanging looks

230

and silent conversation. Clark was watching them, trying to pick up on their man-vibes.

Steele cut his eyes my way. "Nice to have you back, Grey."

Color me confused. "Huh?"

Greg tossed his napkin down next to his dessert plate. "Okay, what's up?"

"I have no idea what you're talking about." I looked down, concentrating on cutting my next bite with the side of my fork.

"Is this normal for her?" Clark asked. "This avoidance routine?"

"Too normal," Greg answered. "Out with it, Odelia. What's cooking in that addled brain of yours?"

"Nothing."

"Nothing, my ass," tossed out Steele. He glanced at Clark. "It's her tell, Littlejohn. Just like in poker. The minute she quick changes a subject or avoids a direct question, turn on your bullshit detector."

Three against one. I didn't like the odds.

"It's like this," I began.

Steele groaned. Greg scowled. Clark looked on with interest, like I was an example in a psych class.

"Stop it right now, guys, or I'll go inside and not tell you a thing."

"Maybe you should come to work with *me* tomorrow, sweetheart."

I narrowed my eyes at my hubby. "Tomorrow is not bring-your-insane-wife-to-work day, Greg. Nor is any other day." I went back to eating my cheesecake, attacking it with the side of the fork in small chops. "It's just that I had an idea." I looked up at Greg again. "You did say we needed to finish this — to find out what happened to Alfred for Joan's sake. And I want to find out why Clarice Hollowell fired me."

"She fired you?" Steele laughed. "Better make sure that gets into your employee file." He took a sip of his coffee, smiling into his cup. "Grey fired from nosiness. That's rich."

"Okay," Greg said to the table in general, "we're getting totally off-track. Let's just back up a moment." He leaned forward and put a hand out to stop my attack on the cheesecake. "What exactly did you have in mind for tomorrow, Odelia?"

"During the day or the evening outing?"

Greg's jaw was clenched so tight, I was sure he'd pop a vein if I didn't tell him my plans for Monday.

"In the morning, I thought I might run by Rambling Rose and see what I can find out from Shirley's assistant, Amber Straight."

Greg's jaw relaxed — a good sign that he didn't think my plan too off-kilter. I tried to be just as nonchalant with the other half of my information. "Then, in the evening, I thought it might be kind of fun to check out drag queen bingo."

EIGHTEEN

Even with the AC running, the inside of my car was growing hot as it sat on a side street just steps from the Rambling Rose office. I was on my cell phone, calling to make sure they were open. They were, but the woman on the phone, who'd introduced herself as Amber, informed me that they were not taking any new bookings at the moment. When I asked why, I was told it was because of the unexpected death of one of the owners. The way she'd said "one of the owners" made me wonder if there were more partners than Clarice.

The call could have been made from home, but I didn't want them to leave in the time it took me to drive from Seal Beach down to Corona del Mar. Satisfied someone was holding down the fort, Clark and I climbed out of the car and made our way into Rambling Rose.

Greg had insisted that if I was going to

run around annoying people, I had to take Clark with me. Clark had backed him up; so had Steele. My protests had fallen on three sets of deaf ears.

Saturday afternoon, Clark had called the car rental place and explained what had happened to the back window of his rental. Sunday morning, he had driven off and returned with a different car, saying not to worry, his insurance covered it. Still, I insisted on taking my car this time. It was old, paid for, and didn't belong to anyone but me.

Before getting out of the car, Clark and I had gone over our cover story. Unless someone in the shop had been at the service and seen the mayhem, there was a good chance we wouldn't be recognized.

Marvin Gunn had made it clear that Rambling Rose represented Shirley's new life, the life after her stint at the club, and those friends had made themselves scarce after her death. It made me wonder what part of her life was covered by the people in the photo. Were the other fugitives part of her post show-biz life, or had they been around during her time at the club, or did they overlap? Either way, the only folks I noticed from the photo who'd attended her service had been Scott Johnson and Marvin

Gunn. Even Clarice had sent an understudy.

The Rambling Rose office was just as frou-frou as its website, if not more. The roomy reception area was furnished with two floral upholstered love seats, French antiques (or reasonable facsimiles), and vases of fresh flowers. The soft tinkling of a bell announced us when we opened the front door and entered. A moment later, a short, perky blond came out of the back room carrying a hefty sample book of invitations. Her compact figure was dressed in a smart summer pantsuit of subdued peach linen, her hair an explosion of short curls. She appeared to be in her mid to late twenties. Her outfit and makeup were immaculate, reminding me of how beautiful Shirley Pearson had kept herself. It appeared to be part of the job requirement, though if this woman was in drag, I was the pope.

She put the sample book down on a white French Provençal desk. "May I help you?" she asked in an upbeat voice with a faint girlish squeak to it. Then she noticed the side of my face. "My goodness, that looks painful. Are you okay?"

Gingerly, I touched the large scrape on my right cheek. I'd done my best to cover it, but it was too big and scabby to do much except wait out the healing process. "Yes,

I'm fine. Thank you. Silly, really. My cat tripped me on Saturday, and I went down face-first on our concrete patio. Hurt like the dickens."

Amber smiled with sympathy, though her own face was scrape-free. She was pretty but not beautiful. With high cheekbones and a slightly upturned nose, it was the sort of face that was very cute when young but might not age well. Just to the left of her upper lip was a mole à la Cindy Crawford. It wasn't a face I'd noticed at the memorial, but it didn't seem totally unfamiliar either.

I stepped up to the desk and got into character for my story pitch. Behind me, Clark nosed around, looking like a bored male dragged into the shop against his will.

"We're here to talk to Shirley," I told the young woman with a smile.

Her face took an immediate nosedive. "I'm sorry, but that's impossible."

I glanced back at Clark, a surprised look on my face. He acted out a sullen shrug. I turned back to the woman. "But I spoke to her a couple of weeks ago. It's about an anniversary party for our parents. They're going to renew their vows." I indicated Clark. "This is my brother."

"I'm Amber Straight, Ms. Pearson's assistant. Former assistant." She flashed us her sad face again. "I'm sorry to have to tell you this, but Ms. Pearson died last Saturday."

I slapped a hand over my heart. "What?" I turned to Clark. "Did you hear that, Donald?"

Clark and I hadn't discussed our undercover names, and from the heated glare he gave me, I'd say *Donald* wasn't sitting well with him.

"Yes, Dorcas, I did. That's a real shame."

I patted the hand over my heart in a small, panicked flutter. "Oh dear, what should we do?"

"This party's your idea, sis. Just make sure I'm home in time for the game."

The game. Doesn't matter what time of year it is, all a man has to say is *the game* and people automatically understand he has places to be, and soon. It could be snail racing from a pub in England, but if it's on ESPN and/or betting is involved, it can officially be called The Game and elevated to a position of must-see TV. In this case, it was Clark's way of making me do the heavy lifting of lying.

I turned back to Amber with a frustrated smile. "Men and sports. What are we going to do, huh?"

In a very professional manner, Amber

moved the conversation along. "Did Ms. Pearson book your event?"

"I'm sure she did."

"What is the name and date?"

A near slip of my tongue almost gave her Grey, but in the end I said, "The name's Cooper. We discussed several dates, but I believe we settled on the second Saturday in September — the weekend after Labor Day weekend."

To the side of the desk was a table holding a computer. Amber put her fingers to the keys. A soft tap, tap, tappity-tap filled the room. A glance over my shoulder showed Clark moving slowly throughout the room, hands shoved deep into his pockets, looking bored to death. I knew better. I knew he was studying everything, including the large groupings of photos from past events that adorned the largest wall.

"I'm sorry," Amber said, returning her attention to me. "But there's nothing in the computer for a Cooper party for any date."

"Oh, dear." I started my fluttery routine again. "I realize you are in mourning, but do you have another planner who could assist us? It's not going to be a big affair," I added quickly, "but we do want it done professionally." I put on my best begging face, learned from living with three animals

and a horny husband. "Mother is so looking forward to it, especially after Dad's
cancer scare last year." I paused for effect.
"Perhaps Ms. Pearson had a partner?"

Amber Straight seemed genuinely touched
by my bogus plight, which made me feel
like a genuine heel. "There are a couple of
other owners, but at this time Rambling
Rose isn't taking on any more events. At
least not until the owners decide how they
are going to proceed in the future. We're
just handling what's already on the books."

"But," I pressed, trying to be firm but not
obnoxious, "I'm sure Mother and Dad's
party not being on the books is just an
oversight."

Amber seemed unsure of what to do.
Event planning is a business where pleasing
the customer isn't just deep-seated in
company policy, it's an obsession. I was
banking on that being the case with Rambling Rose.

Holding up a perfectly manicured finger,
Amber said, "Let me make a call and see
what I can do." She indicated one of the
love seats. "Make yourselves comfortable.
I'll be back in a minute."

After Amber Straight disappeared through
a closed door, Clark called me over to the
photo groupings. "Sis, check this out." He

pointed to a photo dead-center in the display of photos from various events. It was a group photo taken in front of the colorful green and pink awning of Rambling Rose. Amber Straight was there, perky and efficient. Standing next to her was Shirley Pearson. Next to Shirley was Clarice Thomas Hollowell. They were all dressed beautifully, standing with one foot pointed forward, the other back. With shoulders straight, tummies in, boobies out, they beamed like beauty queens awaiting inspection. Behind them was Marvin Gunn. His hair was longer and he was clean shaven, but it was him.

I scanned the other pictures. "Any other photos here with him?"

"Not that I can see. The others seem to be events they've planned."

"You think maybe he killed Shirley and threatened Clarice to get the company?"

"What about Alfred Nunez? I don't see him connected here or at Billie's Holiday. Why was he murdered? And why would Scott Johnson and Roslyn Stevens take off in a fright?"

"Scott was at the service," I pointed out.

"And took off the minute you recognized him."

"You know, Donald . . ."

Clark shot me a death glare.

"What is it with you and that name?"

"Never mind," he snapped, his voice low. "Just say what's on your mind, and don't call me Donald."

"Alrighty then." I adjusted my shoulder bag before continuing. "It seems that while Scott was surprised that I knew who he was, and got angrier as I connected the dots to him and Roslyn, he really went ballistic when I called him Scott Joyce."

"Yeah?" Clark turned away from the photos and looked at me, all ears.

"It's as if all these people have individual private secrets that have nothing to do with each other, except that they somehow know each other." I sighed and sat down on the love seat. "I wish Willie would call with the backgrounds on those names Greg gave him."

Amber returned just as Clark's cell rang. He apologized and went outside to take it.

"Probably his bookie," I said to Amber with a scowl.

"Good news," she told me, once again deftly changing topics. This young woman was well trained in how to handle the public. "One of the other owners said she'd handle your event, as long as it's not too large or elaborate."

I clapped my hands together. "That's wonderful news! And it's not, I can assure you. Just the renewal of vows ceremony, followed by a sit-down luncheon for about fifty people. No band or dancing. We were discussing a place with an ocean view."

"Sounds lovely." She consulted the computer again. "Ms. Thomas said she can meet with you later today around two o'clock. Does that work for you?"

"Yes, of course. I'll try to park Donald in front of the TV and come alone. We girls will get more done that way."

"I have an appointment this afternoon, so if you find the door locked, just ring the bell and Ms. Thomas will answer."

Alone time with Clarice was exactly what I needed — alone, that is, except for me and my shadow brother. I thanked Amber and headed out the door. Just before making a getaway, I stopped and turned back.

"This is going to sound silly, but that man in the photo here." I walked over to the wall of photos and pointed to the one in the middle. "Donald is sure he recognized this man. Is he an event planner, too?"

Amber joined me in front of the wall to see whom I was referring to. "Shirley — Ms. Pearson — did most of the events. Occasionally, Mr. Gunn helped." Her voice did the sad dip of grief again. "This photo was taken last year."

I pointed to Clarice. "Is that Ms. Thomas?"

"Yes. She doesn't usually handle events, but she has impeccable taste and style. I'm sure you'll be happy."

I looked at the photo again and remembered something. "You know, once I called and another young woman answered, but there are just the four of you here."

Amber looked at me oddly. "Someone else? You sure?"

"Yes, I believe so. Does a woman by the name of Ruth or Roslyn work here?"

A flicker of something hard beamed out of Amber's eyes. "She only comes in on occasion when we need extra help."

I smiled at the information and touched Shirley's picture. "So sad about Ms. Pearson. When is the service? I'd like to send flowers. She was so kind to me."

"I'm afraid the service was Saturday."

"The day before yesterday?" When she nodded, I gently touched the young woman's arm. "I'm so sorry. I hope it was lovely."

"Doubtful." Amber Straight's eyes again took on a flinty look. "We had a big wedding on Saturday at eleven o'clock, right during the time they scheduled the service.

Mr. Gunn and I had to be there to handle things since Ms. Pearson was gone." She took a deep breath. "I'm sure it was planned that way, to keep us away."

"Why in the world would anyone want to keep you from attending the memorial service?"

Amber started to say something, then stopped herself, her grief battling with her training. "Forgive me, I've already said too much." She cleared her throat. "Just chalk it up to Ms. Pearson having two very different sets of friends."

Something didn't compute. I had seen Marvin Gunn at the service, but Amber said the two of them were shepherding a wedding at the time. I looked at the photo again, studying Gunn's face.

"Donald is sure he knows Mr. Gunn, but I doubt it. He doesn't usually hang out with wedding planners. Bartenders, maybe, but not refined event coordinators."

"Your brother probably knows Mr. Gunn's brother."

I swung my head in Amber's direction. "His brother?"

She nodded. "Yes, Marvin Gunn. He owns Billie's Holiday, a bar right down the street." She tapped the photo. "Our Mr. Gunn is Aaron Gunn. They're twins."

NINETEEN

Before leaving for work, Greg had suggested I take Clark to the Hotel Laguna for lunch since we'd be down this way. The hotel's Terrace restaurant is one of our favorite and special places to lounge over good food served with a kick-ass view. It sounded great to Clark. We had just over two hours to kill before the two o'clock appointment with Clarice, so off we went to the Hotel Laguna in Laguna Beach.

"Great place," exclaimed Clark as the waiter showed us to a table at the Terrace. It was not quite noon, so the lunch crowd hadn't arrived yet, allowing us to claim not only a table with an unobstructed view of a good stretch of the Pacific Ocean and the California coastline, but one under a shade umbrella as well.

"If it's too warm, we can go inside," I offered.

"Not on your life." He took the seat across

from me.

"The food's very good, though it's no Blue Lobster." I winked at him, referencing a favorite joint in Massachusetts that served fabulous fried seafood. "Greg and I love to come here, though it's been awhile since we've made the trek. We've attended a few weddings here, too."

"Did you and Greg get married here?"

The question brought down a curtain of sadness. "No, we didn't." I looked away, even though I was wearing dark glasses. "We were married poolside at Zee and Seth's. That's where we met."

Clark covered my hand with one of his. "Don't worry about Zee. If you two are as tight as you say, she'll come around."

Even though I was getting tired of hearing that, I clung to the hope it held. "I've never seen her or Seth this angry before."

The waiter came and handed us menus. "There will be three of us," Clark told him after he took our order for two iced teas. With a nod, the waiter placed a third menu in front of one of the empty chairs and took away the fourth place setting.

"Three?" I asked. Who did Clark know besides us? For a fleeting moment I wondered if he and Greg were trying to be peacemakers and had talked Zee into joining us. The Hotel Laguna was one of her favorite places, too, and Greg knew that. If that was the case, I had mixed feelings about it. I wanted to make up with Zee, but I wasn't ready to give in to her demands. I needed to concentrate on the task at hand and finish it. Maybe then I could mend the fences of our friendship and vow to put murder aside as a hobby.

"I've invited —"

He never got the chance to finish.

"Hey, sports fans."

I looked over at the wide doorway leading from the bar to the Terrace to find Dev Frye filling the frame. He wandered over to our table. When he bent to give me a peck on my right check, he halted, then aimed for my undamaged left one.

Clark stood up and shook hands with Dev. "Thanks for coming, Dev."

"No problem. I love this place." Before sitting down, Dev removed his suit coat and hung it over the back of his chair. "Not to mention you promised it would be an eye-opening affair."

Clark looked over at me. "Shut your mouth, sis, before you catch flies."

I snapped my mouth shut, but not for long. "You invited Dev? When did this happen?"

"Gee, Odelia," Dev said to me with his rumbling voice. "I didn't realize I was such an obnoxious party crasher."

"No, Dev, of course not." I patted his arm with affection. "I'm just surprised. Clark didn't say anything about it." I turned to my brother. "That call you received while we were at Rambling Rose — that was Dev?"

Our drinks arrived, and Dev ordered an iced tea of his own.

"No, the call wasn't from Dev. That call is what prompted me to make my own call to Dev. I found out important information about some of the folks in the photo. Might as well tell both of you at the same time."

"Well, while you were out making calls, I discovered important info of my own." I leaned back in my chair, a picture of smugness.

Dev extended a hand to me. "By all means, ladies first." He looked at Clark. "You don't mind, do you?"

"Not at all."

Dev's iced tea arrived just as I told the guys about Marvin Gunn having a twin brother involved with Rambling Rose. "I'll bet Aaron Gunn is the one in the photo Clarice gave me, not Marvin."

Clark studied the surf. There were several

clusters of people lounging on the sand below us. Just to our right, a pair of curly-haired girls played tag with the waves while a young couple looked on with pride.

"And I'd say you'd win that bet hands-down." When Clark looked back at me, I could see my reflection in his sunglasses. "The twin-brother thing is something I learned about the same time you did."

I looked at Dev. "You knew about the twin?" He nodded, bursting my bubble of having an exclusive scoop.

"Okay, but it still doesn't explain how all the people in Clarice's photo tie together. We've only connected Aaron Gunn, Shirley Pearson, and Clarice. From what Marvin told us Saturday, it sounds like Shirley met up with him first and worked at Billie's Holiday. Then, when she became a success-ful event planner, she left the club behind for a better — or at least a more conserva-tive — career. Makes you wonder if Aaron is the one who took Shirley away from Mar-vin. Or was Rambling Rose her idea?" I paused, giving my brain time to catch up with my mouth. "So how do Alfred, Roslyn, and Scott fit in?"

"That's the million-dollar question we keep circling back to." Clark looked back out at the ocean.

"Did —" I stopped just short of saying Willie's name. "Did that guy come through on some of the names Greg gave you?"

"Guy?" Dev looked from Clark to me with raised eyebrows. "Come on, folks, don't play me for a simpleton. It pisses me off."

Clark and I remained silent, our eyes, both shielded by glasses, glued to one another like two sets of dark, magnetic orbs. Dev took another drink before he turned to Clark. "So what did Willie find out?"

Like a stain, a slow grin spread across Clark's face. Our waiter returned to take our food order. When he departed, Clark got down to serious business.

"Roslyn Stevens isn't running from the law," he announced. "She's running from a stalker."

I turned to Dev. "Weren't you trying to locate someone who knew her?"

Dev nodded from behind his own sunglasses. "Yeah. Still no luck. But there are old police reports on the stalker. I finally reached the Chicago PD and talked to a detective about it. Seems some guy back there wasn't too happy when Roslyn spurned his advances. She got a restraining order, but it didn't help. He tried to kill her — beat her pretty bad until someone heard her screams. He vowed he wouldn't stop until she was dead."

"Wow!" I nervously fiddled with a button on the front of my dress while considering Roslyn's reason for beginning anew.

"Takes all kinds." Clark took a drink of his tea. Both he and Dev eschewed straws in favor of drinking straight from the glass.

Dev continued, "I was told the guy did time for the attempted murder but was released right about the time Roslyn Beckworth died in that car accident. That was about six years ago."

Clark nodded, confirming Willie's information matched what Dev had learned.

A thought hit me like a flash flood. "People must think that guy caused the car accident."

"They did," Dev said. "The detective I spoke with told me the cops were all over this creep, but there wasn't any evidence to connect him to Roslyn's death. He seemed relieved that she's alive and well and living here in SoCal, but he said it also meant reopening the case to find out who did die in that car." He shook his head. "He wasn't pleased, to say the least. And when we do find Roslyn, she'll have a lot of explaining to do."

"Not to mention," Clark said, "the stalker to deal with all over again."

"On that point she's clear. Seems Roslyn's stalker was killed in a bar fight last November."

Clark looked at Dev over his glasses and grinned. "Looks like Willie's data isn't complete. We didn't have that bit of info."

"That's a relief," Dev replied with a snort. "Hate to think the cops are always the last to know."

While the boys enjoyed their little cop humor, I remembered something Clarice had told me. "When I asked Clarice about the body that was cremated as Doug Pearson, she said it probably came from a mortuary or coroner's office, something like that. Could be the same for both Roslyn and Alfred's stand-ins."

"That makes three accident cases that will have to be reopened." Dev gave another snort. "Though it wouldn't be the first time someone in a coroner's office sold the body of an indigent — if that's what it turns out to be and not something even more sinister."

We sat in silence, the surf our background music. I didn't know what Clark and Dev were thinking, but I was having a moment's silence for the poor and nameless who didn't have anyone to miss their bodies.

"As for Roslyn," I said, breaking the quiet, "I wouldn't close the door on her safety just yet. For one reason or another, she's afraid and in hiding again."

"Odelia's quite right," Clark added. "Especially after you hear my other tidbits."

While Dev and I waited for the next round of news, our food was delivered. Clark waited until we were alone again.

"Willie's contacts came up with nothing for Alfonso Nunez or even Alfred Nunez. Of course, we know that Shirley Pearson was running from that bank robbery charge. Willie couldn't find out anything about Shirley's partners in the job, only that the money has never been recovered, nor has it been flashed around. It's about half a million."

"Same info we have," Dev confirmed. He started to take a bite of his club sandwich but stopped. "Shirley's place was ransacked after her death. Obviously, someone is looking for something. Might be that cash." Dev turned to me. "You didn't monkey around at her place, did you?"

I huffed in irritation. "Of course not."

"Just checking. Seems you beat us to Roslyn's place. How about Alfred's?"

"I'm guessing you met Roslyn's landlords?"

"Yep. And Alfred's neighbor."

"We learned nothing, just that Scott

254

Johnson was hanging around Roslyn a lot and helped her clear out."

Even through his sunglasses, I could feel Dev's intimidating stare.

"Honest," I told him with emphasis, "that's all we learned."

My mind wandered back to the half-million dollars. "A half-million dollars is a lot of money to sit on. Makes me wonder if that's what funded Rambling Rose's start-up."

"Could be," Dev said, "but didn't Clarice say she helped Pearson with that?"

"Yes, but who knows if we can believe her."

"We questioned the assistant, that Amber Straight," Dev informed us. "She claims she doesn't have a clue where Clarice is and hasn't heard from her since right after Pearson was murdered. Aaron Gunn said the same thing. Both claim Clarice is mostly a silent partner in the biz and only came in on occasion."

Amber was lying to the police and Aaron Gunn probably was, too. It made me wonder why they were protecting Clarice. Was it just loyalty to a boss and partner? Or maybe they were all protecting each other; if one fell, they'd all fall.

Dev looked at me. Even though he was

wearing dark glasses, I could tell he was trying to read my mind. "Did you learn anything of value snooping around Rambling Rose today?"

"I learned about Aaron Gunn, but I seem to be the last to board that train."

"Well," Dev continued, obviously pleased he knew something we didn't, "seems Marvin and Aaron Gunn aren't the only siblings connecting Rambling Rose with Billie's Holiday."

Clark and I stopped eating and gave him our full attention.

"Amber Straight's brother works at the club. His name is Brad Straight." He paused, giving us time to recognize the name. When both Clark and I offered up a shrug, he continued. "You know him as Betty Rumble."

Clark was the first to find his tongue. "That little twit is Amber's brother?"

"I knew there was something familiar about her," I said to my plate. When it didn't respond, I looked up at the men to explain. "I thought her face looked familiar. It was the cheekbones — those high cheekbones. They both have them, and the coloring."

"They're from Arizona," Dev explained. "They moved here together after their mother died about three years ago."

My head snapped toward Clark. "Maybe you were right to follow Betty after the service. You said he was acting funny."

Dev shook his head. "No, Betty's story checked out. His dog really was having a litter during the service."

Humph, back to square one.

The three of us retreated into silence, each chewing and digesting our individual thoughts along with our food.

"Like Nunez," Clark said, breaking the quiet with more information. He held his ahi burger with one hand while he spoke. "Willie found nothing interesting on Clarice under the last name of either Thomas or Hollowell. Nothing bad or dangerous or a reason for her to be in hiding." Clark divided his attention between me, Dev, and his food.

Dev shrugged. "After what happened to her husband and the filthy bastard he was, maybe she simply decided to live quietly. John Hollowell was connected to some nasty characters, and it got him killed. Maybe she's making sure she doesn't catch their attention."

That sounded plausible to me. I waited for Dev to say something more about Clarice. When he didn't, I nudged him.

"Have you been able to question Clarice yet?"

"No," Dev replied. "She's making herself scarce. I was hoping to find her at the service but, as you know, she never showed."

"You think she knows yet about Alfred Nunez being murdered?"

Dev bunched his big shoulders. "Hard to say. If she does, it wasn't through us. In fact, we found nothing at Nunez's apartment linking him to any of those people. The only evidence is that photo, so I'm not sure how Clarice would find out. I'm pretty sure his family hasn't made any public announcement."

"Did you ask Marvin Gunn if he knew him?"

"Yes, we did." Dev's voice was heavy with sarcasm. "We do know how to do our job, Odelia."

Across the table, Clark drowned a short laugh with a large drink of tea.

"After the shooting," Dev continued, "the police questioned Gunn extensively, I can assure you. He claimed he knew nothing about any Alfred Nunez. He just reiterated what he told us at the club — that he knew Shirley and through Shirley, Clarice. He also claims he knew nothing about the shooting."

I screwed up my face at Dev, conveying my doubts. "Do you believe him?"

"My gut tells me he's telling the truth about the drive-by. Not sure about anything else. Frankly, the timing of the shooting was too soon after we left the club to have been Gunn."

"What about the photo?" I pressed, even though I knew it might make Dev mad. "Didn't he point out his brother?"

"Yes, he did. That's how we found out about Aaron Gunn. But Marvin claims he has no idea who his brother hangs out with, though he did know that Aaron knew both Shirley and Clarice. He didn't mention the Rambling Rose connection, however."

Everybody seemed to have half-answers to every question. I found it annoying.

I turned to Clark. "And what about Scott Johnson?"

"I'm saving that for last."

"It's that juicy?"

"It's that disturbing."

I pulled down my sunglasses and stared at my brother.

Clark ignored my stare and continued. "The Gunn twins grew up here in Southern California, someplace called Costa Mesa."

"That's the city just north of Newport Beach," Dev informed him.

"According to Willie, Marvin is quite the successful businessman. Over the years, he's invested in all kinds of property and start-up companies. Some failed, but most didn't." Clark paused briefly, double-checking his memory. "That club is not his main meal ticket. In fact, it's mostly a hobby and the hub from which he runs his little empire. I think Willie said he's divorced, no kids."

"And Aaron?" I asked.

"We didn't ask for info about him, but Willie looked into him once he discovered Marvin had a twin. Seems Aaron does not have his brother's Midas touch. He's had a lot of different careers and gotten into financial trouble from time to time. Although the report didn't say so, I'm guessing brother Marvin has saved his ass on occasion." He took a drink of his tea. "Oh yeah, and like Shirley, Aaron likes to get into drag, but there's nothing to suggest he lived as a woman like she did."

I took a bite or two of my Asian chicken salad as I sorted everything I'd just heard. I was on information overload but still curious about a lot of things. "So," I asked Clark. "You ready to tell us about Scott Johnson?"

Clark took a big bite of his sandwich, chewing slowly. To my right, Dev seemed perfectly happy munching on his own food until Clark was ready to gab again. I was wiggling in my seat in anticipation, which made it difficult to eat.

"Your instincts about Johnson were right, sis," Clark finally began. "He's a serious piece of work." Dev put down his sandwich and gave Clark his full attention. "Using different identities over the years, including Scott Joyce, he's suspected of the kidnapping, sexual assault, and murder of at least three college girls in the Northwest, possibly more."

With a loud clatter, my fork fell from my hand and bounced off my plate, then the table, before finally coming to a sloppy landing on the ground. "Oh my gawd, Roslyn!"

"Yeah, Roslyn," Dev said with deliberation. "Seems she left one threat only to land in the hands of another. Anything else on this Johnson guy?"

"That's about it."

TWENTY

Dev wiped his mouth with his napkin and rose from the table. "Excuse me, folks, but I gotta make a call."

"Where's he going?" I asked Clark.

"Well, if I were him, I'd be calling the station to put out a BOLO on Johnson and Roslyn."

"You mean like on TV when the police put out the news to other cops that they're searching for someone?"

"Yep."

I barely did more than pick at my food. "We have to find her, Clark."

"No, Odelia. Let Dev handle this. That's why I invited him. This Johnson guy is serious business, and the police know how to approach situations like these. You don't."

"Do you think he killed Shirley?"

"Difficult to say. If he did, it wasn't for the same reason he killed those other women. If he knew Shirley at all, he had to know she was really a man."

"What about Alfred or the drive-by? Do you think he did that?"

"Hard to say about Nunez, though Dev told me on the phone the police think it was a hit. But I do know that generally guys like Johnson are loners. That shooting on Saturday was carried out by two people — the driver and the shooter. The shooter looked Latino to me, but I could be wrong. And like Gunn, I don't think Johnson had enough time after leaving the club to arrange a hit."

I held my forehead in my left palm. "Oh joy, that means someone else is mad at me."

"Probably Shirley's real killer."

"Gee, thanks. As if I couldn't figure that out on my own."

I glanced at my watch. We'd have to leave soon to make my two o'clock with Clarice.

Dev returned to the table. In his hand was his cell phone. He slipped it into a pants pocket and grabbed his jacket off the back of his chair. "Sorry to eat and run, folks, but I've got to get back to the office." He started to pull out his wallet.

"No, Dev," Clark said. "I have this."

Dev nodded his thanks.

I breathed a sigh of relief. We could slip out shortly after Dev left. He'd be none the wiser, and I'd still be on time.

I looked up at the big detective. "You guys on the hunt now for Scott Johnson?"

"And Roslyn Stevens. Hopefully she's still alive. It will depend on Johnson's MO. Creeps like him are generally very methodical in how they handle their victims."

I wanted to retch at the thought Roslyn might not be alive and wished we'd been able to grab Johnson at the club on Saturday. Maybe if I hadn't been so bold, he wouldn't have spooked before Dev could get to him.

Dev looked at Clark. "You have any idea which specific jurisdictions those other murders occurred in?"

"No, but I'll find out and let you know as soon as possible."

"Great. It would save us the time to hunt it up. I'd like to give those cops a call. See if they can give us any information that might help us track Johnson."

Dev slipped into his suit jacket, then looked down at me. "What are your plans today? I hope they don't include looking for Roslyn Stevens."

I shook my head, wondering if Dev and Clark had some telepathic connection that came with their calling. "No. I —," I began, then stopped. I couldn't tell him I was meeting Clarice or Dev would be all over it, me, *and* her. I didn't look at Clark, worried he'd say something or that Dev would pick up on my vibes. "I have an appointment," I said as simply as I could and left it at that. I knew Dev would draw his own conclusions, but right now I wasn't going to help him — not until I had my own time with Clarice. Then she was all his.

Dev took off his sunglasses and bore his eyes into my face. "I'd rather you go home. You've already come close to getting killed once in the past few days. Let's not press our luck."

"Don't worry, Dev. Clark will be with me."

"Greg put Odelia under house arrest," Clark explained.

Dev grunted. "If she's under house arrest, then why isn't she home, where she belongs? At least until this blows over."

"She's not allowed to go anywhere without Greg or me," Clark told him. "If she goes to her office, Steele will take over the watch. She's not to go anywhere or do anything on her own."

"It's a start," Dev agreed. "Just stick to her like glue."

I slapped my hand on the table firmly but not so hard I rattled the dishes. "Would you two stop talking about me like I'm not here?

It's really aggravating."

As soon as Dev left the restaurant, Clark powered up his cell phone. Excusing himself, he walked a few feet away to the end of the terrace where there were no other guests. He returned a few minutes later.

"Willie said for you to behave and listen to me and Greg, especially me." He said it with a straight face from behind his shades, looking far too much like a casually dressed secret service agent guarding the president. All he needed was an earpiece.

"When did you and Willie become speed-dial buddies?"

Clark shrugged and took his seat. "I was on the call with Greg after the shooting. We decided I'd be the point man since Greg's so busy at the shop right now. No sense having the calls go to him, then to me, when I'm the one following you around."

My nose twitched of its own accord. I'd always found sitting on the patio of the Terrace a relaxing way to spend time; not so today. "So what did Willie say?"

"I asked him about Scott Johnson — if he knew the names or locations of the cops investigating those Northwest murders. He said he'd look into it and call Dev directly to save time."

I picked at my salad, taking a couple more

half-hearted bites before pushing my plate away.

"Wait a minute." Clark held his iced tea glass halfway to his mouth. "You have a problem with Willie calling me but none with Willie calling Dev Frye? You'd think it would be the opposite. After all, Dev is still a law-and-order boy."

Clark did have a point, but I had an explanation. "Willie and Dev have been in contact before regarding stuff. I mean, it's not like they exchange Christmas cards or anything, but there is some history there."

"By *stuff,* am I to assume you mean your colorful predicaments?"

Again my nose twitched like the Easter Bunny's. "Assume anything you want. It's a free country."

Clark frowned at me, his mouth set into a nearly perfect straight line. "It's a good thing you have all of us watching your ass."

"Speaking of which, why didn't you squeal to Dev about my meeting Clarice after lunch?"

He leaned forward and studied me. Even with both of us wearing sunglasses, I could feel his look piercing my brain. "Why didn't you?"

"You know damn well why. Dev would have made a beeline to Rambling Rose.

Once he has his paws on her, I'll never get the chance to speak to her about Alfred Nunez, or about anything else."

Our check came, and Clark insisted on taking care of it. "Who knows how long I'll be mooching off you and Greg, seeing how this is going. Although I may have to return to Phoenix for a follow-up interview."

"The job looks good?"

"Better than good. I think I'll enjoy working in the private sector for a change."

"Is that why you didn't tell Dev, because your loyalties have changed?"

I watched Clark weigh his answer, telling me he was also wondering about shifting loyalties. Once a cop, always a cop maybe, but something was battling within my big brother. Not a war, but definitely a conflict.

"Not at all, Odelia. I didn't tell Dev about Clarice because I didn't want to waste his time. He needs to be looking for killers." Clark pushed his glasses down the bridge of his nose and peered at me over the top of the frames. "You see, I still have a cop's gut, and my gut is telling me she'll be a no-show."

"And if she's not?"

"We'll question her and I'll do my best to convince her to go to the police, even if we have to hog-tie her and drive her there ourselves."

The front door to Rambling Rose was locked, and the place looked deserted. Taped to the front door was a pink Rambling Rose envelope addressed to Odelia Grey.

Standing in the heat on the stoop in front of Rambling Rose, my gut lurched, telling me Clark's gut was on the money. All the way to the shop I had the sinking feeling he would be right.

I glanced back at Clark. He stood just behind me, reading the envelope over my shoulder. "You going to read that?" he asked. "Or are you afraid it'll bite?"

In answer, I yanked the envelope off the door and tore open the sealed flap. Inside was a note on matching Rambling Rose stationery: *How gullible do you think I am? Shirley never made booking errors. — C*

Crap.

TWENTY-ONE

Slipping a fingernail just under the edge of my wig, I scratched behind my left ear. I hate wigs. They're hot and itchy, especially in June. Although it could be worse. It could be August, and a wig that's hot in June would be unbearable in August.

The inside of Billie's Holiday looked a lot different than it had on Saturday. The change in atmosphere was mostly due to lighting. Monday night the lights were dimmed, but not dark as I imagined they would be during a show. It was just dark enough to show off the neon lights of the signs above the bar — signs that weren't turned on Saturday morning — and the subdued stage lighting, but light enough for folks to read their bingo cards. On the stage, a table with an electronic bingo-ball mixer had been positioned. Behind it was a lit board with all the bingo numbers displayed.

My escorts for the evening were Sally Kipman and Mike Steele.

Last night, when I had announced my intentions for today, the visit to Rambling Rose was met with concern and hemming and hawing from my three keepers. Oh, who am I kidding? My plan to return to Billie's Holiday had been greeted with a full-blown volcano on the part of my husband.

When he realized he couldn't talk me out of going, Greg had been adamant about my not going alone. The discussion had dragged on long after the coffeepot was empty and the remaining cheesecake had been slipped into the fridge. Clark wanted to go, but Greg pointed out that he might be recognized as having been with me at the service. Greg, of course, had volunteered first, but Clark had nixed it, saying there wasn't much clearance for a wheelchair if something bad went down and a quick getaway was needed. No one disputed the fact that it might be a good idea for someone to go and nose around, just that it probably shouldn't be me and especially not on my own.

Steele acted like an antsy kid raising his hand in class for permission to pee. "Let me go," he'd insisted. "I've been there before."

Everyone looked at him with surprise.

Billie's Holiday didn't exactly look like Steele's usual bottle of designer beer.

"Hey, don't be so surprised," Steele said, acting like we'd just found out he'd spent five years in prison. "I live nearby, and bingo night is a fun thing to do with out-of-town guests. It draws quite a crowd." Steele looked at me. "Besides, you can't go alone. You'll stick out. No one goes alone to drag queen bingo — it's something you do with friends for fun, like a bunch of girlfriends or in groups. The only people who come in alone are those sitting at the bar just to drink and watch, and they're usually guys."

"Too bad I can't call Zee. We could officially make it a girls' night out." My voice trailed off in sadness at the thought of the woman who no longer wanted to be my BFF.

"Don't you have other girlfriends, Grey?"

"Of course I do," I snapped. "Kelsey and Joan, for starters, but I don't think I should ask Joan to get involved with this. Plus, she's too timid. And Kelsey's on vacation until Tuesday. She left Friday to attend a wedding in Texas."

Steele nodded. "I did see an e-mail about her being out of the office."

A thought occurred to me. "I know who'd be perfect — Sally. Sally Kipman. She even called me this week asking if she could help."

"And she's teamed up with you before," Greg added. He glanced at my boss. "It was that time you went missing, Steele."

Steele turned to my hubby with raised eyebrows. "Missing? You make it sound like I went on a bender and had a lost weekend."

Clark rubbed his hands together. "This sounds good."

"I was kidnapped, Littlejohn," Steele said, setting the record straight.

Greg straightened his shoulders with pride. "And it was Odelia who found him."

Clark looked up at me. "This I gotta hear."

I waved him off and got up from the table. While Steele told the story with great embellishment, I went into the house and grabbed my cell phone. Sally, a no-nonsense type, accepted her call to duty with her usual aplomb, sounding ready to take on anything thrown at her.

I felt it my duty to give her the small print. "Before you get too enthusiastic, General Patton, you should know that Saturday I was there for a memorial service and ended up being shot at."

"That was you?" The question came out as a laugh choked short by the horror of what could have been.

"Yes, me and Zee Washington. So if you want to back out, I'd certainly understand. Seems I'm not only a corpse magnet but a bullet magnet as well."

"No chance, Odelia. I offered my help and I meant it. Besides, we'll be inside a crowded bar — no room for drive-bys."

I wished I shared her confidence.

"And I've heard," she continued, "that drag queen bingo is a lot of fun. There's a very popular one up in West Hollywood at a place called Hamburger Mary's. Ever been?"

"Afraid not. It's a new thing to me. Guess I've led a sheltered life."

"Jill and I have been talking about going for a long time. All the proceeds go to charity. Too bad she has a French pastry class tomorrow night. It's the first class in a series, so she won't want to miss it."

"I wouldn't want her to miss it either. Her cooking classes usually mean treats the next day at the office."

On Monday night, Sally swung by the house to pick me up. Clark was off to meet Greg at his shop in Huntington Beach to help him out. Steele met us by the front door of Billie's Holiday. He was just a few minutes late, but standing out front, just yards from where the shooting had occurred, gave me the heebie-jeebies. I couldn't wait to go inside and take our seats.

"Quit fiddling with that wig," Sally whispered to me, "or people will *know* it's a wig."

She was seated to my right, Steele to my left. Our table was in a prime spot. Close to the stage, with a clear view of the entire room.

"Yeah, like there's any real doubt."

I'd bought the wig earlier in the day, right after leaving Rambling Rose the second time — the time I left with my tail between my legs and my brother gloating at my side. The wig hung just past my shoulders and had bangs. The color was lighter than my real hair — a very light brown with pale highlights. It was also not very expensive. Clark had wanted me to go platinum blond.

"With the lighting in here, it will do," Sally said out of the corner of her mouth, "so quit fidgeting."

Steele looked very Southern California casual in jeans, a tee shirt sporting a surfing logo, and his topsiders without socks. Of course, the jeans bore a high-end label. I also noticed he hadn't shaved his usual five o'clock shadow. Sally wore navy Dockers and a tucked-in Hawaiian shirt on her tall, slender frame, while I had opted for a green knit tunic over khaki capris and sneakers.

The unmod squad going undercover.

We ate our burgers with onion rings and fries and washed them down with beer and soft drinks. The burgers were, as Corey had claimed, pretty damn good. The place filled up quickly, with most folks arriving by seven thirty to grab some grub before the bingo started. Betty Rumble was one of the waiters, dressed tonight in leather hot pants and a lime-green sequined halter top. There were three waiters, all in drag, all dressed similar to Betty in flashy hooker wear with either platform shoes or go-go boots. Two wore wigs, one didn't. Betty was sporting his own natural blond spikes. I studied him as covertly as I could, comparing his face to my memory of Amber Straight's. They definitely had the same coloring, facial structure, and build, although Amber seemed more sturdy. Our waiter was Corey. I was worried he and Betty would recognize me, but they didn't seem to.

The clientele was pretty eclectic, ranging from middle-aged, older tourists to groups of young adults. In one corner was a gaggle of very young women having a bachelorette party — the bride obvious by the short wedding veil on her head and the tight scoop-neck tee shirt with the word bride printed across her hearty bosom. While he ate his burger, Steele's eyes remained glued to the wedding party. I could almost see him calculating the number of shots the girls were slamming down.

I kicked him under the table and hissed, "You're not here as a scout for *Girls Gone Wild.* Remember that."

He glanced my way, wearing a sappy grin. "I can multitask."

"You're disgusting, Steele. Those girls are about twenty years younger than you. They're barely legal to drink in this state."

"And your point?"

"They are pretty cute," Sally added.

I shot an evil eye her way. "You're not helping, Sally."

"You're right," Sally admitted. She fixed Steele with a serious eye. "Keep your mind off your pecker, Steele, at least for now. After, if you're a good little spy, maybe Odelia will let you pick up a drunk chick in the parking lot."

I took a huge bite from my burger to squelch the obscenities on the tip of my tongue. I knew I should have come alone. Hell, we could've bought Clark a hairpiece and *he* could have made the trip.

Shortly before eight o'clock, Marvin Gunn appeared onstage with a microphone.

277

He thanked everyone for coming and made an enthusiastic pitch for the charity the evening's proceeds would be going to. He also thanked the various sponsors who'd donated the prizes, which ranged from things like dinner for two and bottles of wine to a bay cruise and theatre tickets.

When we first came in, Steele had bought each of us a pack of bingo cards at the door and picked up three bingo daubers — the small plastic bottles of ink with sponge tips for marking the bingo cards — from a box they had on hand. True to his word, Steele did know his away around drag queen bingo. He'd even suggested either the Hawaiian burger with grilled pineapple or the pulled pork sandwich as some of the tastier items on the menu. And he'd insisted we try the onion rings. It was news to me that he even ate fried foods.

When the announcements were over, Gunn introduced Lillian Cherry, the bingo caller for the night. Making his way to the stage was a tall, slender man dressed in a lavish red sleeveless gown edged with green fringe. The gown was slit from the floor almost to the family jewels, revealing a pair of nicely toned legs — legs a lot more shapely than my own thick stumps. On his head he wore a platinum-blond wig adorned with green and pink feathers. His makeup was garish but skillfully applied to elicit maximum laughs. He faced the crowd with wide-open arms as if giving a group hug.

"Hello, bingo babes and bingo boys!" Lillian Cherry announced into the microphone with over-the-top flair. "We've got a great night of bingo ahead with faaaaabulous prizes, so grab your daubers." He gave the crowd a lascivious wink. "And while you're at it, grab those thingies you mark the bingo cards with, too, and let's get balling!"

The crowd went wild. Clearly, Lillian Cherry was a favorite with the regulars.

Standing behind the bingo-ball mixer, Lillian Cherry got the first game rolling, calling out the numbers in a smoky, sexy Lauren Bacall voice. He had it down pat, knowing when to move along and when to pause to give folks time to mark their cards. His comments between numbers were timed perfectly.

The games were raucous and interactive, with the audience calling out smutty references to some of the numbers called. Whenever O-69 was called, the crowd howled and hooted for a full five seconds. The regulars knew what was expected of them and delivered, just as Lillian did his job with expertise. Between dotting my sheets to mark the

279

numbers drawn, I continued to survey the crowd, looking for any faces that might look familiar or suspicious. I found none.

I didn't know what I was hoping for by coming to the club tonight. Maybe the off chance Scott Johnson would return to the club, preferably with Roslyn by his side. Or that Clarice would stop in for a drink. Clarice was toying with me, and I didn't like it one bit. If it weren't for my promise to Joan, I'd walk away and not give a damn. Well, that wasn't true. Knowing what I knew about Scott Johnson, I was as eager as Dev to find Roslyn Stevens.

I was also determined to find out who had put the hit out on me and why. I wanted to personally slug the person who'd nearly killed Zee and shattered our relationship, providing I got to them before my husband did.

TWENTY-TWO

Steele nudged me. "Look, Grey, all you need is O-69 to win."

"Really?" I looked down at my card. I had been so focused on scouting the crowd, I hadn't noticed. Game after game, I had been marking my numbers on autopilot and not paying attention to my progress. But Steele was right. Sally looked my card over and confirmed I was closing in on the prize — dinner for two at La Brisas, a lovely Mexican restaurant in Laguna Beach.

Lillian Cherry continued calling the numbers. I held my breath, sure someone else would get it before the outrageous O-69 could be called.

B-4.

N-35.

G-57

B-10.

O-69.

"Oh my gawd!" I jumped up amidst the

281

wolf whistles and hooting from the crowd. "I have it! I have it!"

Lillian Cherry pointed a ridiculously long fingernail at me. "And what do you have, girlfriend?"

"*Bingo!* I have a bingo!" I hopped up and down on my cushy-soled shoes.

"Well, get that tooshie of yours up here so we can verify it."

Picking up the card, I wiggled my way through the few tables separating me from the stage. Once there, they began repeating the numbers that gave me my win.

"And that's a good *bingo!*" yelled Lillian Cherry to the crowd. Everyone clapped and cheered as they handed me the gift certificate to Las Brisas. Lillian put an arm around me for a photo op, and Sally took the photo with her phone's camera. Done, I turned to Lillian to thank him, but the words didn't come out as smoothly as I had planned. My attention was riveted to his face.

"You okay, sugar?" Lillian asked. "Did winning fry your brain?" He tittered.

I shook it off and laughed. "No, sorry. Just wanted to say thanks."

When Sally and I got back to our table, I spied Steele standing by the bachelorettes' table, chatting them up. As soon as I'd received my prize, Lillian Cherry announced a short intermission, and Steele had wasted no time making his move. Whatever he was peddling to them, it must have been clever, or at least clever to drunken young women, because they were all giggling, especially the bride.

When we sat down, Sally nudged me. "He's exactly as Jill described him, except for the clothes."

"Yeah, those are his slumming togs."

"I thought she was making some of it up."

"Knowing Jill, she's taming it down for your consumption." After a second, I turned to Sally in surprise. "But you've met Steele before. Several times, I'm sure."

"Yeah, but not around his natural hunting ground. It's like watching a hungry hyena on the Discovery Channel."

"Let me see the photo you took, Sally."

Sally pulled out her cell phone and brought up the photo of me with Lillian Cherry. He looked familiar, but I couldn't place him.

Corey showed up at our table. "Can I get you ladies anything?"

The occupants of the table next to us flagged him down. "Hey, our waiter's disappeared," a guy with a military haircut said. "Can you get us drinks?"

Corey turned and flashed a becoming smile. "Be with you in a jiff." How pretty Corey was as a woman was disturbing my female vanity.

We placed orders for another beer for me and Steele and a soft drink for Sally. Before Corey left, I stopped him. "Change my order from beer to a Coke," I told the waiter. "I think I've had enough alcohol tonight." Corey gave me a nod and turned on his platforms to go, but I stopped him again and showed him the photo taken a minute before. "Lillian Cherry looks so familiar. Does he play at other clubs in the area? Or maybe I've seen him on TV?"

"No," Corey replied with a shake of his head. "Lillian doesn't do drag very often anymore. Mostly he calls bingo for the club as a favor to his brother."

Inside my head I heard a spring snap. I looked back at the stage, but Lillian Cherry was gone. "His brother?"

"Marvin Gunn," Corey replied, "the owner of Billie's, is his brother."

Steele returned to our table wearing a grin, pleased as punch with his performance.

"Take it easy, Steele," I whispered to him, "or I'll tell those girls you have an incurable STD."

He winked at me. "And I'll tell them you're my dried-up, old-maid aunt visiting me on a three-day pass from the Betty Ford Center."

He looked across the table at Sally, then at me. "You ladies having fun tonight?"

"We're not here to have fun, Steele," I snapped.

"Oh no? Looked like you were having fun when you collected that prize."

Ignoring him, I poked a nail under the wig at the back of my neck and scratched. "I swear, tonight when I get home, I'm burning this thing."

Intermission was nearly over, and most of the crowd had reclaimed their seats. I handed my dauber to Steele. "I'm going to the ladies' room. Watch my card and stay out of trouble."

"Okay, but if your card wins, I'm keeping the prize."

With a roll of my eyes, I excused myself and made my way through the crowds toward the sign that said Restrooms. The sign led to a long hallway under a lit Exit sign. It was the same corridor through which Scott Johnson had made his escape. The restrooms were on the right-hand side. On the left was a door to the kitchen on which a sign was posted Employees Only. It must have been a service door, because it wasn't the one through which the waiters went back and forth with food and dirty dishes. At the far end on the right, just past the restrooms, was a door over which was another lit red Exit sign. At the very far end of the corridor was a door marked Private. It seemed more than a fifty-fifty chance that door would lead to Marvin Gunn's office, the place from which he ran his kingdom of investments and deals. The door was closed. Glancing to make sure no one was around, I secured my bag higher on my shoulder and tiptoed to it, putting my ear close to the painted wood. Nothing. Not a peep. Hmmm, this might be a good time to have a little chat with Marvin Gunn and see if I could jar some information loose.

I looked at the door to the ladies' room with longing. I really did have to pee. The beer I'd had with dinner was running right through me. I looked back at the closed office door, not wanting to miss a golden opportunity. What to do? What to do?

Telling my bladder to suck it up, I knocked on the office door gently. No answer. I knocked again, a little harder. Again, nothing. "Mr. Gunn," I called, keeping my voice low. I tried the doorknob, expecting to find it locked. It wasn't. With a simple turn, I opened it a few inches and peeked in.

A scream caught in my throat like a chicken wing going down sideways. I looked over my shoulder. No one was in the hall. I could hear Lillian Cherry onstage, calling to customers to get ready to start the next game. Without entering the office, I surveyed the room from the doorway gap. The room had been ransacked. Drawers and cabinets were open, papers were on the floor — the debris was a backdrop of clutter framing the corpse.

Marvin Gunn was sprawled backward in a wooden swivel desk chair, his arms draped over the sides. His eyes were staring at the ceiling, his mouth open in surprise or maybe a last call for help. Stuck directly into his chest was a long, sturdy knife.

Now I *really* had to pee.

Covering my hand with the end of my knit tunic, I grasped the doorknob and closed the door, hoping to wipe my fingerprints clean in the same motion. I backed up, keeping my eyes on the door as if I expected Gunn to become a zombie and follow me. When I reached the ladies' room, I pushed the door open and ducked inside.

There were two stalls — one large handicapped stall and one regular — both empty. The only other items in the room were a small vanity with mirror and sink, a paper-towel dispenser, and a large trash can that was nearly full. With my chest heaving with anxiety, I went into the smaller stall and did my business, worried the whole time the killer was out in the hallway, waiting to pounce on me. The last thing I wanted was to die with my panties around my knees; they weren't even my nice panties.

Finished, I pulled myself together and washed my hands. I looked in the mirror. Terror looked back at me. Pulling a lipstick out of my bag, I applied fresh color to my pale lips, stalling the moment when I had to step out into the hall.

The door to the bathroom popped open just as I was finishing my lower lip. I jumped a foot into the air, leaving a gash of Sunset Mauve from my lips halfway across my lower right cheek. It looked like I was underlining the scabbed-over scrape.

"Are you okay?" It was Sally Kipman. "You've been gone so long, we got worried."

Grabbing Sally by the collar of her shirt, I pulled her into the bathroom. "No, I'm not okay," I said in a hushed voice. "I . . . I found another body."

"What!"

I clamped a hand over her mouth just as I heard footsteps outside the door. With my other hand, I put an index finger to my clownish lips and tugged her into the handicapped stall. Once there, I slowly removed my hand from her mouth and together we listened. The footsteps went away.

"It's Marvin Gunn," I told Sally, my voice barely audible. "He's in his office — dead."

"How do you do this?" Sally plopped down on the toilet and put her head into her hands.

Before I could answer, the bathroom door flung open. Sally stood quickly and we huddled together in the confines of the stall, waiting for whatever came next.

"I'm having such an awesome time," said a woman. I peeked through the slender gap between the stall wall and door. I couldn't see much, but I did see what looked like a veil. Chances were it was the bride from the bachelorette party.

"Yeah, drag queen bingo is so cool," answered her companion.

"I'm totally wasted," the bride giggled. "Hey, what's with that guy at intermission?" The bride went into the stall next to us, and soon we heard tinkling.

"His name's Mike. Says he's a lawyer and asked for my number."

"You gonna give it to him? He's kind of cute for an old guy."

A giggle, totally of its own accord and not remembering the severity of our situation, escaped my lips before I could stop it.

Long hair hit the floor in a silent waterfall as the girl by the vanity looked under our stall door. "There's two girls in the next stall," she whispered to the bride as if we couldn't hear her.

The bride giggled. "Whatever lifts your skirt, literally."

We heard a flush as the bride left her stall, followed by the sound of water at the sink. Her friend quickly peed next. After more hand washing, one of them knocked on our stall. "Next time, ladies, get a room."

After they were gone, we poked our heads out of the stall. "We have to get out of here," I told Sally.

"We have to report the murder, Odelia." Her voice wavered, so I knew she could be persuaded to leave the corpse be.

I was peeking out the door, hoping the coast was clear. I turned back around to find Sally was now in the stall with the door closed, making her own waterworks.

"No," I hissed to her through the door. "Let someone else find this one." With a quick look in the mirror, I grabbed a paper towel and rubbed the lipstick off my face. Then I adjusted my wig.

While Sally washed up, I nodded toward the door. "Let's get the cute old guy and get the hell out of here before the entire police force shows up."

"Did you see anyone?"

"No, and I don't want to."

We opened the door and slid out into the hallway. Sally first, me behind her. "Get Steele," I instructed her. "I'm heading straight out the door."

As Sally trotted off on her mission, I took one final glance back at the office door, gasped, and stopped in my tracks. Like Lot's wife, I was as white and still as a pillar of salt. The door, which I had taken such pains to close, was open — not wide open, but a couple of inches open. I was sure I'd closed it tight. I'd even listened for and heard the soft click of the latch. Finding my feet again, I double-timed it to the front door. Steele and Sally came out moments after.

"What's up, Grey?" Steele asked when I stepped out of the shadows of the building to join them. The summer sun hadn't been down long, but it was dark enough to give some cover.

I was about to say something when we heard a scream, followed by several more.

We all turned to the door. From inside

the club, hysteria was starting to build. I looked at Steele. "My guess is they found the body."

"What body?" Steele asked, his voice a near squeal.

I started walking. "Let's get moving."

Sally had parked her SUV several blocks away. It had been the only parking spot she could find when we arrived. Now I was glad it wasn't close to the club. During the walk, Steele tried several times to find out what was going on.

"You didn't tell him?" I asked Sally as we walked with a quick step. I wanted to run but didn't want to collect any suspicious looks.

"No time."

"Tell me what?" Steele stopped. "I'm not moving another step until you tell me what in the hell is going on."

Sally backtracked to Steele and said something to him while I continued walking.

Behind me, I heard Steele gasp. "What?"

Steele and Sally caught up to me. "This is a joke, right, Grey?"

"No, Steele, it's not. Marvin Gunn is back there in his office deader than a doornail. Trust me on this."

Steele grabbed my upper arm. "Tell me

you didn't do it, Grey. Even in self-defense."

I yanked my arm away. "Are you insane? Of course I didn't. But I'm not sure if anyone saw me find the body. Hopefully no one did, especially the killer."

As Steele studied my face in the glow of a street light, a police car, siren wailing like a lost child, sped by. It came to a screeching halt in front of Billie's Holiday.

"You're right, Grey, we need to get out of here."

Once Steele had us safely bundled in Sally's vehicle, he gave us our marching orders. "Kipman," he barked to Sally. "Take Odelia straight home. Got that?"

Sally saluted, but when she snapped her hand away from her head, I noticed she'd folded all fingers in except her middle one. "I'm not one of your dumb-ass bimbos, Steele. I can take care of Odelia."

Before I had found Gunn's body, the two of them had been getting along fine. Clearly the stress of yet another murder was taking its toll.

"Okay, you two," I snapped from my position wedged between them. "Calm down or I'm calling Greg for a ride home."

I turned to Steele, who was standing outside the SUV, talking to us through my open window. "Where's your car, Steele?"

"Back that way." He tossed his head in the direction of the club.

"Then get in," I instructed. "We'll drop you off at your car, then we'll all go home. It's been a rough night. A good night's sleep and a long talk with Clark will help me decide what to do."

My words seemed to knock some civility back into my sidekicks. With some reluctance, Sally released the locks on the back seat. We heard another police siren. Quickly, Steele climbed in. "My car's just past the club on the same side," he advised her.

We pulled out of the parking space and made our way in the direction of the club. We had to take it slow because traffic had backed up. As we got closer, we saw one of the police cars had parked in the far right lane, forcing the two lanes heading north down to one lane. Traffic was further hampered by cars slowing down to gawk. A uniformed cop was in the street, directing traffic around the scene and telling people to keep it moving.

Unfortunately, one of the police cars had blocked in Steele's Porsche.

"Damn it," Steele swore from the back seat. "Now what am I going to do?"

"You know, Steele," Sally ventured. "It's not like you're guilty of anything but being a lech. You could just tell the cops that's your car and you need to go home. How would they know you've been in the club?"

"Because he was a lech, that's how." I pointed out the window. Standing on the sidewalk was the gaggle of drunk bachelorettes. A police woman was talking to them.

Steele slunk down in the back seat. "I really do not want to spend the rest of my evening being questioned." He looked longingly at his spiffy sports car and sighed. "Take me home, Kipman. I can come back later tonight or even tomorrow morning to get the car."

"Is that an order or a request, Steele?" Sally glared at him in the rear-view mirror. "If it's a request, I didn't hear the word *please.*"

I was beginning to think I should go back to the club and confess to anything just to get taken into police custody and away from Frick and Frack here.

Steele gave in. "All right. *Please,* take me home."

"Now that's more like it." Sally looked in the rear-view mirror again. "A few more *please* and *thank you*s to Jill once in a while wouldn't kill you either."

Steele shot forward. "That's what this shitty attitude of yours is about? You don't think I appreciate Jill?"

"I appreciate her," I said, hoping it would be enough to mollify Sally. It wasn't.

"I didn't say that, Steele," Sally volleyed. "I'm just saying you could be more polite and thoughtful, considering all the bullshit she takes from you. According to her, it's escalated lately."

"I have to agree, Steele," I volunteered. "You've taken snide and snarky to new heights lately in the office. Everyone's noticed."

"Sorry, Grey. I didn't realize part of my job was to enhance your personal employment experience." He turned to Sally. "As for Jill, you tell her if I were polite and thoughtful, there'd be no bullshit. And where's the fun in that?"

Sally slammed on her brakes. If it weren't for the narrowness of the space between the front seats, Steele would have shot into the windshield like a missile. Sally glared at her partner's boss while folks behind us honked.

"Better put your seat belt on, Steele," Sally told him through clenched teeth. "It's gonna be a bumpy ride."

My hand was on the door handle, ready to throw myself at the nearest uniform and beg for mercy.

TWENTY-THREE

Steele's beachside condo was in Laguna Beach — in the opposite direction. Once Sally got the SUV moving again, it seem like forever before we worked our way past the traffic jam caused by police presence at Billie's Holiday. Next, we had to find a suitable place to make a U-turn.

"So, Grey, who do you think killed Gunn?" The question came from Steele. After the word war with Sally, the two of them sulked in silence as we inched our way through the traffic. The quiet, thick as it was, was music to my ears.

"I have no idea. It could be any one of dozens of people. I still don't know how he's tied in with Clarice and her friends, or if he is at all. As of this afternoon, I would have said he wasn't, though while you were making cow eyes at those girls, Sally and I found out that Lillian Cherry is Aaron Gunn, Marvin Gunn's brother."

"Really?"

Sally cut her eyes from the road to me. "Maybe he killed his brother. Didn't you tell me on the way down here that Marvin bailed out his brother financially from time to time?"

"That's what Clark thinks. I do know that Aaron Gunn is one of the partners of Rambling Rose, though I got the impression that Shirley did most of the actual work. And it sounds as if even Clarice was more involved than Aaron."

"So you think it's Aaron, not Marvin, who is in that photo with Clarice and Alfred and the others?" Sally braked for some fool trying to cut into the line of waiting traffic.

"I'm almost positive now. While Marvin owned the club, he doesn't seem to have any connection to the other people, except for Scott Johnson showing up at the service. And his appearance doesn't mean he knew Marvin."

"You know," said Sally, "during intermission, Lillian left the stage and went to the back. He could have killed his brother and made it back onstage with no problem."

I thought about that. "During intermission, there had to be a lot of foot traffic in that hallway because of the bathrooms. Someone had to have seen someone going in or out of the office."

"But," Steele interjected, "no one would think twice about Lillian going back there, would they?"

"You're right," I said, moving that information to the forefront of my brain. "As Lillian Cherry, he was a performer. As Aaron Gunn, he was the owner's brother. No one would think it odd if he were back there. And," I said, raising an index finger high in the air, "from my brief look at the body, it didn't look like Marvin struggled — same as Shirley didn't. I'll wager that whoever killed them, whether it be the same person or two people, both knew their killers and trusted them."

Steele unfastened his seat belt and leaned forward between Sally's seat and mine, totally forgetting Sally's earlier threat. "Assuming for the moment the killer is one and the same, who is common to both in such a capacity?"

I didn't have to give it much thought. "That would have to be Aaron. He was in business with Shirley, and Marvin was his brother. No one else appears to have the same level of familiarity with both."

My head was beginning to hurt from all the suppositions. "But what about Alfred Nunez?" I asked. "He doesn't fit with either.

Nor does Roslyn or Scott. What's their connection?"

Sally gave a little snort. "And here we are again, back at the same question. It would be a fairly cut-and-dried puzzle if not for them."

Finally, Sally spotted a place to legally make a U-turn.

"Rambling Rose is just ahead on the right," I told them as we started south on PCH. "It's a few blocks north of the club."

Traffic going south was just as slow as that going north, thanks to all the cars slowing to watch the police activity. Once we got past Billie's Holiday, it should increase to normal speed. I was thankful it was a Monday and not a weekend, or the traffic would have been twice as bad.

"There it is." I pointed out the window to the cheerful office with the striped awning perched on the corner of PCH and a small side street. "Just ahead."

As we inched past Rambling Rose, my eye caught on something in the back of the building. "Pull over," I yelled.

"What?" Sally shot a look of surprise at me. From the back, Steele leaned forward, all ears at this change of events.

"Pull over. No, wait. Turn right at the next corner."

Sally made the requested turn at the side street.

"Now turn right at the next street," I directed, "then right again."

The turns took us down some narrow, cute residential streets and deposited us on a side street heading back toward Pacific Coast Highway.

"Now slow way down," I cautioned Sally. "Up ahead on the left, on the corner, is Rambling Rose."

"What is it, Grey?" Steele leaned forward again, his mouth close to my ear as he spoke. The smell of onions and beer blew softly past my nostrils.

"I want to check out Rambling Rose. I think someone is in there."

The car edged forward. On the side of the building that didn't face PCH was a small parking lot that only had room for a few cars. The lot was empty. I studied the windows that faced the lot. There were only two of them — rectangular windows near the back of the building. I also spied a back door that opened to the parking lot. It was close to the far end of the building

Steele lowered his window and looked out. "I don't see anything, Grey. And the lot is empty."

As the car rolled past the building, I

301

craned my neck to see if there was any sign of life at the front of the building. "Go around the block again, Sally."

In response, Sally eased her vehicle into a right turn onto Pacific Coast Highway, then took the next right as we retraced our steps back to the side street that held the wedding shop.

Before we got too close to Rambling Rose I told her to pull over. I unbuckled my seat belt. "I'm checking it out."

"Oh no, you're not, Grey." Steele placed a strong hand on my shoulder as I started to open the door.

"Shit, Odelia," snapped Sally. "The car's still moving."

"Then stop it."

"Hang on a minute. There's an open spot just a few feet ahead."

Steele wedged his body so far forward between the seats, he was nearly driving. "Keep the damn car moving, Kipman. Don't let her out."

Sally pulled into the empty spot. "Is that another one of your orders, Steele?"

"She's just going to get into trouble." He turned to me. "Isn't a dead body enough excitement for one night, Grey?"

I aimed a cocked eyebrow at my boss. "I thought you wanted to be part of the excitement, Steele. Well, here's your chance, and all you have to do is sit in the car."

When I opened the door, Sally turned off the engine. "I'm coming with you."

"No need," I told her. "I'm just going to see if I can peek in a window, that's all. Maybe Clarice is sneaking around in there. I still need to question her."

"And maybe Clarice is the killer," Steele said, his voice getting higher with his frustration. "If so, I hardly think she's going to want to have a little chat with you or anyone."

"Relax, Steele, maybe the place is as deserted as it looks. If so, what better time than now to check it out, especially with everyone focused on the club and Marvin?"

"Please say you're not considering breaking and entering." Steele looked about to have a stroke. I didn't answer.

Sally opened a storage area between the two front seats and extracted a small handgun. She checked it and slipped it into her waistband.

The gun kicked Steele over the edge. "Holy shit, Kipman! Do you have a license for that thing?"

"Of course I do, Steele."

Steele didn't look convinced. Me, I'm scared snotless by the sight of any gun —

legal or not.

"A license to carry a concealed weapon?" he pressed. "Because that gun looks concealed to me."

"Relax, Steele. I'm an expert shot with hours of training in firearm safety."

He sat back. "Why am I not surprised?"

"The big surprise," Sally said to Steele with a straight face, "is that I didn't use it on you earlier."

Sally looked at me, her face serious. "Considering the jams you get into, it would do you good to learn how to use one of these."

"Um, no thanks. And I'd prefer it if you'd put that thing away." I got out of the vehicle. "In fact, both of you just stay here. I'll be right back."

Sally got out on her side. "No way I'm letting you go up to that building alone."

"Me neither." Steele opened his door and set a foot on the ground.

"Damn it," I swore, keeping my voice down. "How inconspicuous can I be with a parade following me?"

"I'm coming with you," Sally insisted.

"You can only come if you leave the gun here." I stood on the sidewalk, my hands on my hips, giving her my best Zee stance. I didn't know if it would work, especially in the dark gray of the evening and against a woman with a gun — friend or not.

"But —" Sally started.

"I'm with Grey on this one," added Steele.

I snatched off the wig and tossed it inside the vehicle. Combing my fingers through my flattened hair, I whipped my head around to Steele. "As for you, you keep your butt in the car. If you see anything wrong, call for help. We don't need all three of us tramping around up there. And I'm certainly not putting your law license in jeopardy."

The two of them looked at me, weighing whether I meant what I said. For good measure I added, "Or you can both go home and I'll go it alone on this. Just Sally, no gun, or no dice."

The two of them looked at each other, then at me. Swearing under her breath, Sally removed the gun and put it back into the storage compartment. Stretching across the seat, she popped open the glove box and pulled something else out. "But I'm taking this." It was a flashlight.

I nodded. "Now that's a good idea."

Steele pushed a button on his watch and it lit up. It wasn't the thin, fancy one he usually wore to the office but a serious watch with gadgets. "Okay, but I'm not getting back inside. I can watch you two from here. You have ten minutes."

I protested. "Ten minutes isn't enough time to blink, Steele."

"Make it twenty."

"Thirty," I countered.

"Twenty-five, but not a second more." He pushed another button on his watch. "When my watch buzzes, I'm calling for help."

Steele stuck his hands into his pockets and leaned against the SUV. To someone who didn't know him, Mike Steele looked bored and barely interested, but the silent yet nervous tapping of his shoe against the pavement didn't escape my notice. Nor did the tightness of his jaw. I hoped my crazy mission was a quick one, because if Steele clenched his teeth like that for twenty-five minutes, he was going to crack some caps.

Keeping to the shadows, Sally and I crept back to Rambling Rose and slithered along the wall of the building to the back windows. The sills hit me about the height of my chin, which was great for keeping us out of sight but not so great for snooping. Both windows were covered by semi-closed vertical blinds. A dim light was on inside the building — probably some sort of low-level security light.

Standing on tiptoes, I peeked over the

edge. Being quite a bit taller than me, Sally had an easier go of it.

The dim light we'd noticed seemed to be coming from the hallway. It cast a dull light into the room, leaving most of it in shadows. Gripping the edge of the window, I stretched myself upward as far as possible on my short legs and looked over the sill. It took a second for my eyes to adjust and to piece the scene together through the openings in the blinds. It was a large office with book-cases.

"Do you see anything?" I mouthed to Sally.

"The room looks messy," she whispered, "but it's difficult to tell in this light if it's just clutter." She directed her flashlight through the slits in the blinds. "Really, Odelia, I think this room was ransacked."

That sounded ominous, especially considering Marvin Gunn's office had been tossed and so had Shirley's home.

With stealth, Sally moved over to the next window. I followed. The faded light from the hallway showed us this room was also an office. Although as large as the other, it was more plainly decorated. I didn't notice anything in the low light.

My calves and feet were getting tired of standing on tiptoe. I lowered myself and shook out the muscles, vowing to kick my exercise walking up a notch or two starting next week.

The back door had a small window at a lower height and no blinds. Next to it was planted a well-trimmed bush that matched those at the front of the building. Slinking my way down the length of the wall, I made my way to the door. It was then I saw the car. The parking lot wasn't empty, as we'd thought. There was a wide space between the end of the building and the fence separating the property from the commercial building next door, making a single parking spot unseen from the street. Parked in it now was a dark Lexus, either black or dark blue, I couldn't tell. I had no idea what kind of car Clarice drove, but it was the type of car that would suit her.

I edged to the back door and looked through the window. The small amount of light allowed me to make out a kitchenette with a round table and two chairs, a refrigerator, and what looked like assorted small appliances arranged on a short counter. It was likely the employee break room and where they made refreshments for clients. There was no sign of Clarice or anyone else. I started to put my hand on the doorknob.

"Pssst," hissed Sally, stopping me. Sally

had flattened herself against the end of the building and faced the direction of her SUV, ready to signal Steele if she had to. She scooted closer to me. "Be careful, there's probably a security system."

Great, a little something that had totally slipped my mind. I withdrew my hand and fretted about lost time. I looked at the car again, pointing it out to Sally. "If Clarice or someone is in there, wouldn't it be disarmed?"

"Probably. You ready to take that chance?"

I wasn't sure which would be the lesser evil, breaking in and having a security alarm go off or breaking in and surprising a possible killer. Whoever had killed Shirley and/or Marvin had been skillful with a knife, and it could have been Clarice. I certainly thought years ago she was capable of putting a hit out on her husband. I took a second to weigh whether I wanted to put Clarice's slicing and dicing talents to the test.

Sally edged back along the wall and looked into one of the windows again. She glanced my way and signaled for me to join her.

Hoisting myself up a few inches, I surveyed the plain office again. I didn't see anything. I lowered myself and shrugged at

Sally. She ducked down and indicated for me to look to my right. With a deep breath, I grabbed the sill and stretched up as far as I could, stretching bone, sinew, and skin to their limit. I cast my eyes in the direction she'd directed. Sally joined me and used her flashlight like a spotlight.

Just inside to the right of the door, it appeared a large, long bundle was lying on the floor. It was difficult to see through the narrow vertical slits of the almost-closed blinds, but something was definitely there. I lowered myself, rested, then up again I went like a jack-in-the-box, this time zeroing my eyes immediately in on the target. I dropped to the ground again. It was either a trussed body, a rolled-up rug, or a world-record-holding cigar.

Sally popped up again and stared at the bundle several moments before waving me to join her. Again I pulled myself up. In the small bit of light, I saw the heap moving slightly. It wasn't a cigar or a rug or even, thankfully, a dead body. The light was too dim to get an idea of identity or even sex, but whoever it was, they were still alive but not moving with any speed.

Sally was pantomiming to me again. This time, I think she was scolding me for not letting her bring the gun. I was beginning

310

to think that had been a wrong move on my part myself. Whoever was in there was in trouble. I motioned to Sally that she should return to Steele. I made a calling motion.

"Call for help," I told her. "I'm going in."

"Not without me, you're not."

I hung my head. "Did you bring your cell?"

She shook her head. "I was worried it might ring. Even the vibration is loud. You didn't bring yours?"

I patted down the pockets of my capri pants and shook my head. "It's back in my purse."

Our options were to go back to Steele and the SUV and call for help or go in and help whoever was inside now. "It makes more sense," I reasoned with Sally, still keeping my voice in a whisper, "for one of us to go call for help and the other to check on whoever is inside."

Sally didn't budge. "There might still be someone in there, Odelia."

"Well, alarm or not, I'm going in." I moved toward the back door. Sally followed, sending a pantomime message to Steele to make a call, though it was so dark and he was a half-block away, I doubt he noticed anything.

I tried the back door's knob. It didn't

move. I was looking around for a rock or something with which to break the back window when Sally noticed that we didn't need to break anything. The back door was an old-fashioned kitchen door, probably left over from when the building was a private residence. The window had a screen over it, and the bottom portion of the window had been raised to allow fresh air to come in. Now I just needed something to cut the screen.

Like magic, Sally produced a Swiss army knife and opened it, revealing a nasty-looking serrated blade. "If that window is open like that, chances are the alarm isn't armed."

I was beginning to worry about Sally.

Taking the knife, I ran the blade along the lower edge of the old screen. It parted like butter left in the sun. After running the blade along both sides, I was able to curl the screen upward. I handed Sally back her knife and slipped my hand through the opening, feeling it scratch my arm as I blindly reached for the door lock. It only took a few seconds to unlatch the door, but it felt like an hour. I half expected to hear Steele's watch alarm go off in my ear.

Once inside, I made tracks for the plain office. It was the one nearest the kitchen.

Behind me was Sally with her knife in one hand and her flashlight in the other, though we didn't need the flashlight. The hall light was plenty. Then I noticed Sally was holding the flashlight like a club.

I felt for a light switch in the office, then changed my mind. If anyone other than Steele wandered by, they might notice the increased light. At my feet, the bundle grunted and moved with more energy, scooting toward me like an inchworm. I knelt down, and Sally swept the bound figure with her light. When the beam landed on the face, I gasped.

It was Clarice.

TWENTY-FOUR

"Sally, check to see if anyone else is here."

Before leaving, Sally flashed the light around the room. Seeing no obvious threats, she grasped the flashlight tighter and went on her mission.

Not caring now about the light, I snapped it on, making Clarice flinch. Her hands were tied behind her, and her ankles were bound. Her nose was splotched with dried blood and there was a gash on her lip, which the gag in her mouth was pulling in a painful direction. Her eyes were huge, but I couldn't tell if Clarice was pissed off or scared. One shoe was missing. She wore a cream-colored linen tunic with matching pants, both dotted with blood.

Sally returned a few seconds later. "No one else is here," she reported. "But I was right about that other office. Someone ransacked it good." We looked around the room we were in. It also looked worked over.

Spotting a phone on the desk, I picked it up. The line was dead. Damn.

I undid Clarice's gag, then worked on her hands. Sally undid her ankles. Clarice moaned when we moved her but was alert.

"Go away, you stupid cow." The words were harsh, softened only by the weakness of her exhausted voice. "I fired you."

"That's a nice way to thank someone." Sally matched Clarice's tone snit for snit.

"Who did this to you, Clarice?" I asked. She didn't answer.

I assisted Clarice into a nearby chair.

"Go away," Clarice ordered again through cracked lips. "Get it through that fat, thick skull of yours: I don't want your help."

Sally left and was back in a jiffy with a bottle of water. "Here," she said, twisting the top off and handing it to Clarice. "I found it in the fridge. Not that you deserve it."

Clarice took the plastic bottle within two shaking hands and gingerly held it to her lips. I cupped her hands in one of mine to hold the water steady.

"Who did this, Clarice?" I asked again. "Was it Shirley's killer?"

She didn't look up. She took another drink of water. It dribbled down her chin and onto her ruined pantsuit. After a couple more sips and a few deep breaths, she looked me in the eye and said, "I told you to leave, and I mean it. I don't want you here."

I put my hands on my hips. "We just saved your snotty ass, and you're throwing us out?"

Clarice started to say something, but Sally cut her off. "Doesn't anyone say *thank you* anymore?"

Clarice took another drink, making a point of ignoring the comment.

I put a hand on each arm of the chair, trapping Clarice in her seat. "Tell me who killed Shirley Pearson," I demanded.

"That's none of your business, Odelia. Not anymore."

Sally stood nearby, feet slightly apart, the flashlight once again gripped like a weapon. I could tell she was as enamored of Clarice as I was. "Humor us."

Clarice mustered her strength to shoot Sally a death ray of a look before turning her bruised, hard eyes to me. "Who the hell is she?"

"A friend of mine. She can be trusted."

"I said, it's none of your business." Clarice shot a dagger at Sally. "That goes for both of you."

Sally glanced at her watch, then reached

out and tapped me on my shoulder. "Let's get out of here, Odelia. Leave the bitch to her own devices. It's worked so well for her so far."

Clarice indicated Sally with her chin. "She's obviously the smart one."

I was a finger snap away from throwing Clarice to the floor and tying her back up, starting with the gag to her mouth. Needing answers for Joan stopped me.

"Shirley may not be my business, but Alfred Nunez is. Remember Alfred? Or I guess you knew him as Alfonso."

"He's none of your business either, not anymore."

Taking my hands off the arms of the chair, I stood up straight. "That's where you're wrong, Clarice. The death of Alfred Nunez is very important to me."

Clarice let out a gasp. A hand went to her swollen mouth. "He's dead?"

"For a second time." I crossed my arms. "You see, I recognized him from your photo. Several years ago, I attended that man's funeral — or should I say the funeral for the man burned in the car accident in his place. I'm a close friend of Alfred's daughter."

"You know Joan?" The splash of surprise

on her blood-splattered face came off as lurid.

"Yes, quite well. And her mother. When Alfred was found murdered recently, Joan asked me to look into his life, specifically what he'd been doing for all these years. I haven't been working for you, Clarice, but doing a favor for a friend."

Clarice let out what might pass for a muffled sob, squelching it before it turned to more. "How? How did he die?"

"Gunshot. Dumped in a dumpster in Santa Ana with no ID." I loosened my tough stance. Being a badass was uncomfortable. "The police identified him from finger-prints. Imagine how surprised his family was when they got the call."

After staring at the wall for a minute, Clarice said in a shaky voice, "If I tell you about Alfred Nunez, will you go and leave me be?"

I stepped forward, wary but all ears. "We'll see."

Clarice shot a hand out and grabbed my forearm with surprising strength. "Promise me, Odelia. I'll not have you on my con-science, too." Her eyes grazed over my scraped cheek. "It looks as if you've already had a brush with something . . . or some-one."

Sally looked at her watch again. Clarice noticed. "You have a bus to catch, blondie?"

Ignoring Clarice, Sally said, "Dump her and let's go. She's not worth it."

But I couldn't leave just yet.

Pulling up a chair, I sat in front of Clarice. "We have a friend who is going to call for help if we don't show soon. So tell me what you know and do it fast."

Clarice looked at the wall behind me, struggling with her decision. She cleared her throat, filling the room with the sound of loose, soggy mucus. "Alfonso — or, rather, Alfred — came to us after he got into trouble with a bunch of hoods." Her eyes left the wall and moved to my face. "He had a gambling problem, Odelia. I don't know if Joan knew that or not. Mostly horses."

I had asked Joan if her father had any reason to disappear. She'd said she hadn't known of anything. Lying didn't come naturally to Joan, so I was going with the assumption that she didn't know. But it might explain why Alfred and Joan's mother had been on the outs.

"He'd kicked it in the past several years," Clarice continued, "but at that time he had a bad gambling addiction. He'd also gotten in deep with an organized group out of

Bakersfield, and they threatened him. That's when he decided to disappear. It was to save himself and protect his family."

Dev had said the killing of Alfred looked like an execution, making me wonder if some if his old Bakersfield pals had finally caught up to him. If so, how had they found him? Through tireless due diligence, happenstance, or did someone squeal?

"What do you mean by 'he came to us'? Who is 'us'?"

"No one."

"Don't screw with me, Clarice. I'm really not in the mood." I leaned back in my chair, my eyes boring into her face. I tried to look menacing, though I'm sure I merely looked exhausted and foolish.

Sally leaned toward me. "We need to get going, Odelia, before Steele calls in the cavalry."

I nodded but kept my eyes on Clarice. Willie came to mind. "Tell me, Clarice, are you and your buddies here at Rambling Rose running some sort of private protection scheme? You know, like a witness protection program, but for anyone with enough cash to disappear?"

From the way Clarice looked at me, I knew I had hit a bullseye or at least come close.

"Was it you and Shirley? Is that why she was killed? Was someone trying to find someone else, or did Shirley's old pals from the bank heist find her?"

At the mention of Shirley, Clarice didn't look so cocky. She looked sad and tired. "I met Shirley after she'd started her new life. One night over drinks she confessed to me who she really was and how Marvin Gunn had helped her start over. She was indebted to him for it."

"He was draining her financially?"

"Not in debt to him," Clarice clarified, "but indebted, grateful for the opportunity. Not only to start over but to start over as her true self — as a woman. That's why she agreed to help with the bank job in the first place. She was a very young and unhappy man and wanted even then to be a woman. Her cut of the money was going to help her start over."

"What happened to the money from the bank job?"

"She didn't know. When the police broke up the robbery, they all took off. One of the other guys might have taken it, but it wasn't Shirley. She hitchhiked to California, drifted around, and eventually found Marvin. He took a young Douglas Pearson under his wing and nurtured him into Shirley Pearson."

"Someone broke into Shirley's place after she was killed and ransacked it," I told Clarice. "Did you know about that? Or have something to do with it?"

"No, on both counts. Though I'm not surprised."

I looked around the trashed office. "Obviously, someone is still looking for something."

Clarice remained silent. Out of the corner of my eye, I could see Sally getting antsy.

I went back to questioning Clarice. "How did Shirley's new life tie in with these people in hiding — with Alfred, Scott Johnson, Roslyn Stevens, and who knows who else?"

Once again, Clarice held back a strangled sob but at the last minute sniffed it back under control. "Shirley wanted to help others in her predicament. She was like that, always thinking of other people. Maybe that's why she was so wonderful with clients. Alfred and I had met many years ago. Back then, he worked for my first husband, Kenneth Woodall, and we'd kept in touch over the years. He came to me for a loan to get the thugs off his back. I gave him the money, but they weren't satisfied. They hounded him for more. That's when he came to us. He wanted to start over, like Shirley did. He didn't know about Shirley's past with the bank thing, only that she'd left behind a life she hated for a new one she loved. Alfred's only stipulation was he wanted to stay close to Joan, even if he couldn't talk to her and be a part of her life. We helped him, imposing our own condition: he had to stop gambling. We found him a new job, a new identity, a place to live."

"Who was the dead guy in the car?"

"The what?"

We'd had this conversation before about Shirley's stand-in corpse. Obviously, Clarice still didn't think it important. "Someone died in the car and was buried as Alfred Nunez. Who was it?"

"No one died in that car, Odelia, I can assure you. The body was that of a homeless person, a John Doe rotting at the county morgue."

"That means you had accomplices beyond your little group."

She clammed up.

Remembering back to when Steele went missing, I recalled what Willie had taught me. "Disappearing like that takes money for a decent fake ID and documents — money and special connections. And if you were paying for someone at the county to slip you a body from time to time, that had to be expensive. Where did the money come from? Was Marvin Gunn a partner in this?"

Clarice gave us a slow nod. "Yes. After we helped Alfred, it was Marvin's idea to turn it into a business. He has a head for such things, knowing when there's a need and then supplying it."

"*Had* a head for such things, you mean," Sally added.

We both turned to look at Sally. Me with a scowl, Clarice in horror. Slowly Clarice turned her head in my direction. "Marvin?"

"Marvin was killed at the club just a short while ago," I told her without sugarcoating it. "And his office was torn up. The police are there now."

Clarice hung her head. "Shirley, Alfred . . . and now Marvin."

I felt bad for Clarice and the others, but it wasn't going to stop me from getting to the bottom of things. In my head I was doing some tricky math using the timeline of Shirley and Alfred's disappearances.

"You were already in the hiding biz when I first met you a few years back, weren't you?"

She snapped her head up, surprised, no

324

doubt, that I had figured out that little tidbit. But then, Clarice always did underestimate me.

"Yes. John knew nothing about it." Her cut lip melted into a small smirk. "It was my secret. Money made and saved and invested without his knowledge. When I needed to take off after that situation with John and Sophie, it was easy. I knew how, and I had the funds to tide me over until his murder was sorted out."

This chat with Clarice was an information smorgasbord, but time was running out.

TWENTY-FIVE

"What about Scott and Roslyn?" I pushed to get more answers, willing Clarice to accelerate since she was unwilling to budge physically. "Did you find them or did they find you?"

"A bit of both." Clarice sniffed. "Either of you have a tissue?"

Sally took off and returned with a roll of toilet paper from the bathroom across the hall. She tore off a length and handed it to Clarice, who took it and said nothing. Sally shot her an evil eye until Clarice grudgingly squeaked out, "Thank you."

Clarice blew her nose. "Marvin got the word out about our . . . um . . . *assistance program* through some underground methods. Sometimes we'd read a news story about someone like an abused wife who sounded like they could use protection and made the contact. We had to be discreet, of course, when we did. In Roslyn's case, someone told someone we know about her. Shirley flew to Chicago and offered our help. Scott contacted Marvin."

"Who paid for your services?"

"Sometimes their family. Mostly they did themselves. Some came with enough cash to pay us and start new lives. Others, like Roslyn and Alfred, paid our expenses over time, like an installment loan."

"That photo you gave me — those are all people you helped start over?"

"Yes, most of them. We became like a small family of our own over the years."

"Even Aaron Gunn?"

She looked up. "Marvin insisted as part of our partnership that we use his brother in the party business, more to give him something to do and keep him out of trouble. He doesn't have quite the same drive as Marvin. Over time, Aaron got involved in the other business, too, but only peripherally."

I thought about the club. "Would there be any reason for Aaron to kill Marvin? Maybe he was jealous or something like that?"

Clarice looked horrified at the thought. "No, he loved his brother. Aaron isn't the smartest tool in the shed, but he has a good heart — almost too good and too trusting."

Sally stepped forward. "Did you ever

bother to investigate the backgrounds of any of these people?"

"Marvin did most of the interviewing and had the contacts for the documents and such. Shirley and I did the setups like housing and finding them employment. We helped them get settled and adjust. It was rather fun."

I closed one eye in irritation. "Is it fun now?"

Clarice jerked as if I'd slapped her but returned quickly to her stony face. I ran a hand through my still-flat hair. It felt gummy from being trapped under the hot wig.

"Marvin should have vetted your clients better. Scott Johnson is wanted for the murder of several young women."

It took a few seconds for the meaning of my words to sink in, then Clarice stood up quickly. "Roslyn." She staggered. Both Sally and I moved to steady her, then resettled her back in the chair.

"What about Roslyn?" I asked, even though I had a good idea of Clarice's concern.

"When all this trouble started, we put the word out to our people to be careful. Then some started disappearing. We didn't know if it was because they went into hiding or if," she hesitated and swallowed, "something had happened to them. Eventually, they all checked in — all but Scott, Roslyn, and Alfred. That's when I came to you. I needed someone who could nose about without a known connection to me. Shortly after, Scott called me to let me know both he and Roslyn were safe. He told me he was taking care of her and not to worry. Roslyn worked for him, so it seemed natural they would look out for each other. That's why I didn't need your services any longer. Everyone was accounted for except Alfred." Her voice tailed off as if losing steam. "I figured he would turn up on his own." She lowered her head.

Both Sally and I leaned in with interest. "Did Scott tell you where they were?"

Keeping her head down, Clarice closed her eyes and shook her head slowly.

I turned to Sally. "Why don't you go tell Steele we're fine and will be out soon. He probably has ants in his pants by now."

She gave her head a fast jerk in agreement and left the room.

I returned my attention to Clarice. "Why, Clarice, were people disappearing? What scared them?"

She took a deep breath, finally resigned to telling the story, or maybe she realized I was going nowhere without it. "It started several weeks ago." She looked at me, her eyes, once challenging, now dull. "We received an envelope. It wasn't mailed but slipped under the door here at the shop. Amber found it one morning when she came in. It was addressed to Shirley, sealed and marked *Personal.* The note inside said unless we gave them the money from the bank robbery, they would start letting certain people know where our clients . . . our special clients . . . were."

"But I thought Shirley didn't have the money."

"She didn't." The response came out of Clarice hurried and chopped.

"Are you sure?"

She gave me a look that dared me to doubt her.

"Then why, after all these years, are people looking for it?" I paced the room. "Seems odd, doesn't it? And how would whoever sent that note know that Shirley was involved in the robbery in the first place?" A conclusion as distasteful and nasty as moldy bread formed in my skull. "This has to be an inside job." I pointed a finger in Clarice's face as I said the words. "Did you keep records on these people? Not just who and where they were, but why they were running and from whom?"

"Yes. We insisted on knowing, although I don't know why Marvin didn't get the right story on Scott Johnson."

"If he had, would you have accepted him as a client?"

Clarice shook her head. "No. Not in a million years. Some of our clients might be a bit shady, but we would never harbor a murderer. Scott must have made something up, and Marv bought it. Scott seemed like a harmless sort of guy."

Harmless. I snorted but kept my thoughts to myself. "Scott was at Shirley's memorial service. Does that seem odd to you? Especially if he was in re-hiding."

"Not at all. Everyone loved Shirley." Clarice looked worried. "Was Roslyn with him?"

"No sign of her."

"You know, maybe you have him mixed up with someone else. It's a common name."

"I don't think so." My lip curled in disgust. "He dumped a chafing dish of meatballs on me and took off when I approached him. A few minutes later, I was being shot at while standing on the sidewalk." I gently touched my injured cheek. "When I hit the pavement, I got this." I moved so close to

331

Clarice that she backed up in her chair. "You know anything about the shooting?"

"I heard about it from Marvin, but that's it. Although, Odelia," she added, getting her courage back, "I'm sure there's a long list of people who would like to take a shot at you."

I backed away. "Very funny."

Stealing over to the side of the window, I peered out through the last narrow opening in the slats. From here I couldn't see Sally's SUV. It was only visible from the end of the building. I couldn't see any sign of Sally either. Knowing Sally and Steele, they were probably arguing.

"Amber said something about Shirley's service being held on Saturday morning to keep people away." I kept an eye on the outside while I spoke. "I got the feeling she meant people from Rambling Rose. Any reason why she'd feel that way?"

"Truthfully, it was the only time the service could be held when the most people could come. But we also put up the pretense that Shirley and I had nothing to do with Marvin and his business outside of being friends and acquaintances. We never conducted our mutual business here or at the club."

I nodded, remembering that Marvin had

told the police he barely knew Clarice and that Shirley spent more time these days at Rambling Rose.

I turned away from the window. I was restless — the hair on my neck tingling with anxiety. It was taking far too long for Sally to run to the SUV and come back. Then I realized I hadn't made myself clear about her returning. She was probably waiting with Steele for me to come out with Clarice. Whatever it was Clarice was waiting for, we had to do it now and get the hell out of here. Whoever tied her up would be returning. Otherwise, they'd have killed her outright.

Clarice started to rise from her chair, but I spun around and stopped her. "Oh no, you don't. You're not going anywhere unless it's out the door with me."

Clarice was no dummy. I might have been unarmed, but I was younger than her by about ten years and outweighed her by close to a hundred pounds. Not to mention I was pumped up with nervous tension. There was no way she was overpowering me, and she knew it. It would be like pitting Paris Hilton against the Hulk.

She sat back down with a dull thud. "I have to use the bathroom, Odelia. I've been . . . incapacitated for a while."

I wished Sally was here. One of us could watch the place while the other took Clarice to the potty.

"In a minute," I told Clarice and returned to my questions, hoping Sally would return in the meantime.

"If Shirley, Marvin, and Alfred are dead, that only leaves you and Aaron who knew about the side business. Or does it?" I narrowed my eyes at her. "Who else knew about it? Did Amber?"

"I didn't think so."

Finally, some progress. "You didn't think so? Meaning, you're pretty sure now she did?"

"She knows now."

"Did you or Shirley tell her?"

Clarice shook her head and offered a blunt no.

"That envelope slipped under the door that she supposedly found — maybe she wrote that herself. Maybe she found out about your little business and saw a potential cash cow."

I stopped verbalizing my thoughts. Something wasn't computing. I backed away from Clarice and put my brain through its paces. Even if Amber knew about the side business, she might not have known about Shirley and the bank robbery.

"Who slapped you around and tied you up, Clarice? I've met Amber. You might be older, but she didn't look like she could do all that on her own. And the police think Shirley's killer was either a man or a strong woman."

The name of the probable killer was on the tip of my tongue, no matter how much Clarice claimed it wasn't possible. "Was it Aaron?"

Aaron Gunn could have been at Hannah's wedding helping Shirley. He could have been the one I heard call to her. If he'd met her in the cloakroom, Shirley wouldn't have suspected anything, just that he needed to discuss something with her. And Aaron might have learned about the bank robbery from his brother.

I thought about Marvin Gunn. Had there been time during intermission for Aaron to slip off the stage as Lillian Cherry and kill his brother and search his office?

"No," Clarice protested again. "Aaron had nothing to do with Shirley's death or his brother's. I'm sure of it."

I tried a different route. "Tell me, Clarice, why did they leave you alive when they'd killed the others? Seems kind of odd, doesn't it?" Clarice's name was starting to climb its way to the top of my suspects list, at least as an accomplice.

"Odd or not, Odelia, go find your surly friend and get out of here. I'll be right behind you."

"Leave with me now, Clarice. What's stopping you?"

"I can't, Odelia, not until I get something. Don't worry, I'll leave right after that."

"Get what, Clarice — the stolen money?"

"No!" Her protest seemed genuine, but it was getting so I barely trusted myself any longer, let alone her.

She took a deep breath and stood. "The list, Odelia. The master list of everyone we helped. I have to get to it before they do." Clarice swept the room with an arm. "That's what this is about. They were looking for the money but found none. But now they want that list. It's perfect blackmail fodder. People would pay big money to find some of those people, and some of them would pay to remain hidden. It also contains updated information about where some of them are now."

"That's why they spared your life, isn't it? They know you have it or know where it is? They probably thought Marvin knew, too."

Clarice spotted her missing shoe over by the desk and pointed to it. I nodded my okay. While I watched, she crossed the floor in an uneven gait and slipped it on. After that, she stood fidgeting on her feet. I took pity on her. "Okay," I told her, "let's hit the bathroom — both of us."

"I beg your pardon?"

"If you need to pee, you're going to have to do it in front of me. I'm not letting you out of my sight for an instant."

Resigned, she started for the door, but I stopped her and pointed at the roll of toilet tissue she'd been using on her nose. "You might want to grab that on your way out."

The bathroom was across the hall. Roomy and gleaming with white and rose tile, they'd left most of it as it had been when the building had been a private residence, except for removing the tub and installing a large modern shower enclosure. Guest towels and fancy soaps were in abundance, matching the cutesiness of the front office. There was one small window, but it was set high with opaque glass. It would be difficult for Clarice to maneuver if she got it in her head to crawl through it. We entered the bathroom, me after her.

"Do you mind?" Clarice asked, plunking the toilet tissue on the counter.

"Go right ahead." I gestured toward the toilet like a model on a game show showing off a prize.

Clarice crossed her arms and stared at me. I caved slightly. After all, I wouldn't want someone watching me in such a delicate moment. I moved just outside, closing the door but not all the way. "This is as much privacy as you're getting," I told her. "Live with it."

In short order, I heard her urinating and wondered how many women I would have to hear pee before the night was over.

A flush and running water told me Clarice was washing up. The water continued running. And running. And running. Didn't she believe in water conservation? I opened the door to find her on her hands and knees halfway under the sink cabinet.

"What in the hell are you doing?"

Clarice poked her head out and looked up at me. "Getting a manicure, what do you think?" Her head disappeared. "I hid the list under here," her muffled voice called out, "but it appears caught on something."

I wanted to scream with frustration. "Why didn't you just tell me that before? We could have gotten it and been out of here."

She poked her head out again and sat back on her haunches. "Because I didn't want you to know this much, Odelia. That's why I fired you and blew off that fake meeting. I wanted you to get so mad you'd go away for good." She took a deep breath. "Once I learned how dangerous this could get, I was sorry I got you involved. But you're so pigheaded, you wouldn't take the hint. Maybe I should have hired someone to shoot at you." She started to duck her head back under, then hesitated to swipe a strand of hair behind an ear. I thought she was done with her rant, but she wasn't. Instead, she tacked on one more assault. "But even that didn't deter you, did it? Whoever shot at you was wasting their time."

With her head under the sink and her linen-clad ass in the air, I was sorely tempted to kick her. Instead, I patted myself on the back for showing remarkable restraint.

"There, I've got it." Clarice's head popped back out. In her hand was a small padded manila envelope with a crunched corner. Clarice opened the flap and pulled out a small flash drive. Without ceremony, she slipped a hand into the neckline of her pant-suit jacket and tucked it into her bra.

"My guess is," I said to her, "that Marvin also has a copy of that, just to be safe, and that's what his killer was looking for."

"If they found it, they won't be back. If they didn't, they will be."

"They?" It was the first time Clarice had

referenced more than one person. "Who's *they,* Clarice?"

Ignoring my question, Clarice stuck her hand back inside the cabinet and used it as leverage as she slowly got to her feet, emitting a very unladylike grunt and groan as her legs unfolded. "My joints aren't what they used to be."

"Tell me about it." I glanced back out into the hallway. "Now can we get out of here?"

"You can go, Odelia, but I'm not going with you."

When I turned back around, I saw the gun in her hand, the hand she'd stuck back into the cabinet. What was with all the guns?

"Aw, geez, come on, Clarice. You're not going to shoot me, and you know it."

"Not if you leave right now, I won't."

"We can leave right now together. I don't even care about that list." It wasn't the truth, but it was a lie I could live with.

"It's not that simple, Odelia. First, people have murdered my friends, and I'm probably next. Second, I have these people to protect." She patted her chest with her free hand. "And third, I'm pretty sure some of what I've done is a crime."

"Ya think?"

She made a face at me. "So you tell the police whatever you want, but I'm disap-

340

pearing. I did it once before. I'll do it again. After all," she said, smiling as wide as her split lip would allow, "I'm a professional."

She pointed the gun at my gut. I really didn't think Clarice would kill me, but I wasn't so sure she wouldn't shoot a limb just to keep me occupied while she fled. I backed up, Clarice following, until we were in the hallway.

"Keep going," Clarice told me, "back into the room. I need to grab my purse."

I turned and marched back into the room where Clarice had been held hostage. Once we were there, we heard the back door open.

"Must be Sally," I said to Clarice. "Finally. Maybe she can talk some sense into you."

Clarice rolled her eyes. She kept the gun on me while she moved toward the desk where her handbag had been dumped during the ransacking, its contents scattered across the desk. With her free hand, she started gathering her things.

"Hey, Sal," I called. "We're in here."

TWENTY-SIX

No one had told the drag queen that I didn't like guns. Nor did I think it the right time to tell him myself.

Sally stood in front of him, a gun to her back as they came through the door from the hallway. I stood in front of Clarice, a gun at my back. We were the cream filling in a deadly sandwich cookie. Make that expendable filling. After all, to a killer, what were a couple more bodies? It would be like shooting fish in a barrel. And now that Clarice had uncovered the list, there would be no reason to keep her alive. The flash drive snuggled against Clarice's boobies had changed it from a standoff to a massacre.

Sally looked straight ahead, not at me, not at Clarice. She looked shell-shocked but, knowing her, it was a façade. Inside, she was probably calculating every detail.

"Move over there," the drag queen ordered, his voice normal and not the breathy, high pitch he'd used before. He poked Sally in the back. "Next to her."

Obeying, Sally moved forward until she stood next to me.

I took note of the pink tee shirt the gunman was wearing. Across the front was the slogan *Boy-Girls Wanna Have Fun.* "What happened to your halter top?" I asked. "Too much blood on it?"

"Shut up," he snapped.

"That's going be a nightmare to get out," I continued. "It's hard to launder sequins properly. Can't toss it either — someone might find it."

"I said shut up!"

We heard soft footsteps in the hallway, followed by the appearance of Amber Straight. She was dressed in jeans and a tight black tee shirt. Her curly hair had been pulled back away from her face and secured with a dark do-rag. She looked like an elfin ninja. Her presence didn't surprise me, though Betty Rumble's did. Since they worked together at Rambling Rose, I was expecting Amber and Aaron to be in cahoots. Maybe Aaron was the softie Clarice claimed.

"Mrs. Cooper?" Amber seemed as surprised to see me as I was Betty.

"Her name isn't Cooper," Betty Rumble told his sister without taking his eyes off of us. "It's Odelia something-or-other. I don't know who the other one is, but they were at the club tonight together."

Without checking the time, I knew Steele should be on the phone by now calling the police, especially if from his perch down the street he had seen Betty and Amber grab Sally. I just prayed everyone got here in time and Betty wasn't trigger-happy.

"Get out of my way," Clarice demanded, speaking to Betty and Amber, "or I'll shoot these two." She'd stopped fussing with her purse and moved up closer behind me.

Um, it seemed Clarice hadn't reached the same conclusion I had about our lack of worth to anyone. I could tell by the smirk on Betty's face that he had. So had Sally. She'd given up her stoicism and replaced it with fright.

"Go ahead," Betty told Clarice with a giggle. "Shoot them — less bullets for me to waste."

I needed to stall for time. "Nothing spells *discretion* like the sound of gunfire." When everyone, including Sally, looked at me like I was crazy, I added, "With all the cops just a couple of blocks away at Billie's, they should find their way here in record time."

"Hardly," answered Amber with a sneer. "They're too tied up playing cop to pay attention to us."

"Don't be too sure of that," I told her. "Because of Gunn's murder, they'll be especially on guard for anything suspicious. I'm sure they even have officers walking the streets right now looking for anything out of the ordinary. And gunshots are out of the norm for this neighborhood." I didn't know if the bull I was slinging was true or not, but on TV the cops always canvass the neighborhood around a crime scene. I hoped Amber and Betty watched the same shows I did.

Everyone went mute while considering my words. Betty broke the silence. "Hand over the list, Clarice, and we'll let you all live."

"Are you nuts?" Amber asked him. Obviously, she wasn't as worried about cops swarming the place. "Just kill them, grab the info, and let's get out of here."

He shook his head. "Fatso here might have a point. When I ducked out of the club, the cops were thick up and down the whole street."

"Then let me do it." Amber pulled a knife.

I backed up and felt Clarice's gun dig into my back. "So you're the one with the killer knife skills," I said to Amber, wondering if the cops had got it wrong about Shirley's murder. Amber was neither strong or a man.

Crazy as a hoot owl, yes.

"Actually," interjected Betty with some pride, "we're both pretty handy with a blade. Something our daddy taught us a long time ago."

"That's right," I said. "You're brother and sister. I heard that tidbit from my friend on the police force."

Betty giggled again. "Name's Brad Straight. Can you imagine a gay drag queen with the name of Straight?"

Amber took a step forward with her knife. Sally and I backed up together until I again felt Clarice's gun in my back. I wasn't sure which I preferred — the quick death of a gunshot (providing Clarice could hit a vital organ) or the slow, painful death of a knife. There was something unsettling going on behind Amber's blue eyes, something that told me, given her druthers, she would rather take her time with a blade.

"So, did you share the honors?" I asked them. "Did one of you do Shirley and the other Marvin?"

"You're a smart cookie," said Betty.

I shrugged. "Not really. The cops are pretty sure a very strong woman or a man killed Shirley. Handy with a knife or not, Amber is neither of those."

"And you'd be right," confirmed Betty.

"We gave Shirley plenty of opportunities to hand over the money. I told her what had happened to Nunez — how we sold his whereabouts to those thugs from Bakersfield. Told her it was just the beginning."

"But how did you know about Alfred?" The question came from Clarice. It was one of the questions on my own lips.

Betty laughed. "There's that old saying: loose lips sink ships. In this case, it was loose pillow talk."

I looked at Amber. Had she had an affair with Marvin or Aaron? She stared at us in silence, eyes impatient with bloodlust. In her other clothes she'd seemed perky, a former cheerleader who loved weddings, but now she was a cold and calculating killer. "Marvin told you?" I asked her.

Betty laughed again. "Of course you'd think it was the cute blond girl who did the undercover work."

I had gone for the obvious and been wrong. I latched my eyes onto Betty, looking beyond the makeup and false eyelashes. "It was you he told?"

"Not Marvin. Aaron." The comment came from behind me, from Clarice. "Marvin was straight. Shirley told me not too long ago that she suspected Aaron had a new boyfriend but was being close-mouthed about it."

"That would be *moi.*" Betty seemed pleased with himself. "Marvin didn't like him dating employees at the club. He'd done it before and it hadn't gone well."

"So Aaron told you about Alfred and the others?"

"Yep, it was one night at a romantic little cabin in Big Bear. We were celebrating two months together. Amazing what kinds of secrets come out after a bottle of wine and lovemaking. He even told me about big bad Shirley and the bank robbery. Now Aaron's over at Billie's blubbering over a brother who treated him like an indentured servant. What a waste."

It was becoming clear to me. "Tonight," I said to Betty, "you disappeared before intermission. I know because your tables were clamoring for drinks but you'd gone AWOL. You went to the back door and let Amber in. While everyone was carrying on over bingo games, you were probably threatening Marvin and destroying his office looking for the list and the money. When you didn't find it, you killed him."

"Very nice deduction," Betty told me, "and mostly true."

"Shirley didn't take that money," Clarice

shot off.

"I'm inclined to believe you . . . now." Betty pointed dramatically at Clarice. "The bank money was a surprise, doll, let me tell you. I was more interested in the *witless* protection program you were running."

Amber added, "We both were. That's why we came here."

Sally found her voice. "You two wanted to go into hiding, so you started killing people? Hardly seems like a way to avoid attention."

"Jesus, no." Betty Rumble clearly thought we were imbeciles. "We're trying to locate someone we believe is in hiding. It has taken Sis and I some time, but we finally traced him here."

Hearing Betty call Amber sis made me want to see and touch Clark. I wanted to hear him call me sis again and worried I might never get the chance.

"We took these stupid jobs," Betty continued, "just to find out what we could, but Clarice keeps those records shut tighter than her hoochie. So I seduced Aaron and got him to talk. When he said he wasn't privy to the list, we had no choice but to start with the threats and follow through."

In a kooky way, it was starting to come together. "You used the idea of the bank money to try and cover up the fact that it's really the list you wanted?"

"Close but no cigar, creampuff. If we'd managed to squeeze the bank money out of Shirley, it would have been a bonus. But what we're really after is the information about all those new identities."

Clarice edged out from behind me. She still held the gun up, but it was pointed at Betty now instead of me. "Who are you looking for? If he is one of ours and I tell you, will you leave us and the others be?"

Sally and I stole glances at each other. I could tell she believed as well as I did that no matter what information was shared, our lives would end as soon as Betty and Amber received it. I kept my ears cocked, praying for the sound of cops summoned by Steele. Twenty-five minutes had come and gone. Where in the hell was the help he'd threatened to call?

"We're looking for our father." Amber's eyes sparkled with madness. "When our mother got sick, he took everything we had and vanished, leaving us alone and broke, with medical debts out our ass and more on the way. When she died, we promised each other we'd hunt him down and make him pay."

"Too bad Shirley and Marvin weren't as cooperative as you're willing to be." Betty shook his head with sadness. "I don't feel bad about Marvin; he was an ass. But Shirley was a nice lady. I confronted her Saturday at that wedding. Asked her where he was. Demanded to know. She refused to tell me — kept trying to snow me, telling me Dad was dead."

Clarice's eyes went wide and darted from Betty to Amber. "Was your father Homer Randolph?"

"Yes," Amber confirmed, gripping the knife until her knuckles went white. "He and Mom never married. We were given her family name — Straight." She raised the knife. "Where is he?"

"This was all so pointless," Clarice wailed. "Shirley wasn't snowing you. Homer really is dead. He had a heart attack about two or two and a half years ago. Died almost instantly."

"You're lying," Amber spit out.

"I'm not," Clarice insisted. "Homer went into hiding, what, five years ago? Right?"

Betty and Amber nodded in unison.

"He told Marvin his ex-wife was squeezing him for support. He paid cash for our services."

"That was our money you took!" shouted Amber.

"Listen," Clarice tried to explain. "We

don't know anything about where the money comes from. We listen to people, make a judgment call, and either accept them or don't."

"A judgment call," I scoffed. "You mean like Scott Johnson?"

Clarice shot me one of her death-ray looks, but I was immune to them. I shot one of my own back, canceling hers out.

"You're sure our father, Homer, didn't die in pain?" asked Amber.

"Yes," Clarice answered. "The doctor said it was quick. Apparently he had a bad heart and didn't know it."

Amber shook the knife in our direction. "Too bad. I was looking forward to gutting him."

It was pretty clear to all of us whose mind had jumped the track in a big way.

"If you'll let me," Clarice said, "I can prove to you Homer is dead. I have his records. He was the only one of our people who'd ever died, so we kept a copy of his death certificate just in case."

"Drop the gun!" a voice yelled from just outside the doorway.

It was Steele.

I didn't know whether to be happy or petrified.

TWENTY-SEVEN

"I said drop the gun or I'll shoot." Steele's voice was steady and authoritative. It was his legal voice — the one he used when calling opposing counsel out on bullshit tactics. He stepped into view in the doorway and stood a few feet away from Amber and Betty. He glanced at Sally and me. "You two okay?"

I nodded for both of us.

Clutched in Steele's right hand and aimed at Betty was Sally's gun. In his left hand was my phone.

Steele with a handgun. Geez. And so much for not letting him get involved. Double geez.

Quickly, I glanced at Sally. She looked as surprised and terrified as I felt. It was a standoff, and we were the only ones unarmed. Not good odds.

"Who you gonna shoot, cowboy?" asked Betty of Steele. "You shoot me, I'll fire. You shoot my sister, I'll fire. Either way, one of your gal pals is gonna wind up in the morgue."

"We have no complaint with you," Steele said, now switching to his negotiating voice.

Actually, I did have a complaint with Betty and Amber, but I wisely understood now was not the time to raise my hand and voice it.

"Let Odelia and Sally go," Steele continued. "This is between the three of you. It doesn't involve them." He held up the phone. "Odelia has a family emergency. I beg you, please let her go."

My eyes shot open. I stared at the phone. Was Steele bluffing?

Betty's eyes widened, too, but for a different reason. "Are you insane? Who gives a shit about *her* problems?"

"What's going on, Steele?" I asked in a shaky voice.

He ignored me and kept his baby blues trained on Betty and Amber. "There's enough time for the two of you to take off before the police arrive. No one here will stop you, I promise. But if you stay, you'll be leaving either in cuffs or a body bag."

A body bag? I couldn't believe those words were coming out of Steele's mouth. And I thought *I* watched too much TV.

"The list," Amber said to her brother.

Betty two-stepped a couple steps to his right so he could watch us and Steele better. Amber stayed where she was, close to me and Clarice, with her deadly blade at the ready.

Betty glanced at Steele. "Tell Clarice to give us the list."

"No," cried Clarice. "If they get the list, a lot of people could get killed."

Her gun dug deeper into my back, but my mind was on what Steele had said about an emergency. Was it Greg? Clark? If Steele was bluffing, I was going to tie him up and drag him down Pacific Coast Highway behind my car, providing we got out of this alive.

"What about the gun in my back, Clarice?" I asked. "A lot of people *here* could get killed if you don't cooperate, including yourself."

"Give us the list and we'll go," Betty said to Clarice. Amber held out her hand, palm up, toward Clarice.

"It's gone," Clarice explained.

"I don't believe you," answered Amber, who moved forward, her knife just inches from my gut. It was a toss-up which would enter my soft middle first, the blade or a bullet.

"Time is ticking, folks," Steele reminded everyone. He shot a look at Clarice. "Quit playing games and give them what they want so we can all go about our business. You folks need to get out of here, and we need to get Odelia to the hospital."

"The hospital!" I yelled. "Is it Greg?" Next to me, Sally reached out and put an arm around my waist.

Steele shook his head. "It's not Greg. Dev Frye called you." Steele held up my cell phone to make his point. "Zee Washington's been shot. She's in surgery at Hoag."

My breath came in big gulps as I tried to understand what Steele had just told me. My legs felt like rubber. I staggered and would have fallen if not for Sally's support.

With tears streaming down my face, I pleaded with Betty Rumble and Amber. "Please let me go. I have to get to the hospital."

"Give us the list and we'll take off," Betty repeated.

I shook off Sally and turned on Clarice, not caring about the gun in her hand. "Give them the damn list!"

Surprised by my outburst, Clarice took a step backward. She seemed confused. Her eyes darted from me to Amber and Betty.

"Give it to them!" My voice bounced off

the walls.

Unsure of what to do, Clarice let the gun in her hand waver. Taking advantage of her moment of weakness, I slammed my left arm against her right hand, sending it wide and high. The gun went off, the bullet destroying the window before she dropped it. Sally took a dive for the dropped gun.

"Not so fast," shouted Betty, his gun aimed at Sally's head. She stayed crouched by the gun but put her hands up in the air. Steele didn't move a muscle, keeping his gun tight on Betty.

I had Clarice pinned backwards on the desk. With one hand, I tore open the front of her jacket and reached into her bra, digging out the flash drive. I held it up for everyone to see. "This for our freedom."

"Take it," Steele encouraged Betty and Amber. "And get the hell out of here while you still have time."

Betty exchanged looks with his sister, then nodded to her. Amber stepped forward, one hand out, the other still grasping her knife. I handed her the flash drive and pulled my hand back, lest she get the urge to slice me just for good measure.

Steele stepped farther into the room, continuing to keep the gun trained on Betty and the cell in his hand. "Now slowly back out of the room and leave. We'll stay here until you're gone."

Betty jerked his head at Amber, and the diminutive killer backed up until she was next to him. Slowly, they edged toward the door, while Steele shifted farther away from it to give them room to make their getaway. He stayed away from us, keeping Betty's gun occupied. The men kept their guns aimed at each other while the delicate dance played out.

I shifted from foot to foot, worried about Zee, going mad at the excruciatingly slow progress of the Straights.

"Could you move a little faster, please?" I urged. "I have to get out of here."

"All in good time, Grey," Steele told me, his voice calm.

Amber was the first out the door. Once in the hallway, we heard her pick up her pace. Behind her was Betty. As soon as he edged out into the hallway, Steele said to us in a rushed whisper, "Get down behind the desk and stay there. All of you."

Without question, I grabbed Clarice by her jacket, hauled her ass down to the floor, and shoved her behind the large desk. Sally grabbed Clarice's gun and joined us. Clarice was weeping but compliant.

Steele moved quickly to the door. He shut

and locked it, then moved off to the side, away from it, and kept his gun on it. It was clear anyone coming through the doorway was going to get a bullet for their trouble. It was barely shut when we heard shouts and someone throwing themselves at the office door. Two shots hit the door in succession, splintering the thin wood but ineffective in opening it or hurting anyone. Curled up behind the desk like defensive armadillos, the blast of each bullet caused both me and Clarice to flinch.

Sally and Steele kept their guns trained on the door. Through the shattered window, we could hear many voices, but there were no more gunshots.

Looking up at Steele, I asked, "The police were here the whole time?"

He shook his head. "I'm guessing just the last few minutes."

I started to get up, but Steele waved me back down. We stayed that way until there was a solid knock on the door.

"Open up, it's Dev."

I let out a cry of joy and relief, followed by a cry of anguish for Zee.

TWENTY-EIGHT

As soon as Steele unlocked the door and Dev entered, I threw myself at the big detective. "What's happened to Zee?"

Behind him were other cops, guns drawn. When they entered the room, Dev pointed to Clarice. "That's Clarice Thomas Hollowell. Cuff her with the others."

A uniformed cop aimed his gun at Sally. She'd forgotten she still had hold of Clarice's gun. Slowly, she raised her hands above her head until an officer relieved her of the weapon. "That's Clarice's gun, not mine," she told him.

Her hands still in the air, Sally staggered to a nearby chair and dropped heavily into it, suddenly turning so pale I worried for her.

"Are you okay, Sally?" I asked.

"Just a little bingo, huh?" She lowered her head between her legs and took deep breaths.

"You were great, Sally, really." It was Steele. He still had the gun in his hand, but it was lowered.

One of the uniformed cops held out a hand for Steele's gun. Steele finally remembered he was holding it. He still had my cell phone in his other hand. "This is her gun," he told the cop, indicating Sally. "It hasn't been fired." He handed it off to the police, who assured Sally it would be returned to her after the investigation.

After giving me my cell phone, Steele walked over to Sally and placed a hand on her back, gently rubbing it in a comforting motion. "It's just the adrenaline rush leaving. You'll be fine in a minute."

I stared at my boss in wonder. He'd saved our lives. If he got cocky and insufferable about it later, I'd let him. He deserved it.

I looked down at my cell. It was on, connected to Dev's phone. "You were on the phone the whole time?" I looked up at Dev.

"Yeah. I tried calling you several times about Zee. I tried Greg and Clark, too, but got no answer there either. Finally, Steele answered your phone and told me what was going on." He looked over at Steele. "I told him to stay put until we got here, but, like you, he doesn't listen. At least he had the good sense to keep the phone on speaker while he played hero."

"And Zee?" It took everything I had not to dissolve into a pile of sobbing mush, and even more restraint not to grab Dev and shake an explanation out of him.

"Too early to tell. She's still in surgery. She was coming out of a restaurant with Seth when someone fired from a car. Seth's fine."

"Another drive-by?" I gasped, both my hands shooting to my face to cover my mouth.

Dev grasped my shoulders. "We were wrong, Odelia. That bullet the other day was never meant for you. It was meant for Zee."

A uniformed officer came up and asked Dev a question. I wanted to snap at him and tell him to go the hell away. Instead, I waited, not believing what I was hearing. Who would want to hurt Zee? Some disgruntled Bible study buddy?

After giving instructions to the officer, Dev returned to his explanation. "Apparently, Seth handled a very messy divorce recently. His client was the wife. The husband blamed Seth and went after Zee. His plan was to take Seth's wife away from him, as he imagined Seth had taken his."

My eyes exploded out of my head in

surprise. "Are you kidding?"

"Not at all. The husband paid for the hit. We have both him and the driver in custody. Both have confessed. We don't have the shooter yet, but it's just a matter of time."

The thought of a professional hit man going after my best and dearest friend nearly stopped my heart. It was funny — although I wouldn't want it, I could live with one going after me, but not Zee. I took deep breaths to slow down my pounding heart.

"I have to get to Zee, Dev. Right now."

He gently touched my face. "I know." He looked over to where Steele was comforting Sally. She looked more her old self now. At least her color was back. "Guys," he called over to them, "do you mind if I send Odelia to the hospital while you two tell me what happened here?"

They shook their heads, but another plain-clothes officer, a tall, slim woman with short hair, wasn't so sure. "We need to get her statement, Detective."

"And we will, Detective," Dev assured his colleague. "I'll vouch for her in the meantime. But right now she needs to get to Hoag."

The other detective looked tough but understanding. "How about I drive you to the hospital, ma'am? You can give me your statement there."

I looked up at Dev.

"Sounds good to me, Odelia. You'll be in good hands."

I nodded and walked over to Sally and Steele. I gave them a quick summary of Zee's situation, followed by a big hug. "Thanks for everything."

"Don't worry, Grey," Steele said to me. "You look in on Zee — I've got your back."

I snuffled back tears. "I know you do."

TWENTY-NINE

I walked into the private room at Hoag Hospital with a lighter heart than I'd had in a couple of days. Vases of flowers covered almost every flat surface. Dev was standing by the window. I looked down at Greg. He looked up and nodded encouragement as he rolled through the door. Without looking at Zee, I found a small spot and set the flowers in my hand with the others on the counter.

"Those are beautiful, Odelia." Zee's voice, though weak, was music to my ears.

Next to her bed, Seth sat clutching her hand. He looked gray and bedraggled. He gave Greg and me a small, reassuring smile. "The doctor was just in. He told us she'll be fine soon. They got the bullet, and it doesn't appear that it did any permanent damage."

I nearly fainted with relief.

I took a step toward Zee's bed, still wor-

365

ried in spite of the doctor's report. After kissing his wife's hand, Seth got up from his seat and offered it to me.

"No," I protested. "I'm fine right here."

"Take it, Odelia," Zee insisted.

I sat down next to Zee's bed and took her hand, which was still warm from her husband's. "I'm so sorry, Zee. You know if I could trade places with you, I would."

"I know that, sweetie, but it's not your fault."

"I'd still trade places."

"I owe you an apology, Odelia," Seth said softly. "A big one."

Zee coughed slightly. "No, Seth, *we* owe Odelia a big apology." She squeezed my hand, and I could feel how weak she was. My heart was heavy watching her struggle to speak.

"Shh," I said to her. "Whatever it is, it can wait."

Seth shook his head. "No, Odelia, it can't. We have to say it now." From her bed, Zee nodded in agreement.

Seth sat on the edge of his wife's bed and took her other hand. "The shooting, Odelia, wasn't your fault. Not now, not the first time."

"I know that, Seth."

"We shouldn't have been so quick to

blame you."

"Why not? I did. I was sure those bullets were meant for me." I paused. "And it doesn't matter now because Zee's going to be fine." I looked at Zee and gave her a big, dopey smile. "And it's a good thing Dev's people found the guy who did this," I told her, "or I'd be tracking his sorry ass down myself."

"Actually, we didn't find him," Dev said. His cell phone vibrated. He pulled it from his pocket and glanced at it before continuing. "The shooter was brought in by a private citizen — someone who took great pains to locate him and take him down. He actually arrived trussed like a rolled roast and quite worse for wear. His story matched that of the driver's."

"Who did that?" I turned toward the Washingtons.

"This is the first time we've heard that part," Seth said with interest.

"Who? Dammit. Who?" I demanded, sounding like an owl with Tourette's.

Dev waved his cell at us. "Sorry, folks, but I have to go. So glad you're doing fine, Zee. I've been shot myself. Take it easy, do everything the doctor tells you, and you'll be up and around in no time."

When Dev took his leave, I followed. On

the way out, Greg grabbed my hand. "Some things don't need a full-blown disclosure, sweetheart."

I couldn't have disagreed more.

"What was that all about?" I asked Dev when I caught up to him by the elevator.

"I got a call. I have to leave."

"Not that and you know it." The elevator came, but I pulled Dev away from it. "Who brought the shooter in? Was it Willie?"

"Not to my knowledge."

"Then who?"

"Look closer to home, Odelia." Dev's eyes traveled down the hall to where Greg was seated, watching us.

Greg had said he would take care of the shooter, and I knew he had meant it. I just didn't think he'd be able to find him. If I had, I would have been more scared at that than standing between two guns.

Another elevator came. This one Dev got on. I was too stunned to stop him.

I walked the length of the hallway to Greg. "You?" I asked my husband, shaking my head. "You brought in the shooter?"

"I was simply the wheel man, sweetheart."

"Wheel man?" I put my hands on my hips and stood facing Greg, my face set in stone. "What in the hell does that mean?"

"It means I drove the car — or in this

case, my van. I'm just sorry we didn't find the bastard before he shot Zee."

I walked away from Greg to think. Turning around, I leaned against the wall and stared at him. Around us, nurses, doctors, and various hospital staff bustled about, doing their jobs.

"It was you and Clark, wasn't it?"

Greg didn't say anything but just continued to look at me, his face set in determination, his mouth hard, his shoulders straight.

"You two hunted that creep down, hogtied him, and delivered him to Dev, didn't you?"

He simply nodded.

I wanted to both kiss and slap him — at the same time.

Returning to Greg's side, I lifted his right hand and studied it. It was scraped and bruised, not unlike my right cheek. I'd seen the scratches the day before but dismissed them. Greg was always scraping his hands and arms at work.

"You beat the bastard raw, just as you said you would."

"Nah, Clark would only let me punch him a few times."

"This is something I'd expect from Willie and his thugs, not from you and Clark."

"Speaking of Willie . . ."

"I knew it!" I dropped Greg's hand and walked away a few steps, then returned. "I knew his fingerprints were all over this."

"Actually, they're not. At least not like you'd think."

"Huh?"

Greg took my hand. "Clark wanted to tell you this himself, but he got called back to Phoenix before he could. He told me he'd call you as soon as he got back home, but I think you should know now. And this is something Dev doesn't know and probably shouldn't."

Hearing that last phrase told me I was in for a lulu piece of information. I stood in the hallway of the hospital half wishing someone was waiting to throw me into a wheelchair and take me to the psych ward.

"What is it?" I asked Greg, bracing myself.

"That job in Phoenix? The one Clark's taking?"

I narrowed my eyes at my hubby. "Yeah?"

Greg indicated for me to bend down. I did. When my ear was near his mouth, he whispered, "The job is with Willie's company. Clark works for Willie now."

Without saying a word, I strode down the long hallway. When I reached the end, I turned on my heel and strode back, ignoring the curious looks I got along the way.

When I reached Greg, I bent down again.

"And what about you?" I asked. "Are you going to tell me next that *you* work for Willie, too?"

"No, I don't." Greg got an excited gleam in his eye. "Why? Do you think he'd ask?"

THIRTY

Steele and I seldom ate lunch together, so when he'd asked if I'd join him at Morton's, I knew something was up. Not that I minded. Morton's, a wonderful upscale restaurant, was certainly a lot nicer than my usual brown-bag lunch.

Even though we work literally yards from each other, Steele had said the day before, when he'd suggested the lunch meeting, that he'd meet me at the restaurant at one o'clock. In fact, I hadn't seen him all morning. I arrived on time and was shown our table. Steele hadn't arrived yet.

The deal with Lori Ogle's firm had closed on schedule the week after the Rambling Rose situation. We had worked on it twelve to fifteen hours a day, which helped me keep my mind off of what had happened.

There was a lot of fallout from the service Clarice and her pals had been running, not to mention emotional scars left on those involved on the fringes.

Brad and Amber Straight were facing two murder charges, along with kidnapping and extortion. Clarice and Aaron Gunn were facing their own legal woes. Billie's Holiday and Rambling Rose were both shut down. Sadly, numerous brides and drag queens were left in the lurch.

With Clarice's flash drive in their hands, the police were able to find almost all of the people Clarice and her friends had helped to disappear. A few were wanted on various charges in their home states, but some were in hiding for protection. I'm not sure what will happen with those people and hope they can continue to remain safely out of harm's way.

Through the police BOLO, Scott Johnson was spotted and arrested while picking up supplies at a convenience store. Roslyn Stevens was found imprisoned in a storage unit not far away, drugged almost into unconsciousness and severely dehydrated. Dev told us that when she was informed her stalker in Chicago was dead, she immediately wanted to return home to her family and resume her former life. Although I never got to meet Roslyn, I was thrilled for her happy outcome. I even heard a rumor she might be offered a book deal about her experience.

Joan's family buried Alfred Nunez for the second and final time in a private graveside service. Steele and I wanted to go, but Joan said her mother requested no one but she and Joan and Joan's stepfather attend. Joan told me that as soon as the priest put Alfred to rest, he remarried her mother and stepfather. Steele is still working with the insurance company to end the fraud investigation, though he told us that even if they drop the fraud charges, they will insist on getting their money back with interest. He has it in his head to sue Clarice and the estates of Marvin Gunn and Shirley Pearson for the insurance money with interest, along with other damages. I say, go for it.

"Sorry I'm late, Grey."

I put aside my thoughts and greeted my boss, who looked ultra snazzy in a new suit.

"I had an appointment this morning that took longer than expected."

He took the seat across from me. When a waiter approached, he motioned toward my iced tea, indicating he wanted the same, but at the last minute asked to see the wine list instead.

"Wine during lunch hour?" I raised an eyebrow. "Then again, you're a partner; why not?"

Steele scanned the wine list. "You know what you're having for lunch?"

"I was thinking the grilled shrimp and sea scallops."

He placed an order for a bottle of wine I'd never heard of and handed the wine list back to the waiter.

I leaned forward. "A whole bottle? You think that's wise?"

"It's for both of us, Grey." He seemed amused.

"Um, I don't know about you, but I have a pile of work waiting for me back at the office." After a slight pause, I added, "And my boss won't like it if I slur over the phone to clients."

The comment earned me a chuckle. "Don't worry about any of that today, Grey. Today, you and I will be returning to the office when we're good and ready — maybe not at all."

Huh?

I bent down and looked under the table.

"What are you doing?"

I brought my head back up. "Looking for alien pods. I don't know who you are or what you've done with Mike Steele, but it's okay by me."

That brought a bigger laugh.

"Seriously, Steele, what's going on? You're

freaking me out."

The wine came. The waiter and Steele went through the uncorking and tasting ritual while I squirmed in my seat. After pouring us each a glass, Steele raised his and asked me to join him in a toast.

I lifted my glass. "What are we toasting? Your disbarment?"

He shook his head with a smile.

"Your last sexual conquest decided you're not the father of her child after all?"

"No, not even close." He leaned forward. "You're looking at the newest partner in Templin and Tobin's Orange County office."

Templin and Tobin was Lori Ogle's firm.

Steele tried to clink his glass against mine, but I pulled it back.

"Templin and Tobin doesn't have an Orange County office."

"They will soon enough, and I'm its managing partner, providing I take the job."

My head was swimming, and I hadn't even had a sip of wine yet. "Providing you take it? So you haven't accepted?"

The waiter showed up at our table to take our food order. Steele waved him off.

"Not yet. I was just made the offer this morning." He lowered his glass. "Funny thing is, after my name was in the paper connected to that showdown at Rambling Rose, I thought for sure they'd withdraw their courtship. Instead, it only heightened their interest. They told me they could use a partner with guts."

Steele winked at me. He actually *winked* at me. Now I knew I was dealing with a doppelganger.

He gestured with his wine glass again. "Come on now, let's celebrate possibilities."

Following orders, I held my glass out. Steele gave it a tap with his own. The two thin glasses meeting in midair gave off a pleasant musical tinkle. Steele took a sip of his wine. I knocked back half of mine.

"Is that why you've been grumpier than usual lately, because you're leaving?" I stared across the table at the man who was soon not to be my boss. "I thought it was because of Lori Ogle — because you had ants in your pants for her."

Steele let out a solid laugh. "Lori's gorgeous, but she plays for the same team as Sally and Jill."

"Really? I'm surprised Jill didn't pick up on that."

"I wouldn't have known either if I hadn't asked her out after the deal was done."

I played with the fine stem of my glass. "Maybe she only told you that to get you off her scent."

"Very funny, but she has a partner — a doctor at the UCLA Medical Center." He took another drink of his wine. "I'm sorry I've been a bigger ass than usual, Grey. Really, I am. Between the stress of the deal and Templin making overtures, I was on overload."

My brows scrunched to punctuate the serious nature of my next question. "Do you want to leave Woobie?"

"That's the struggle I'm having. I really like the firm and the work I do. I wasn't out shopping my résumé, Grey, believe me. The partners over at Templin took notice of me during this deal and tested the waters. They'd been thinking of opening an Orange County office for some time. I've weighed all the pros and cons, even the financial ones, and I still am not sure which way I'll go."

He waved the waiter back over and looked at me. "Still going with the shrimp and scallops?" I nodded, and he gave the waiter the order, tacking on the salmon entrée for himself.

The idea of Steele leaving Woobie threw a monkey wrench into my little self-centered world. On one hand, it would be nice to get him out of my hair. On the other hand, if I

378

were truthful with myself, I would miss working with him. We'd become friends over the years, and I took a small amount of sick enjoyment in our surly banter. Okay, I took a lot of enjoyment in it. I wasn't worried about my job at Woobie. I'd been there forever and would have plenty of work even without Steele monopolizing my time. Someone else would be assigned as my supervising partner, and life would go on.

"If I go, Grey, I want you to come with me."

I shook my head, uncertain if I heard him correctly. "I'm sorry, Steele, what was that?"

The waiter came by with our salads and refilled our wine glasses.

"I said, if I leave Woobie and go to work for Templin and Tobin, I want you to come with me. Jill, too. They told me I could bring over or hire any staff members I'd like. We even discussed you at length."

"You discussed *me?"*

"Yes, of course. They were quite impressed with your work on this deal. And, of course, I sang your praises."

"And did you sing my praises as a corpse magnet?"

"They know all about you, Grey." He laughed. "Your name was in the news along with mine, remember?"

Not once in all my years at Woobie had I ever considered changing jobs. Well, upon reflection, that wasn't true. I had threatened to leave once. That was the day they assigned Michael Steele as my supervising attorney. Instead, they offered a raise and a private office as a bribe to stay.

"Think of it, Grey. You could set up the office from scratch. Have a hand in the hiring. You'd be the office manager of the OC branch of T & T, in addition to doing paralegal work."

I swallowed the lettuce in my mouth. "I know you think that should tempt me, but it doesn't. It's just more work and responsibility."

"But you're not totally opposed to it, are you?"

"Where would the offices be?"

"In that new building right across from Woobie."

We'd all watched that new high-rise go up. It was glossy and modern and filled with amenities like its own cafe and Starbucks, even a dry cleaner and a florist.

"I'd have to talk to Greg about it." I pointed an index finger at Steele. "That doesn't mean I'm interested, just that it's a decision he and I would have to discuss."

"Of course."

"And it's all really moot if you decide not to take the position, isn't it?"

"Yes."

"So when will you be doing that?"

"They gave me until Labor Day to decide."

Labor Day was about seven weeks away. "That's a long time, isn't it?"

"Not really. Not for making a decision of this caliber, especially when I wasn't looking for a new job in the first place. There's a lot to consider when a partner leaves a firm. They want the new office opened just after the new year."

He started to eat again, then stopped. "By the way, please understand this is totally confidential. No sense ruffling people when I don't know yet which way I'm going to go."

I nodded my understanding.

"And, Grey, I hope you do come with me if I decide to take the position. I've gotten quite used to your adventures and would miss them terribly."

"Oh, but not the quality of my work?"

In response, Steele smiled and lifted his wine glass again. "Here's to our futures. May our professional paths continue to travel the same trail, whatever that may be."

I felt blindsided. This latest development,

on the heels of the situation with Clarice and Joan and being held yet again at gunpoint, was about to collapse both my brain and emotions. I wasn't a creature of change.

We clinked glasses again. Steele took a sip of his wine. I knocked back the rest of mine like a shot of tequila.

ABOUT THE AUTHOR

Like the character Odelia Grey, **Sue Ann Jaffarian** is a middle-aged, plus-size paralegal. In addition to the Odelia Grey mystery series, she is the author of the paranormal Ghost of Granny Apples mystery series and the Madison Rose Vampire mystery series. Sue Ann is also nationally sought after as a motivational and humorous speaker. She lives and works in Los Angeles, California.

Other titles in the Odelia Grey series include *Too Big to Miss* (2006), *The Curse of the Holy Pail* (2007), *Thugs and Kisses* (2008), *Booby Trap* (2009), and *Corpse on the Cob* (2010).

Visit Sue Ann on the Internet at
WWW.SUEANNJAFFARIAN.COM
and
WWW.SUEANNJAFFARIAN.BLOGSPOT.COM

We hope you have enjoyed this Large Print book. Other Thorndike, Wheeler, Kennebec, and Chivers Press Large Print books are available at your library or directly from the publishers.

For information about current and upcoming titles, please call or write, without obligation, to:

Publisher
Thorndike Press
10 Water St., Suite 310
Waterville, ME 04901
Tel. (800) 223-1244

or visit our Web site at:

http://gale.cengage.com/thorndike

OR

Chivers Large Print
published by AudioGO Ltd
St James House, The Square
Lower Bristol Road
Bath BA2 3SB
England
Tel. +44(0) 800 136919
email: info@audiogo.co.uk
www.audiogo.co.uk

All our Large Print titles are designed for easy reading, and all our books are made to last.